BOOM TOWN

Brad Dennison

Author of
THE LONG TRAIL and THUNDER

Published by Pine Bookshelf
Buford, Georgia

Boom Town is a work of fiction. Names, characters, places, and incidents are either the product of the author's imagination or are used fictitiously. Any resemblance to actual persons, living or dead, events or locales is entirely coincidental.

Copyright 2014 by Bradley A. Dennison.

All Rights Reserved

Cover Design: Donna Dennison
Cover Art: Fall of the Cowboy, by Frederic Remington

Editors: Donna Dennison
        Loretta Yike

THE McCABES

The Long Trail
One Man's Shadow
Return of the Gunhawk
Boom Town
Trail Drive
Johnny McCabe
Shoshone Valley
Thunder
Wandering Man

JUBILEE

Preacher With A Gun
Gunhawk Blood (Coming Soon)

THE TEXAS RANGER

Tremain
Wardtown
Jericho (Coming Soon)

*To my munchkins, Megan and Seth,
who are growing up way too fast.*

PART ONE

The McCabe Trail

1

June, 1880

Jessica said, "Oh, Johnny. You were right. It is so incredibly beautiful here."

They were knee-deep in grass. It was early summer, and the grass was still green from the spring run-off. Johnny and Jessica stood on a low, rounded ridge, and below them the land stretched away in a canopy of green. Flowers showing pink or red or white swayed in the wind, and the grass rippled like waves in an ocean.

Jessica leaned into Johnny the way a woman does with the man she loves, and he had one arm about her shoulders.

Behind them, about a hundred yards away, were the wagons. This was where they had camped the previous night. Behind the wagons was the trail that cut north from the Bozeman trail to McCabe Gap.

Johnny felt small arms wrap around his leg, and he looked down to see Cora. He lifted Cora, and slid one arm underneath her so she could sort of sit in the crook of his elbow.

"What do you think, sweetie?" he said. "Do you think you'll be happy here?"

She nodded. "It's nice here. But it's different than home was. It's colder and windier."

Johnny grinned and nodded. "Windier. It sure is. It'll be a little less windy when we get into the valley. But it'll be cold in the winter, and with lots of snow."

"Snow? Really?"

He had told her this before, but she apparently liked to hear it.

He said, "There'll be snow drifts as tall as you are."
"Will I be able to build a snowman?"
"You bet you will, sweetie."
"How much longer till we're there?"

Johnny said, "We should be there before dark. We'll get moving once the boys are back."

Jessica said, "Looks like they're coming now."

Five riders had topped a low hill maybe a mile off and were coming toward them.

Johnny figured they were eight miles south and east of the valley, near land that was claimed by Zack Johnsons' ranch. The herd they had brought with them officially belonged to the Swan-McCabe Cattle Company, meaning the critters belonged to Matt and Jessica, and to Johnny through marriage to Jessica. Since Johnny and Zack shared range with each other and their herds were often mingled, Zack saw no reason why they couldn't leave the Swan-McCabe herd on his range for a while.

Matt and Peddie walked up to them, hand-in-hand. Like young lovers, Johnny thought. Josh and Temperence often walked like that. And Jack and Nina. Even though Matt was forty-five, something about love can bring out the youth in a man.

Matt said, "Looks like that's Joe and the boys. Time to get these wagons moving again."

The riders topped the hill and reined up by Johnny and the others.

Johnny said, "Any problems?"

Joe shook his head. "None."

Zack said, "Ramon is there at the line shack. He and the boys'll watch out for his herd."

Johnny nodded. "Let's get moving, then."

"One thing," Joe said. "I think this is where we should part company."

This had Johnny curious.

Dusty said, "There's a man in a Mexican prison we owe a debt to."

Johnny said, "I thought we were going to take care of that after we got everyone settled in the valley."

"Not *we*," Joe said. "We talked about it, the three of us. You and Matt ain't coming."

"Now, hold on."

Joe shook his head. "You're not allowed. You both have bigger responsibilities. You, to Jessica and Cora. And Matt, to Peddie."

Matt said, "I don't like the idea of you all fighting our battles for us."

Zack said, "It's not like that at all. It's just that you and Johnny have more important things to take care of."

Johnny looked at Jessica. She hadn't liked the idea of him riding down to Mexico. Breaking a man out of a prison was no easy thing, and it was likely any who weren't killed in the process would have a price on his head. If Johnny didn't get himself killed trying to break Sam out of prison, he would have to be on the run. Either way, he wouldn't be here with Jessica and Cora. She understood he felt obliged to go, but she was mighty glad Zack and Joe and Dusty were taking the stance they were.

The look in her eyes and the arch of her brows conveyed all of this. Such was the magic of a woman, Johnny thought. He reached out and took her hand. She knew he had lost this battle, but she allowed a grateful smile.

Johnny said, "You should at least all come to the valley first. I know Ginny would like to see you both before you light out again," he directed this at Dusty and Zack, and to Joe he said, "And she hasn't seen you in a coon's age."

Dusty said, "If we do that, then Josh will want to ride with us. He can't. Jack will probably want to come too. They're good men, but they're not outlaws. For what we have ahead of us, you need an outlaw."

Johnny looked long at his son. Johnny knew he was right.

Tom had come strolling up, too. The preacher with a gun at his side. Lettie was back at the wagon with Mercy.

Tom said to the men on horseback, "Be safe. Do what you have to do and return to us."

Matt said to the men, "Do you have any plan in mind?"

Joe said, "None at all. We don't even know where he's being held."

Zack said, "Time to ride. We'll be back when we can."

If they can, Johnny thought. Of all of the adventures he had been involved in throughout his life, nothing was as big as breaking a man out of a Mexican prison. He knew there was a good chance he would never see any of them again.

Johnny extended his hand up to Dusty, who reached

down to take it.

Johnny said, "You do me proud. I only wish I had known of you sooner."

Dusty looked like he was about to say something. Maybe offer some sort of light-hearted thing like, *Oh, you'll see me again. We'll be back before you know it.* But he knew his father fully understood the immensity of the job ahead of them, and so he said nothing.

Johnny in turn shook hands with each of them.

To Joe he said, "You've been gone so long. It's been great riding with you again, these past few months."

Joe nodded, shaking Johnny's hand but saying nothing. A man of few words. He always had been.

Zack said, "You take care of my spread while I'm gone. Check in on Ramon once in a while, see if he needs anything."

Johnny nodded. "You know I will."

There was a round of hand-shaking with Matt and Tom, and then Zack said, "Let's ride."

They started out cutting directly south. Johnny and Jessica stood, watching them plow a path through the tall grass along the slope. She slipped her hand back into his.

At the base of the slope, the riders began following a low area between two grassy rises, and then were gone from sight.

Jessica said, "Sam Middleton was right. You men are the stuff of legends."

Johnny snorted a chuckle. "I don't know about that. We're just men who see something that has to be done, and we're blessed enough to have the ability to do it. Blessed or cursed. I'm not sure which, sometimes."

Jessica gave his hand a squeeze.

Tom stood silently a few moments, his eyes shut. When he opened his eyes, Johnny said, "Offering a prayer?"

Tom shrugged. "For all the good it'll do. One thing I've learned the hard way this past year—God doesn't always listen."

The broken preacher, Johnny thought.

Johnny said, "God always listens."

"Let's hope you're right." Tom turned and headed back to the wagon where Lettie and Mercy waited for him.

Johnny said to anyone within listening range, "Come on. Let's get going."

But Jessica threw her arms around him. She said, "I'm so glad you're not going."

He returned the hug, squeezing her like he couldn't pull her close enough to him.

"I've never let another man fight a battle for me," he said. "This is the first time, and it doesn't set well. But they're right. I have a greater responsibility."

Then Jessica said, "Come on. I can't wait to meet everyone."

2

The Bozeman Trail swung more or less north from Cheyenne to Montana Territory, where it curved westward toward the town bearing its name. Shortly after the point where it began curving, another trail split off and headed north. This trail came to within a short riding distance of McCabe Gap, and was coming to be called the McCabe Trail. Johnny felt a little embarrassed by the thought of a trail bearing his name, so he often just called it *the main trail*, or *the trail down to Bozeman*.

The wagons were now moving along this trail. Johnny was on the wagon seat, reins in his hands. Not that Jessica couldn't drive the wagon well enough. It was just that he felt like sitting beside her and Cora. He knew he might never see Dusty again, and since Jessica and Cora were now family too, he found he wanted to keep his family close.

Cora was too young to have developed an appreciation for the world around her, and was lying on the wagon seat with her head in Jessica's lap.

Jessica, however, was staring in awe at the ridges. Most were covered with pine, but some rose to jagged rocky summits. Overhead, an eagle circled about.

"Johnny," she said. "How is it possible to live in a land like this and not simply stare in wonder all day long?"

He shrugged. "You sort of get used to it, I guess. Though I will admit, I'm glad to be home."

"I don't see how anyone could ever get used to this."

Cora murmured, "Are we there yet?"

"Soon, little one," Johnny said. "Soon."

They stopped after a time to rest the teams. Matt got down on one knee to look under the wagon. He had a questionable axle and was hoping it would hold out until they reached Johnny's ranch.

Johnny said from behind him, "How is it?"

"Got a small crack. I'm glad we're near that town of yours. I don't know how much longer this is going to last."

He straightened up. "Once we get moving, we're going to have to take it slow."

"We're close enough. We'll be there by tonight."

Wagons were approaching from the south. A line of

freight wagons, looked like. Buckboards with cargo in the back and canvas stretched over it and tied down. A line of freight wagons had passed them the afternoon before, when they had stopped to make camp.

"Never knew this stretch to be so busy," Johnny said. "There's not a whole lot north of here."

After the teams of mules were rested to Johnny's satisfaction, he climbed back up into the wagon seat. Jessica had climbed back up also, along with Cora.

"We're going to have to take it slow," Johnny said to Jessica. "Matt's axel is not looking good."

A man called from off to one side and behind them a bit. "Ahoy, there! Hello, the wagons!"

Johnny looked at Jessica. "Ahoy?"

A covered wagon pulled up beside them. It was being pulled by a team of mules. A man was in the seat, and a woman. The man looked to be maybe thirty, long and thin and with a floppy felt hat. He wore lace-up boots and homespun trousers. *Farmer*, Johnny immediately thought. Beside the man on the seat was a woman who looked to be a fair bit younger, and she had an infant in her arms.

"You folks bound for Jubilee?" the man said, his brows arched with enthusiasm.

"Jubilee?" Johnny said. He wasn't sure what the man meant. He had used the word like it was a destination. A town, or something. But there was no place north of here that Johnny knew of by that name, and he had been living in these mountains for a long time.

"You bet-cha," the man said. "Jubilee. There's land for the taking. And there's gold!"

He snapped the reins and gave a "giddyup, there!" And he was off.

Johnny sat for a moment beside Jessica and Cora watching the wagon bump its way along the trail. The man was working the team much too hard. Looked like he was in a hurry to get where he was going.

"Jubilee?" Jessica asked. "What's that?"

Johnny shrugged his shoulders. "I have no idea."

He gave a light snap to the reins, and their own team of mules started forward.

They had put three miles of trail behind them when a stagecoach came up behind them. The horses weren't moving at a full gallop, like the stagecoach teams always seemed to be doing in dime novels. Rather, the driver was keeping them to a light trot.

Johnny saw the driver was old Hank.

Hank raised an arm and waved at him. "Johnny! Good to see you!"

"You too, Hank!" Johnny called back.

And the stage continued along.

"It's not Wednesday, is it?" Johnny said. "When you're on the trail, one day seems pretty much like another and it's easy to lose count."

"No," she said, counting the days in her mind to make sure. "It's Monday."

"The stage into town only arrives on Wednesdays. There's not enough people in McCabe Gap for anything more."

They rode for another two hours, stopping to rest the teams again.

Matt crawled under his wagon for another look at his axel, and announced it seemed to be holding.

They began moving again, and after a time Johnny said to Jessica, "See that low rise up ahead? Once we're over that, we'll be within sight of the town."

She was smiling. "I can't wait to meet everyone."

Johnny had told her in detail of the little town that bore his name. It was in a wide expanse between two ridges. Not really a pass, but Johnny had named it McCabe Gap, using the old name for a pass.

Johnny had told Jessica how the first building in McCabe Gap was put up by the man called Hunter. A large building made of logs that served as a saloon. It became a gathering place, and eventually a man named Frank Shapleigh came in and built a hotel, and then the stagecoach from Bozeman began stopping once a week. A man by the name of Charlie Franklin built a general store. A woman by the name of Alisha Summers came in, setting up a business to tend to the needs of the local cowhands. A small church was built, which served during the week as a small school for local children. Not that there were that many children, because there were very few people living in and around McCabe Gap. At last count, there were twelve children attending school regularly.

But as the wagon Johnny was driving topped the low ridge and they came within view of the town, Johnny saw buildings that hadn't been there the summer before. Buildings stood facing each other, forming a small street that headed toward Hunter's. There were two buildings partially completed. One was no more than a framework of two-by-fours, with a couple of men Johnny didn't recognize swinging hammers and pounding nails. A buckboard filled with lumber rested near them.

"Johnny," Jessica said, "this isn't quite what you described."

"No, it's not."

The livery barn was still there. And the church. And Hunter's saloon. But now there were a number of newer buildings between them all.

The street seemed to lead directly to Hunter's, where it was met with another street, forming a sort of L shape. As Johnny approached Hunter's, a man stepped down from the boardwalk and walked toward them.

He was smiling as though the sight of Johnny and Jessica was the grandest thing he had ever seen in his life. He was tall with a long face, and wore a jacket and string tie, and his hat was not the wider-brimmed type you usually saw in the West, but a bowler like they wore back east.

"Greetings," he said, walking up to Johnny.

Johnny gave the reins a small tug to halt the team, and the man held his hand up for Johnny to shake.

"Welcome to Jubilee," the man said. "My name's Aloysius Randall. I'm the proprietor of the hotel here in town."

Johnny then noticed the sign. Where there had once been a hand-painted sign that read HOTEL, now there was a sign with artfully painted letters that read JUBILEE HOTEL.

Johnny said, "What happened to Frank Shapleigh?"

"Mister Shapleigh sold his enterprise to me over the winter. We still have some rooms available. Are you planning to stay in the area? Perhaps homestead, or even try your hand at a gold claim, if you're feeling lucky?"

"Do I look like a homesteader?" Before the man could reply, Johnny said, "No thanks. Not interested."

That was when Johnny saw Hunter stepping out of his saloon. At least that building hadn't changed. It was still an oversized log cabin. And Hunter was still an oversized man with a thick, black beard.

"Johnny!" Hunter called out. Then he looked back to the open doorway. "Jack! Your pa's here!"

Johnny clicked the team forward, toward Hunter's. Not that Johnny meant to be rude to this Randall fella, but he had the disorienting feeling that he was in some sort of insane dream.

He stopped the team in front of the saloon just as Jack stepped out. Like Dusty had told him earlier, Jack was now wearing a badge.

Johnny climbed down from the wagon and he and his son locked in a hardy embrace.

"Pa," Jack said. "I have so much to tell you."

Johnny gave the tin badge a little flip with one finger. "Dusty told me everything. And I'm fine with it all, as long as you are. I don't want you to live my dream, I want you to live yours. But we can talk more about it after we're settled in."

Jack gave a quick glance back at the wagons. "Where *is* Dusty?"

"He's not with us. It's a long story. I'll tell you all about it over dinner." Johnny gave a perplexed glance down the street at the buildings. Another saloon down past Miss Alisha's. A grain warehouse. A seamstress's shop. A bank, for goodness sake.

He said, "What in the name of sanity is going on here?"

Jack shook his head. "It's a long story."

PART TWO

The First Chinook

3

Six Months Earlier

The first chinook of the season hit two weeks before Christmas. Ginny didn't really understand or even want to understand the causes of it. John had tried to explain it to her once. Something about the warm water of the south Pacific making its way up the coast and somehow affecting the mountain winds. It was all Greek to her. All she knew was that she was grateful for the chinooks, because otherwise winter in these mountains would be dreadfully long.

Ginny had been born and raised in San Francisco. Lived there until she was forty, when she closed up the house to move in with John and help him raise her niece's children. Not long after, they had all moved north to this valley. She had lived her first forty years experiencing winters that were cool and rainy, but she could at least get out of the house and take a walk down the street. Here, in these mountains, when the snow piled sometimes three feet high by Thanksgiving, you couldn't really get out of the house at all.

The family did have a sleigh, kept in a small barn out behind the house. They would hitch up a team every so often and take a ride up the stretch to Zack's, or into McCabe Gap to visit Hunter. Ginny so loved a sleigh ride. She had read about them when she lived in San Francisco, but she had never actually experienced one until she moved to these mountains. But they were small compensation for the sometimes weeks that she was cooped up in the house.

If not for the chinooks, then she would have been snowed in from late October until early May.

She didn't care to understand the why of the chinook. All she knew was the chinook brought unseasonably warm weather. Snow would melt and she could step out of the house. True, the ground would be muddy and the stuff would cake onto her shoes and have to be scraped off afterward, but this was a small price to pay for taking a simple walk outside.

The chinook could last a day, or sometimes even as long as a week. This chinook was in its second day when Ginny stepped outside and walked toward the fenced off corral the boys had built.

The snow between the house and the corral was almost entirely gone. Only a small patch in the shade of the house still remained. The grass was wet and flattened down, but the breeze was warm. Ginny wore a shawl over her shoulders and was perfectly comfortable.

Joshua had taken advantage of the weather to ride off and do a quick reconnaissance of the grazing lands beyond the valley. He used the word *reconnaissance*, which he had gotten from his father. The McCabe men seemed to speak forever in military terms. Something that Johnny had picked up while riding with the Texas Rangers, but which he told her once actually stretched back to the father of the first John McCabe. A somewhat mysterious character named Peter McCabe, who came from the old country. Very little was known about which *old country* was meant when the McCabes referred to the old country, but because of the *Mc* in the name McCabe, Ginny figured it must have been Scotland. Peter McCabe was good with a sword and came to the new world under mysterious circumstances and became a frontiersman. He ran with the Huron Indians and eventually became the father of the original John McCabe. It was said that he often spoke in military terms, and the tradition still lived on.

Ginny had cautioned Josh to be careful. The last thing he wanted was to spend the night at a line cabin and become snowed in when the chinook winds passed. But he assured her that he thought they had a full four or five days remaining before winter weather returned. He had grown up in these mountains and had a feel for these things. Something about the direction of the wind and the look of the clouds.

"Even still," she had said to him. "Be home by dinner tonight and let an old woman rest easier."

As she walked up to the corral, she realized she had referred to herself as an *old woman*. She was only in her early fifties. Well, okay, mid-fifties. But her father had been a young man at sixty. *Youth is not in the number of years,* he had often said. *It's in the attitude.* And yet, calling herself an old woman had flowed out of her so easily, and she hadn't even noticed it until now.

Am I letting myself get old? She asked herself, as she leaned her elbows on the top rail of the fence.

One of the men was there, also, sitting on the top rail a few feet from Ginny. One of the few men Johnny retained over the winter. Generally you hired in the spring and cut the payroll in the fall. This allowed the cowhands to go south for the winter and find work there. Around this ranch, there was very little work for a cowhand to do when the land was belt-deep in snow.

This cowhand was probably the tallest man on the ranch and built like a fence pole, and was known by the improbable name of Fatty Cole. Or just plain Fat, as most of the men called him.

Ginny could never quite bring herself to call a man by that name, so she said, "Good morning, Mister Cole."

"'Mornin', Miss Ginny," he said, touching the brim of his hat in the frontier equivalent to the gentleman's tip of the hat to a lady.

Fred Ketchum was in there, twirling a loop over his head as easily as Ginny might swat a fly. In the far corner, a dark colored stallion with two blond-ish stockings pulled back, looking at Fred like he thought he was crazy.

Fred let the loop fly and dropped it over the horse's head and neck. The horse stood and looked at him. Fred walked up to him slowly, saying things like, "Easy boy." And, "You're okay."

He then reached one hand up to stroke the horse's nose.

Ginny was no rancher and had no interest in it. She left those duties entirely to John and the boys. But she knew they had gone mustanging in October before the snows and caught a few. This was one of them.

She also knew Johnny didn't approve of the traditional way of breaking a horse. Climbing onto the back of a wild stallion and trying to hang on while the stallion tried to buck you off and kill you. He had learned a different method during his time with the Shoshone. Approach the horse gradually. Let it get to know you and learn to trust you. Eventually get a blanket on its back. Sometime after that, you introduce it to a saddle.

They called this breaking a horse Indian style, but John had said it wasn't really about breaking a horse at all. It was about letting the horse learn to trust you and get used to being ridden.

"It's all about trust," John had said. "But then again, aren't most things? Marriage? Friendships?"

This method had no allotted schedule. Each horse learned trust and got used to being ridden in its own time. Ginny had seen Johnny do this with the stallion he now called Thunder. The horse he had ridden when he left the previous summer to go to California. When Johnny had finally climbed up and onto Thunder's back for the first time, Thunder hadn't bucked him once.

Johnny had said once he really doubted Thunder could have been broken the cowboy way. He said any attempt to do this would have resulted in a dead rider. And this brought a thought to Ginny's mind.

"Fred," Ginny said, "when you and the boys were out mustanging, did you see that stallion? The one Josh was so fixated on?"

Fred looked over at her and shook his head. "No, ma'am. We ain't seen him in almost two years."

She nodded. "Thank you. I'm always concerned."

Fat grinned. "You think Josh might try to ride him again?"

She said, "The horse almost killed him the first two times. I'm afraid the third one might finish the job."

This stallion was one Josh and Dusty had happened across when they were out mustanging a couple summers ago, and they hadn't even been able to catch him. The horse had trampled Josh nearly to death the first time, and then later on when Josh got a rope on him, the stallion had nearly dragged him to death.

"Mister Cole," Ginny said casually, even though the question she was about to ask was her primary reason for being out here, "have you seen Bree?"

He nodded. "Yes'm. Miss Bree had me saddle her horse

an hour ago. She said a day like this calls for a ride through the hills."

Ginny nodded. This was what she figured. Bree had called to her, *Aunt Ginny, I'm going out.* But with that girl, *going out* could constitute a stroll about the ranch or a ride into town to see Jack, as much as it could mean a day of riding in the mountains.

"I trust she took her Winchester?"

Mister Cole nodded again. "Yes'm. I asked if she wanted me to make sure it was loaded, but she said there wasn't a need."

Mister Cole hadn't just been attempting to be a gentleman, Ginny knew. He had been trying to get her attention. Most of the young men found Bree to be uncommonly pretty. Bree was also one of the only unmarried women of marrying age within a day's ride. True, Temperance was unmarried, but she had eyes only for Josh. And there was Nina Harding, who was focused solely on Jack.

But Mister Cole's efforts had been wasted. When it came to a rifle, Bree could handle one as well as any man, and she knew when her gun was loaded and when it was not. Which brought Ginny back to her primary reason for being out here.

She said, "Fred, Temperance and I are going into town to run a few errands. And to just get out of the house for a few hours, before winter returns. When you're finished, could you hitch a buggy for us?"

Fred glanced over to the cowhand on the fence. "Hey, Fat. Could you hitch one up now for the ladies?"

"Yes, sir, you bet I could," he said as he hopped down to the wet grass.

Temperance couldn't quite handle a horse like Bree, but she had been raised on an Army post and knew how to drive a team. With the reins in her fingers and Ginny at her side, they set out for town.

Fred had said, "Would you ladies like me or Fat to come along?"

"Thank you, Fred, but no," Ginny had said. "I think we can manage a ride to town without getting ourselves into too much trouble."

The ride to the little hamlet of McCabe Gap was three miles by the long route. There was a shorter horse trail, but Ginny knew this wagon wouldn't be able to manage it.

"My, but it's a beautiful day," Temperance said as they rode along.

"Indeed it is," Ginny said.

The sky overhead was almost cloudless. The day was warm. Not quite summer-time warm, but more like late spring. A light breeze blew from the west and brought with it earthy smells. Loam, and wet grass. An occasional draught of balsam from the ridges that surrounded this little valley. Here and there were small patches of snow, reminding them of reality. That it was really winter, and soon the snow would be descending on them again.

Temperance said, "I do hope Josh is right and we have a few more days before winter returns."

Ginny nodded.

Temperance said, "Christmas is coming soon. I'm so excited. I just love Christmas so. I always did when I was growing up. I'm so glad that now that I live with you and your family, I have Christmas again."

Ginny nodded. "That's one of the things we're going into town for. I still haven't found a suitable gift for Bree."

"Really?" Temperance threw her a look of surprise, then tried to cover it up by snapping her gaze toward the trail ahead of them.

Ginny was certain she appeared to most as one who lived a carefully ordered life. It was but a mere illusion. She thought they would all be shocked to discover the disarray her life was usually in.

One who would not be surprised, who could somehow see behind her proper air of formality and sometimes stern ways, was John himself. Even as a young cowhand who wore his gun like he knew how to use it, he had seen through her charade. And another had been the young man she gave her heart to, all those years ago. A man she seldom talked of, and of whom she had even told Johnny only a little. The man who had been lost at sea, on one of her father's ships.

She said, "I have long thought about one thing Bree needs in her life. Something no young woman in the high society of San Francisco would have, and would probably pale at the thought of it. But Bree is unlike any young woman I have ever known."

Temperance nodded. "She sure is."

"That's because of who her father is. And the line of people she descends from. Being a McCabe and all it entails is something that simply runs in the bloodline. Sometimes it's a lot for them to live up to. But the results are always worth the effort."

Jack was standing outside the log cabin that served the small community as the marshal's office and jail. Not that the town actually had an official lawman. The town wasn't even an official town. Just a small unincorporated community. It had begun when Hunter built a saloon near the wide mountain pass known as McCabe Gap, and then a stagecoach began traveling through once or twice a month. Eventually a hotel went up, and a general store, and other businesses like Alisha Summer's house of ill repute. Henry Freeman was the town blacksmith. The folks in town pitched some money together and now they had a building to serve as a jail, and had hired Jack to be their unofficial peace officer.

Jack stood by the door, enjoying the morning sun. He wasn't wearing a coat, for the first time in weeks. He had a cup of coffee in his hand and his gunbelt was in place. The little tin badge Henry Freeman had hammered out on his anvil was pinned to his vest, and his hat was tipped back so he could feel the sun and its welcoming warmth on his face. He had been thinking he should probably walk his rounds, which essentially meant strolling about the town and making sure everything was all right. But the stretch of dirt that constituted the town's single street was now maybe six inches deep in mud because of all of the snow that had melted so quickly when the chinook hit. To get from the cabin, which stood by itself and was not connected anywhere by a boardwalk, he would have to step down into the mess and try to navigate through it. Not that he was afraid of a little mud, but it wouldn't work too kindly on his riding boots.

So he stood on the small deck in front of the cabin, enjoying the sun and drinking his coffee. This was how Aunt

Ginny and Temperance found him.

Temperance pulled the team to a halt in front of the cabin. The steel rims of the wheels were covered in mud.

"Good morning, ladies," he said, reaching to the brim of his hat that was tipped back and making an effort to touch it, but then giving up.

"Good morning, Marshal," Aunt Ginny said.

"And what brings you ladies to town?"

"I need your advice on something."

"I would invite you inside," Jack said, "but I could play host better at Hunter's. How would you like me to treat you to a taste of tea?"

"I would enthusiastically accept the invitation," she said with a smile.

Jack set his cup of coffee on a bench by the front wall, then took a wide step from the edge of the deck to the wagon wheel, and pulled himself up and onto the wagon seat without having to step into the mud.

Though Hunter's was a saloon, it was quickly turning into a morning meeting place for the town residents. Hunter kept a tin of tea on hand for the occasional morning when Aunt Ginny paid him a visit, and for Granny Tate.

Ginny found Granny Tate and Henry sitting at a table along with Charlie Franklin, who owned the general store. At another table, reading a newspaper, was Frank Shapleigh, the owner of the hotel. Shapleigh was maybe forty, with a rumpled jacket and a crooked string tie, which was normal for him. He had a fleshy face, and a thick mustache that seemed to swallow his entire mouth.

Mustaches were the new fashion, Ginny knew, but she hated them. She always had. She was glad Johnny and the boys didn't take to them.

They all offered their greetings, the men standing and touching the brims of their hats. Granny Tate invited Ginny and Temperance to join her for tea. Granny Tate had a taste for fine tea, which Ginny always appreciated in a person.

Mister Chen, the Chinese man Hunter had hired, was pushing a broom off to the side. Ginny couldn't begin to even guess at his age. His face said the latter side of eighty, but he moved like a much younger man. Jack had said there was not a man in town who could beat him wrestling.

He said, "Good morning, Miss Ginny."

"Good morning, Mister Chen. Would you care to take a break from your duties and join me for tea?"

"I would love to," he said, "but Hunter wants the place as clean as possible for tonight."

Hunter was bringing a pot of hot water and a tray of tea fixings to their table.

He said, "It's Friday. I'm figuring because of the weather we may get some business. Maybe not as much as we get in the summer, because the ranches all run with a low payroll this time of year."

Jack said, "I'll tell Darby and we'll make sure we're around."

Shapleigh looked over to Jack and said, "You want to see part of the paper? It's only three days old. I went down to Bozeman yesterday for a business meeting. I figured I'd take advantage of the weather. I also took the opportunity to grab a recent copy of the paper."

Jack said, "Absolutely."

Shapleigh pulled the first page out of the fold and handed it across from his table to Jack.

Jack scanned the front of the page. Ginny knew they normally didn't see a recent newspaper in this town until spring. Even with the chinook, the stage wouldn't start running through here until probably May. Then they would get a newspaper every week.

"So," Hunter said to Shapleigh. "A business meeting in Bozeman, huh?"

Franklin had a cup of coffee in his hand. "Must be coming up in the world."

Shapleigh looked up from his page of the newspaper. "Nothing worth mentioning, really. Probably nothing'll come of it."

Ginny took a sip of her tea. "Jack, I need some help from you. I need to find a Christmas gift for Bree."

Jack looked up with a grin. "I'm probably the last one to ask about things a girl might be interested in. Maybe Temperance is the better one to ask. Or Nina."

"No, you would be the better one to ask. Or Josh, but he's off with the herd."

This had Jack's attention.
Ginny said, "I want to buy Bree a pistol."

4

Now she had the full attention of a lot of people. Hunter had gone to the stove fixing another pot of coffee, but now he was looking over with full interest. Jack was staring at her with surprise. Temperance was staring too, and not even trying to disguise it this time.

Jack said, "Now, weren't you the one who always said a pistol didn't belong in the hands of a woman? Weren't you the one who said you would allow her to be taught how to shoot a rifle as long as Pa didn't try to teach her how to shoot a pistol?"

"Yes," Ginny said with resignation.

"Weren't you the one who said..."

"Yes," she cut him off. "I'm the one who said it."

Jack looked at Hunter, who was staring with disbelief. He decided to wait Aunt Ginny out.

Finally, she said, "At first I had hopes of possibly introducing Bree to San Francisco society. I felt any niece of mine would be a very sought-after debutante in the city. But I've resigned myself to the reality that she belongs here. She's truly her father's daughter."

Hunter said, "What convinced you?"

"Last summer, when Nina was lost in the mountains and you men were all trying to find her. It was Bree who saddled up and rode out there and brought her in."

Jack nodded. "And we're forever grateful to her for that."

Temperance said, "And it was Bree who beat up that outlaw. What was his name?"

"White-Eye. I don't think I ever knew his last name."

Ginny shuddered. "That horrible man. The thought of Bree even in the same room with him makes me cringe."

"But she beat the stuffing out of him," Jack said.

Hunter was grinning. "She beat him up but good. Had his face all cut up."

"It was last summer that convinced me," Ginny said. "My insistence that she not be taught to use a handgun was erroneous."

Chen had stopped sweeping. "In my country, many

women are taught to defend themselves. One of our best fighting styles was created by a woman. Her name was Ng Mui."

"Do you think," Ginny said to Jack, "that you and Joshua could teach her to shoot properly and effectively, the way your father taught you? That is, until he returns and can take over the lessons himself?"

"Sure," Jack said. "I have no doubt. She's as good a shot with a rifle as anyone I've ever seen."

"One question I have," Ginny glanced from Jack to Hunter, "do you think a woman's hand is strong enough to handle a pistol?"

Jack shrugged. "Depends on the pistol."

Hunter nodded in agreement.

"Then that's where I will need your help, in choosing the right one. Mister Franklin, when we're done here, we will be going over to your place to look at your guns."

Charlie Franklin was the proverbial jack-of-all-trades. You had to be, to survive in these mountains. He was a carpenter, at times a cobbler, and a mostly self-taught gunsmith. At his general store, he had a small line of pistols, rifles and shotguns. Nothing new. Mostly items that had been traded in for other goods.

He pulled from his counter a small derringer. Two barrels, what they called an over-under.

"This here's a Remington," he said. "A fine hide-away gun for a lady."

Ginny shook her head. "No, I think what she needs is the type of gun you can fire from a horse. The kind of gun you wear on your hip."

He had eight revolvers. One of them was a short-barreled Colt.

Ginny said, "What about that one?"

Franklin lifted it and handed it to Jack.

Jack spun the cylinder quickly to make sure it wasn't loaded and then aimed it at an imaginary target across the room.

While he was doing this, Franklin said, "It's a forty-four. Five inch barrel. I got it in trade last summer."

Jack shook his head. "Too large a caliber. Bree's not

very big and has small hands."

Ginny looked at him questioningly. Knowledge of guns was something she left to Johnny and the boys.

Jack said, as he handed the Colt back to Franklin, "When a gun is fired, it has recoil. A rifle actually pushes back into your shoulder. A pistol does a similar thing, but it snaps your hand up and back. I don't know if Bree would have the strength in her hands to fire it with any control."

Franklin shrugged and said, "I have a twenty-two."

"Let me see it."

Franklin handed it to him, and said, "Peacemaker model. Got a seven and a half inch barrel. Twenty-two rimfire."

Jack spun the cylinder. Something Pa had taught him to do long ago. When you pick up a gun, always check to see if it's loaded. Pa said that every accidental shooting was the result of carelessness. Make it a habit to check the loads every time you pick a gun up.

He then held it out at arm's length, hauled the hammer back until it clicked into place, then pulled the trigger. The hammer snapped down on the firing pin.

He said, "You got some cartridges for it?"

Franklin nodded. "A whole box full."

"Let's take it out back and see how it fires."

When Ginny and Temperance returned to the ranch, the sun was trailing low in the winter sky. They found Bree in the parlor, oiling down her Winchester. Pa let her have full access to any of the rifles in the rack, but there was one in particular she preferred. She found the balance to be just right. No two guns, even of the same model, will have the exact same balance and feel.

She was sitting in her father's chair, and a fire was crackling away in the hearth. Her gun cleaning equipment was spread out on the coffee table. A rod, a scattering of cleaning patches which were really small squares of cloth cut from a bed sheet, and a small can of gun oil.

Bree was still in levis. They were a pair of Josh's she had confiscated. Since he stood two inches taller, she had to roll the cuffs up.

"There you are," Bree said. "Fred mentioned you had

ridden into town. I did some target practice on an old pine, today. Pa always said to keep your guns clean. Someday your life might depend on it."

Ginny was again struck by just how much Bree was her father's daughter. She wondered if the old man himself, the original John McCabe, would have been proud had he been able to look ahead through the strands of time and see his granddaughter. *His granddaughter the gunhawk*, Ginny thought.

Johnny used the term *gunhawk* a lot, Ginny knew. One of the many terms for a man who lived by the gun. *Gunman* was another. And *gunfighter*, and *gunslinger*. Ginny hated all of them. Johnny had been one at one time. He had left those years behind him, but somehow his past had a way of catching up with him. She supposed it always did.

Gunhawk was the term Johnny seemed to prefer, but he often used it in a way that meant more than simply a man who lived by the gun. Probably without fully realizing it, he used the term for a man who was sort of a latter day knight. Fighting the good fight, for the right reasons. And John was certainly a man like that.

Bree said, "What's that?"

Ginny followed her gaze to the package Ginny held in her hand. It was a box wrapped up in cheesecloth, which was all Franklin had available in his store at the moment, and tied together with twine.

Ginny said, "Christmas is coming up, young lady. Don't you know not to ask questions?"

This got a smile out of Bree that wasn't all that different than the smile she had when she was a young girl. The smile the thought of Christmas brings out in so many people.

"So," Bree said, in her little-girl teasing voice, "did you get me something good?"

"You, young lady, will have to wait two more weeks to find out."

Ginny went to the room to put the package away. But in the doorway she looked back at Bree. The girl was sitting quietly with firelight dancing on her as she ran the rod down the barrel of the Winchester. A cleaning patch was tied to the end of the rod, and she was scrubbing away gunpowder residue.

    The little girl who had been asking about Christmas with pure, innocent delight was gone, and a gunhawk sat in her place.

5

He sat in a small saloon in Wichita. He had a beard and it wasn't a fashion statement. He just hadn't shaved in more than a year. His hair was long, falling past his collar. He hadn't cut his hair in more than a year, either. The beard was largely a dark brown in color, but was so filled with white strands, especially around his chin, that it looked like it had one large white stripe in the middle.

He wore tattered clothes. An old shirt he had pulled from a clothes line outside a farmhouse months ago. A pair of trousers he had taken off a dead man in a funeral parlor in Dodge. The man's name had been unknown. He had died in a gunfight on a drunken Saturday night and was waiting for burial in boot hill. The place wandering gunmen and cowhands who were relatively anonymous and got themselves liquored-up and killed went to be buried.

Buckled at the man's side was a revolver. A Colt forty-four he had taken off a cowhand he had jumped in an alley in Cheyenne a couple of months ago. He needed money, and hit a drunken cowhand over the head and found two dollars and forty-two cents in the man's wallet. He also took the pistol and gunbelt.

The man had little more than the clothes on his back, and a nickel in his pocket. The cartridges in the gunbelt. He had a horse outside, at the hitching rail. The horse wasn't stolen. It was about the only thing he had that wasn't.

In front of him was a bottle of Kentucky whiskey. At least that was what the label said. He had poured himself a glass and it rested on the table in front of him, waiting to be consumed. Waiting to numb him, to make the pain ease off. To take him to a land where he just didn't care.

And yet, he let the glass stand there. The liquid was a sort of golden brown. He stared at the glass and it stared back. But he didn't reach for it. After all, it was alcohol that had gotten him into this situation.

He realized a man was standing in front of his table looking at him. He hadn't seen the man walk up. He just realized the man was standing there. He looked up and saw the man was rather tall, in a dark gray jacket and trousers, a checkered vest and a bolo tie. The man looked to be not quite middle aged. On his head was a bowler like you saw worn back east.

"What can I do for you?" the man at the table asked.

He had once spoken with precision and eloquence. He had been a teacher once. But now the words sort of fell out of him. Flat and not very distinct.

The man in front of the table said, "I have a business proposition for you."

The man at the table gave a bitter snicker. "You have the wrong man, then."

"No, I don't think so. Your name is Victor Falcone."

The man at the table stared at him from tired eyes. Eyes in a tired face, a tired face held up by tired bones.

He said, "Not anymore."

The man standing chuckled, and said, "Mind if I sit down?"

He didn't wait for a reply, but slid out a chair and dropped into it.

"Want to share a drink?" the man in the bowler said.

Falcone said, "I don't drink anymore. You have it."

Falcone slid the glass over to him.

The man said, "Then why did you buy the bottle?"

"Because I still drank then. But as I sit here and look at it, I realized I just can't have anymore. It's why I'm here in the first place. It's why I'm not Victor Falcone anymore."

The man said, "My name is Aloysius Randall. I run a saloon in St. Louis, and a small shipping company out of Galveston. And a few other smaller businesses not worth mentioning."

Falcone looked at him. "Gambling halls. Brothels."

The man called Randall gave a look of surprised innocence.

Falcone didn't even give him time to speak. He said, "I know the type, mister. You have a look of propriety that disguises what you really are."

Randall stared at him, caught between a smile and a little bit of wonder. "You really are everything they say you are."

"And who says I'm anything at all?"

"People who have known you. You see, Mister Falcone,

I've been looking for you. I heard you were in this area."

"Who knows I'm here? I don't go by the name Falcone anymore. In fact, I don't go by any name at all. I'm just a wandering drifter."

"Oh no, Mister Falcone. You're much more than that. Maybe you're beaten and broken. I don't know just what happened to you to make you this way, but I have a job offer for you."

"Not interested."

"It's not anything like your old line of work at all."

Falcone said, "You know what I could go for? A cup of coffee. But I'm down to my last nickel. I wasted my money on this bottle that I'm not even going to drink."

Randall rose to his feet and called to the barkeep and asked for a cup of coffee.

"It won't be very good, I'm sure," Randall said to Falcone. "But it's coffee."

The barkeep came over and set a tin cup in front of Falcone. Randall handed him the nickel it cost for a cup of coffee in this place.

"Much obliged," Falcone said. "But it doesn't mean I'm taking the job. Whatever job you're offering."

"How's the coffee?"

Falcone took a sip. "Like you said, it's coffee."

Randall reached for the glass of whiskey and knocked back a mouthful. "Now, this is much more than coffee."

Falcone gave a weary sigh. "I've had enough of that to last a lifetime. Look where it's gotten me."

"Do you know where I've been recently, Mister Falcone?"

Falcone shook his head. "Don't much care, either."

Randall chuckled. "I appreciate your honesty. I've just come from a corner of the country I believe you're familiar with. Montana Territory. The town of Bozeman. Within riding distance of a place called McCabe Gap."

Falcone visibly winced. "I don't care if I ever hear that name again."

"Let me see if I have this right. Two summers ago, you and a group of outlaws you led attacked the McCabe ranch. Attempting to raid it, I presume. You attacked it in broad daylight, and there, of course, was your mistake. A man like

Johnny McCabe. Presuming everything they say about him is even half true, then it was practically a suicide mission."

"It wasn't broad daylight. It was nighttime." Falcone took a sip of coffee. "But I would wager more than half of what they say about him is true."

"It was indeed a suicide mission?"

Falcone shrugged. "Everything seems clearer in hindsight."

Randall nodded. "All too true."

Randall took a sip of the whiskey. He grimaced a little. "Not the best stuff."

"Mister...Randall, is it? Just what do you want with me?"

"Partly I want a man of your abilities. And partly I want a man of education. And a man of vision."

"Well, I have the education, but I think my abilities right now would be in serious question. And my vision?" He gave another bitter chuckle. "I think history speaks for itself."

"I just came from Bozeman, Montana. I had a meeting with a man from McCabe Gap. A man by the name of Frank Shapleigh. Do you know the name?"

Falcone shook his head. "Should I?"

"He owns the hotel in that little town."

"Good for him."

"They're having unseasonably warm weather right now. What they call a chinook. I decided to take advantage of it and see to some business."

Falcone said, "Thanks for the coffee. But I think you've come to the wrong man. There's not much left of me."

"I think you're wrong." Randall held the glass in his hand and gave what was left of the whiskey a final glance, decided it wasn't worth finishing and set it back on the table.

He got to his feet. "I'll pay you twenty thousand a year."

That got Falcone's attention. He looked at the man, really looking at him for the first time.

"That's more than most cowhands will make in ten years. I'll pay you that every year."

"You'll pay me twenty *thousand*? A *year*?"

"I need a man intelligent enough to see the large picture. A man capable enough to get things done, and experienced enough to know how to do them. I'm staying at the hotel down the street. Room six. If you're interested, we'll talk more there."

Falcone sat and watched Randall walk across the floor and then push his way out through the swinging doors.

Men sat at the tables. Mostly young men, in wide hats and wearing spurs on their boots and guns at their sides. They had watched Randall walk across the room because he walked like he was somebody important. No one looked at Falcone, though. To them he was just a nameless saddle bum who was a few too many days removed from his last bath. Falcone had to admit his last bath was the last time it had rained.

He sat and drank his coffee.

He had once been the right-hand man of Sam Patterson. He had once commanded a group of guerilla raiders, himself. And now he was a whiskey-soaked saddle bum who couldn't even afford a cup of coffee.

He didn't know what Aloysius Randall could possibly expect of him. He didn't know if his hand was steady enough to shoot straight, any longer. But twenty thousand dollars was nothing to sneeze at.

He finished the rest of his coffee in one gulp and got to his feet. He crossed the room, heading for the door, leaving the bottle behind for whoever wanted it. He pushed through the swinging doors and to the street outside.

It was getting dark. Windows along the street were lighted. Riders made their way along the street, in one direction or the other. A buckboard jingled and creaked its way along.

He looked up the street to the hotel. Randall hadn't mentioned the name of the hotel he was staying at, but he had said it was *up the street*. This was not the best part of town. There was only one hotel on this street.

Falcone started along, heading toward the hotel, and room number six.

6

Bree stood in her robe looking at the tree, a cup of hot tea steaming away in her hand. Her chocolate brown hair was in a braid and flipped over one shoulder.

It was Christmas morning, just after sunrise. Bree had been awake only long enough to come down the stairs and fix herself a cup of tea, but the candles on the tree were already lighted. Somehow, every Christmas, Aunt Ginny managed to be up before anyone and got the tree lighted, and got the water boiling for tea and the trail coffee Pa and the boys drank.

Except Pa wasn't here. Neither was Dusty. Pa had ridden off the previous summer, heading to California to visit Ma's grave. Dusty and Zack had ridden out a couple months ago before the first snow, to go and join him.

Bree had started wondering the previous winter if the whole family would ever be together for Christmas again. Jack had been in school back east every year since she was eleven. The previous Christmas, Josh and Dusty had gone to Oregon to look for a girl named Haley, who Dusty knew. They had searched for three months but never found her. Now this year, Jack was back and Josh was here, but Pa and Dusty were gone.

And really, even if everyone was here, everyone would still not be here. Ma would never be here.

Bree felt a twang of sadness deep inside her. But then she shook it off. Aunt Ginny had said once that Ma's way had been to focus on the good and the bright, and turn away from the bad and the dark. This was what Bree was going to do. She was not only her father's daughter, she was also her mother's daughter. And even though Ma had died before Bree was old enough to remember, Aunt Ginny and Pa had worked hard to make sure Bree knew her.

Bree looked at the tree, forcing herself to see it not as a symbol of loss, but a symbol of family and love. And even though Bree wasn't one to talk much about religion and hardly ever set foot in a church, she saw the tree as a symbol of God reaching into everyone's lives and touching everyone's heart. Everyone who was willing to let him in.

And it was indeed a grand tree. Jack and Josh had gone up into the hills and cut a blue spruce. The tree stood seven feet tall, which brought it almost to the ceiling. It had to be placed between two exposed timbers. They had spent a day decorating it. Placing the candles on it, and hanging the decorations. Some from the childhood of Bree and her brothers. Some from Ma's childhood. Some from Aunt Ginny's. There was nothing from Pa's childhood Christmases on the tree, as those decorations were all back east, but Pa had once gone to the mountains and come back with a pine cone and an eagle feather. Bree made a decoration from it, attaching a metal hook to the pine cone and the feather to the cone with a string. She thought it had a little of an Indian feel to it, which Pa liked because of his days with the Shoshone. It had been on every Christmas tree since. It brought a little of Pa's presence to the tree.

A small stack of gifts was spread beneath the tree, but it was the decorations and the candles that kept Bree's eye.

Aunt Ginny stepped from the kitchen, a cup of tea in her hand, too.

Bree said, "It's a beautiful tree, isn't it?"

Aunt Ginny said, "It surely is."

They sat on the sofa and drank their tea, and looked at the tree and watched the fire.

It wasn't long before Josh came down the stairs, his feet sounding to Bree like hammers on every step. Josh didn't just enter a room, he took it like a force of nature.

"Merry Christmas, everyone!" Josh was not a big man, but he had the kind of voice you would be able to hear all the way off in the mountains.

Josh was fully dressed in a range shirt and jeans, and his riding boots pounded on the pinewood floorboards of the parlor as he crossed the room and placed a kiss on Aunt Ginny's cheek.

"Good morning, Joshua," she said with a laugh. "Merry Christmas."

Josh grabbed Bree's braid and gave it a flip. "Merry Christmas, little sister."

Bree was shaking her head with a smile. "Same to you, loudmouth."

Temperance came down the stairs almost directly behind him, but it was easy not to notice because she moved so gently, taking soft graceful steps. Such a calm, quiet presence in contrast to Josh who had all the subtlety of a thunderstorm. But Bree thought it might be partly that contrast that made them such an interesting couple. They were so deeply in love, and she was sure they had shared a kiss at the top of the stairs before coming down.

A couple of nights before, Bree had been stepping out of her room when she caught them at the top of the stairs.

Josh was saying, "There really should be a mistletoe here."

Temperance looked up at the ceiling. "Well, there's not. Kind of too bad."

"We can pretend, can't we?"

And he took her in his arms.

Bree said, "Come on, you two. You're gonna steam up the windows."

Temperance was in her robe and slippers, her lighter colored braid falling almost to her waist. Josh stopped in front of the tree, and she sidled up to him and slipped her hand in his.

"Now that's what I call a fine looking tree," Josh said.

Jack had spent the night, and it wasn't long before he was downstairs, too.

Josh said, "Good. We're all here. Let's get to the presents."

"Joshua," Aunt Ginny said, peering at him from over her glasses and fixing him with the Gaze. "Breakfast, first."

They gathered around the table. Jack led the family in prayer, thanking the Almighty for their bounty, and asking him to keep Pa and Dusty safe on their journey. Then they dug in. Hot cakes and bacon, and Texas toast oozing with butter.

Josh's long hair, so blonde it was almost white, was tied back in a tail. The way it had been for years.

He said, "I'm thinking on cutting my hair short, like Jack's. Most of the men wear their hair short, these days. Zack does. Darby does."

Jack swallowed a piece of toast and reached for his

coffee. "Don't. You'd look like a chicken."

Bree laughed. Temperance was smiling widely, looking from Jack to Josh. "A chicken?"

Aunt Ginny gave Jack a playfully admonishing look and said, "Jackson."

Josh said, "No, I don't."

"When you used to have short hair, back when we were kids, you looked like a chicken."

"I never looked like a chicken."

Jack looked at Temperance and mouthed the words, Y*es, he did.*

There was more laughter. There was talk of Christmases gone by. Like when Josh tried to sneak downstairs to be the first one down. He was twelve years old and was finally going to beat Aunt Ginny or Pa. He was wearing only socks on his feet, and his socks slipped on the stairs and down he went, crashing to the bottom. Bruised his backside and woke up Bree and Jack with the noise. And Pa and Aunt Ginny were already downstairs, anyway.

After breakfast they went to the parlor. The chinook had passed like it had never been there at all, and the snow was falling and the wind was rattling the windows.

Josh sat on the sofa and Temperance sat beside him.

She said, "I so love this family."

This took the bluster out of Josh. He looked at her tenderly and then pulled her in for a hug, and said, "We all love you too."

Aunt Ginny took to her rocker, and said, "So, who's going to hand out the gifts?"

Jack said, "My turn. This is my first Christmas home in too many years."

Temperance opened a package that contained a new dress.

Josh said, "I went all the way to Bozeman for that."

"Josh, it's so lovely. Thank you so much."

Bree then got a box, also from Josh. She was sitting on the sofa beside Josh and Temperance. She opened and found a gunbelt and holster, both hand-cut and sewn together with buckskin.

She looked at Jack with puzzlement. If Jack had known what was in the box, he would have held it till later.

He looked at Aunt Ginny, with a silent question in his eyes. *Should I get her your gift now?* She smiled and nodded, and Jack got her the box Aunt Ginny had bought in town.

Bree opened it, and found a .22 Colt revolver.

Aunt Ginny said, "It's time. Though, I trust you'll use it responsibly, and not wear it at times when a lady should be wearing a dress."

Bree said, "I don't know what to say. I've always wanted one of these. But you always said no."

"Like I said, it's time. After all, you are your father's daughter."

"Thank you so much."

Josh said, "And I made that holster myself."

She held it up, looking at it. Josh had freshly oiled it, so it gleamed in the light from the candles and the hearth.

"Let me see it," Josh said.

She handed the gun to Josh, and he said, "Pa said the first thing you do when you take a gun is check and see if it's loaded. You do it like this."

He flipped open the loading gate, then squeezed the trigger a bit and pulled the hammer back a bit, and spun the cylinder one chamber at time. Bree sat, watching and learning.

As Ginny sat and watched them, she couldn't help but think about how Johnny and the boys wore their guns so naturally, like their gun was somehow a part of them, but she had always thought a gun would look so unnatural on a woman. As she watched Bree take the gun and check the cylinder the way Josh had shown her, she realized she was wrong. Bree was a natural born gunhawk. She was a McCabe.

PART THREE

The Second Chinook

7

In the McCabe family, there was a saying. It was said to have been originally spoken by the first John McCabe, the frontiersman who fought in the American Revolution and eventually helped settle some of the mountains of western Pennsylvania. He was a man who lived to be nigh onto a hundred and was surrounded by grandchildren, but he still stood ramrod straight and moved with strength. Even as an old man he was often dressed in buckskins, and his old flintlock rifle was never far from reach.

The family saying he had started was, "If you want something done right, don't depend on the government for it. You gotta find a way to do it yourself."

Thomas Peter McCabe had been one of the grandchildren that surrounded the old man. He claimed to have heard the old man say it at least once.

Thomas McCabe ended up marrying a girl named Elizabeth and the two started a farm on the edge of the very mountains the old man had scouted, and raised a small passel of children themselves. Their second-born was named for the old man, and was often called *Johnny*.

Johnny McCabe had said more than once to Aunt Ginny that the old man, the original John McCabe, had been a hero to him when he was growing up, even though Johnny had never the pleasure of actually meeting him. As a boy, Johnny had prowled the woods out behind the farm pretending to be John McCabe, scouting the frontier and watching out for warlike Indians. He would have in his hands a long stick that served as an imaginary flintlock. Even as a man of forty, Johnny had said the old man cast a shadow that stretched over the generations, and was sometimes a lot to live up to.

Aunt Ginny found this kind of amusing, since his children could tell you a thing or two about living in the shadow of a great man.

The old man's saying survived, from one generation to

another. *If you want something done right, don't depend on the government for it. You gotta find a way to do it yourself.* Of course, the old man had been a revolutionary. Born under the rule of England. He had been maybe a small player in the casting off of British rule and starting their own government. But he had been there. He had not signed the Constitution, but he had been an acquaintance of Thomas Jefferson, and had been there when the document was signed. That generation was based on self-reliance and independence, not only in daily life but in the way the government should be run.

Johnny said once, "Another thing the old man used to say is, the government has to be run by the people, not the other way around."

Those sentiments were being taken for granted today, Aunt Ginny thought. Maybe too much so. But it was thanks to the works of the old man's generation that today's people were able to take it for granted.

Johnny McCabe took the old man's philosophies seriously. As much shaped by living in his shadow as Johnny's children were by living in his own shadow. And he put those philosophies to practical use in everything he did. Not the least of which was finding a way to circumvent the mail service.

One thing Ginny found about living in a remote area like this little valley in Montana was that mail service was dreadful. Simply to get a letter from here to her native San Francisco sometimes took months. When she had been a child, to get a letter all the way from the west coast to her late mother's family in Maryland could take close to a year.

But Johnny found ways of getting around delays and inconveniences. In this case, the obstacle was the Postal Service.

The second chinook of the season hit the second week of March. They were in their third day of it as Ginny stood on the porch enjoying a mid-morning cup of tea. Snow that had drifted high against the house and partially covered the parlor windows was now reduced to just a few snowbanks here and there. Ginny stood without even a shawl as she watched a rider approach from the small horse trail off to the west of the valley that led to town.

Ginny knew it was Jack before he even got near the house. She could tell by the way he rode. Every rider has his own unique way of sitting in the saddle, as distinct as the way a person walks.

Some riders never quite got used to it and bumped and bounced along in the saddle, but this rider moved as though he and the horse were one. A tin star was pinned to his vest, and she could see the sunlight gleaming against it even from this distance. A gun was tied down low at his right side. He was, after all, a McCabe.

He reined up at the corral that was a short distance from the barn. Fred Mitchum, the wrangler, walked over to meet him. They chatted a bit, and then Jack walked toward the porch.

"Mornin'," he said.

"Good morning. Have you come to join us for lunch?"

"Actually, I'm playing messenger this morning. Letter from Pa. But as long as you're offering..."

She grinned. "You're always welcome, Jackson. In fact, it's been too long since we've seen you."

He climbed the stairs. "It was hard traveling, with the snow as deep as it was. The snow came late this year, but when it started falling, it really started falling."

He gave his aunt a peck on the cheek, and handed her the letter.

He said, "This came from Pa. A freight wagon came up from Bozeman yesterday. The road is still really muddy, but they wanted to chance a run while this weather lasted. They said it had arrived by train weeks ago, but this is the first anyone has been able to make the trail between Bozeman and here since before Christmas. Apparently Pa and Uncle Matt gave the letter to a train conductor out in California. If they had relied on the postal service, we wouldn't have the letter for a couple more months."

She smiled. Old John McCabe's saying came to mind. She said, "Leave it to your father to find a way."

She looked at the letter. Addressed to:
The McCabe Family
McCabe Gap
Montana

Jack said, "Uncle Matt is a minority owner in the

railroad. When an owner makes a request, I suppose you don't say no."

She noticed the letter was still sealed. "You didn't read it? It's addressed to all of us."

He smiled. "I figured I'd let you have the pleasure of seeing it first."

They walked through the parlor, the central feature of which was a huge stone hearth, tall enough that you could almost walk into it, with an old timber as the mantelpiece.

They passed through an open doorway into the kitchen.

Jack said, "Where is everyone?"

"Well, Josh is off with the herd. He expects this chinook to last three more days. He wants to check range conditions. He may not get another chance for a month, because he expects more snow after this weather passes."

"He's probably right."

"Bree is off riding in the hills, and she took Temperance with her. I think Bree was feeling a little cooped up in here. It was only a few days ago the snow melted enough that they could go riding."

"Four walls do seem to make Bree feel hemmed in."

"And you know your sister. If she's doesn't have her nose in a book, she wants to be on the back of a horse. So, it's just the two of us today."

She poured each of them a cup of tea, and they sat at the table. She tore the letter open.

It was written in Johnny's unmistakable hand. A little jittery, like he wasn't used to using a pen. He wrote it with a quill, and some of the words were a little faded as the pen ran out of ink, and others a little too full after he had dipped the pen. He might have been a master with a gun, but he was surely not one with a pen. But he used words well when he wrote.

Ginny began reading while Jack took a sip of the tea.

Ginny said, "Goodness."

"What's he say?"

She looked up at him over her spectacles. "He writes that he's staying with your Uncle Matt. Some things are going on and Matt needs some help, so your father is staying for the winter. He will be home sometime in the spring."

Jack said, "No mention of Dusty or Zack arriving?"

She looked at the letter. "It's dated from before Christmas. I suppose they hadn't had time to get there, yet."

She became silent. She took a sip of tea and set the cup back down.

"What is it?" Jack said.

"What is what?"

"You're worried about something."

She sighed. "You know me all too well. It's just that your father very vaguely wrote that some things are going on. Knowing your father and the trouble that seems to come into his life, I have to wonder just how dangerous those things are."

"It might be nothing at all."

She gave Josh a look that said, *be serious*. She said, "I know your father all too well."

"You might have a point. But Dusty and Zack are on their way. Very likely they arrived some time ago. You won't find two more capable men than Dusty or Zack."

She nodded in acquiescence. "Too true."

"But you're not satisfied. You're going to worry, anyway."

She let out another sigh. This one was long and slow. "I don't think I'll be fully satisfied until all of our family is together again under one roof."

Jack took a sip of tea, letting her words ruminate for a moment. "It does seem the McCabe way to wander, though. The old man wandered from Lake Huron all the way south to Kentucky before he settled in Pennsylvania. His son, Pa's Uncle Jake, left Pennsylvania to fight the Mexican War. Joined the Texas Rangers."

Ginny nodded. She had heard the story more than once.

Jack continued, anyway. "He brought back the first pair of pistols Pa had. He learned to shoot with them. And they say the first McCabe in this country came from the old country. And my own Uncle Joe. We haven't seen him since I was in diapers."

She gave him a cynical grin. "And you know what?"

Jack returned the grin. "Regardless, you won't be happy until this entire family is safe under one roof."

She nodded and took another sip of tea.

After a second cup of tea, Ginny threw together some chicken sandwiches for lunch.

She said, "Are you sure the town will be safe with you gone so long?"

She meant it with some humor. The town was so incredibly small. Except for the first Saturday night after payday, when things could get a bit out of control, McCabe Gap was so quiet it was sometimes all Jack could do to stay awake.

He said, "Oh, if a crime wave starts up, I think Darby can handle it."

She grinned. "How are Darby and Jessica doing?"

"They're doing great. The baby's due soon. Henry is bringing Granny Tate in every day now to check on her."

They ate in silence for a few moments. Ginny's thoughts drifted to the thought of Johnny making his way by horseback all the way to California. Too stubborn to take a stagecoach. He could have taken the stage to Cheyenne, then hopped a train for San Francisco. But, no. He had to ride the whole way on a horse, and he had to go overland, paying no heed to trails.

She said, "They say the railroad will be here in a few years."

Jack nodded. "I think it's probably inevitable."

"Then, visits to California will be a lot easier for us to make. I haven't seen my family home now for over sixteen years."

"Do you miss the place?"

"Yes. Yes, I do." She was a little surprised at her own answer. She said quickly, "But I have no regrets, mind you. Being here, helping your father raise all of you, was a choice I made willingly and would do so again. I do have one regret, and only one. That I didn't realize what it was you really wanted out of life."

He rolled his eyes. "Now, Aunt Ginny, we've been over this already."

"I know. I just can't help thinking about it every so often. You were off in those classrooms in the east, when apparently you belonged here. I should have seen it."

"You have said before, all's well that ends well. I'm here, now. Right where I want to be. Marshal of the little town of McCabe Gap. I get to visit the ranch any time I want. Except when the snow's too deep. And Nina's in my life. I might not have met her if I hadn't been in Cheyenne last summer. I wouldn't have been in Cheyenne if I hadn't been coming home from school. And if I hadn't gone to medical school, then Nina's father would have lost his leg last summer."

She gave a smile. "You seem to always know the right thing to say."

He returned the smile. "Well, I *am* your nephew."

"How are things going with Nina?"

He smiled. He was making an effort not to blush. "Really well."

They sat and ate, then went to the porch for another cup of tea. They chatted about events going on in town. Gossip Jack had overheard at Hunter's. How business was going for Franklin's general store. Word of things going on in Cheyenne and points in between that he had gotten from Old Hank. They talked of Darby and Jessica. What a fine deputy he was turning out to be. He had been a good friend when Jack had known him at college but had always had a lack of direction, and now that seemed to be gone. He now seemed focused. He acted with purpose.

Ginny talked about how they were running low on lye soap, so she would have to ride out to the Freeman's cabin. Ginny bought her soap from Henry Freeman's wife, Lola.

And then the conversation drifted off to silence, and Ginny's gaze fell wistfully onto grassy flatland that led off toward the center of the valley, and the skies above. Clouds hung lazily.

"You'd think it was early summer," she said.

He nodded. "I tried to explain the chinook weather patterns to other kids when I was at school, but I think everyone thought I was making it up. Chinook winds can be strong, but the ridges here protect the valley. Serve as a wind break. Old Hank said the winds further out were catching the stage and making it hard on the horses."

Ginny drew a deep breath and let it out slowly.

Jack said, "Is something bothering you?"

She thought about that for a moment. "No. I wouldn't say *bothering* me, exactly."

"I'm not going to leave until you tell me. And if I don't leave, then poor Darby will have to handle that crime wave all by himself."

She grinned. "All right. I suppose it's just a feel of change in the air."

"A premonition?" he asked. She had always believed that she seemed to have them. Jack knew nothing of such things and believed much of it to be nothing more than coincidence, but he wasn't about to debate her. Especially on something she felt so strongly about.

She said, "Not really, I don't think. Just a feeling. Maybe it's just because your father has been gone all winter, and now it looks like he'll be gone a while longer. And I have a feeling marriage won't be far away in the future for Josh and Temperence, and I'm sure they'll want to build their own house somewhere in the valley. And then there's the railroad that's coming. It's bound to open up the area. More settlers. The town is bound to grow."

He shrugged. "Change happens. One of the constants of life. The only thing that doesn't change about life is change itself."

She smiled. "Aptly put."

"See? All that schooling didn't go to waste."

After a time, he saddled up and rode off, heading back to town.

She stood on the porch and watched him ride away. She had work that needed to be done. When you run a household, there's always work ahead of you. But instead of returning to that work, she stood and watched while he grew tiny in the distance, and then turned his horse onto the small trail that cut through the woods, and was gone from her sight.

She then looked off toward the center of the valley. Not that much different from any other unseasonably warm day. A *chinook* day. Teases you a little with a taste of spring before the winter winds hit again and drop more snow by the bucketful. But there was something different about this day. Something she couldn't quite put her finger on. Something that brought with it a feeling of change.

And something about that change left her feeling a little unsettled.

8

The weather brought on by the chinook lasted another three days, just like Josh had thought it would. When it ended, it did so in grand style. Temperatures dropped below freezing, and snow clouds flooded the skies from the north. By nightfall, the snow was coming down fast and drifting against the front door, and the winds were whistling under the eaves.

Josh was now home, and was bringing in armloads of firewood, filling up the wood box in the kitchen.

Ginny sat in her rocker by the stone hearth in the parlor. A log was on, and flames were rising two feet high. The warmth radiated out into the room, though every so often the wind would pick up outside and Ginny would feel a cold draft that worked its way in through a window.

Josh stepped into the room. He had shaken the snow off in the kitchen, and left his coat hanging over a chair. A habit Ginny had never been able to break him of. He held his hands out to the heat.

"Cold out," he said. Kind of an obvious thing, but it seemed to be what most people said when they experienced bone-chilling weather.

Bree was on one end of the sofa, and Temperance at the other.

Temperance looked at him, and he at her. Without a word, their love for each other was fully expressed. Ginny had once said you could feel it in the air when these two were in the room.

Seeing a young couple in love always warmed her heart, especially since she had experienced it herself, but these two were like none she had ever seen.

Temperance had a background that would make you think she would never find the life she now seemed to be building. Girls in her place were usually in the throes of old age by forty, and seldom saw fifty. Many died of what those in the business called *old whores disease*. Some sort of venereal thing. The fine ladies Ginny used to have tea with before she moved to Montana would turn pale to hear Ginny use that term, or because she was even aware of it, but she had assisted Granny Tate when a couple of the women who worked for Alisha Summers came down with it. Granny Tate found Ginny to have a good touch for healing, and often called on her when she needed a nurse to assist.

Temperance had pulled away from that sort of life. A lot of folks would credit the McCabe family for taking her in, and the love she felt for Josh. But if she didn't have the spark already in her, then you wouldn't be able to nurture the flames.

Josh was someone Ginny had never seen as one to fall in love. Josh had always been a practical thinker. Too pragmatic to concern himself with abstract ideals. His concerns had always been about the well-being of the herd, range conditions and stock prices. But when he looked at Temperance, Ginny saw the light of love in his eyes.

Ginny was starting to wonder if she knew these children at all, considering how wrong she had been about Jack.

The following morning, two feet of snow blanketed the land. Josh was shoveling off the front porch with a flat-pointed shovel when Ginny stepped out, a coat buttoned tight and a scarf tied up and over her head. She had a cup of tea in one hand, and a steaming mug of coffee in the other.

"Here," she said. "Take a little break and drink this."

He nodded. "You don't have to tell me twice. Thank you."

The cup was made of tin. One of the cups the boys usually took with them when they were going to be drinking coffee at a campfire. She used it this morning because the tin held the heat better than one of her ceramic or glass cups would have.

Josh was in a heavy woolen coat, and a coonskin cap was perched atop his head. His hair was tied back in a tail that fell beside the tail of his cap.

They stood and chatted while he drank his coffee. She took a sip of tea. She still cringed a little at how he and the other men on this ranch could drink their coffee so thick and strong.

"How cold do you think it is?" she said.

There was no thermometer, but Josh could make a guess. "Five above, maybe."

"It doesn't seem as cold."

"That's because the wind died down."

Overhead, the sky was a clear blue and the sun was shining.

She said, "I've now lived through sixteen winters in these mountains, but I'll never get used to it. Yesterday morning, it felt like late spring. Today it's the dead of winter again. Where I grew up, the winters could be cool and rainy, but you seldom saw snow. And the weather didn't change nearly as drastically, from one day to another."

"Sounds like you're missing home a little."

The boy could be as perceptive as Jack.

She shrugged. "This place is now my home. But lately I have found myself thinking about the life I had in San Francisco. I haven't seen the family house, the house I was raised in, for such a long time. Maybe when the train comes through, I'll think about making a visit. See some of the friends I grew up with."

Once the mug was empty, Ginny took it and went back inside. She could smell the scent of bread baking from the kitchen. Something about the smell of good bread in the oven just warmed her. And Temperance was turning out to make some of the best bread Ginny had ever tasted.

Ginny hung her coat and kerchief on a rack by the door and then crossed the parlor floor and stopped in the kitchen doorway. The bread was in the oven and Temperance was cutting up chicken, already preparing for the evening meal. She had done so without asking, and was simply working away. She had an apron tied about her, and a kerchief was tied up and over her hair.

Temperance had been a bit bony when she first moved in over a year and a half ago. She was now by no means fat, but her cheeks no longer looked hollow. Ginny had thought Temperance's eyes had a sort of haunted look when the girl first moved in, but that was now gone. It was as though her past was so far behind her it no longer had much effect on who she was now. Temperance was quite remarkable, really.

Ginny wasn't really surprised. It would take quite a girl to win Joshua's heart.

Ginny now thought of Temperance as family. Temperance belonged here as much as anyone else under this roof. And Josh would probably be making a move soon that would make her even more family.

Ginny then found a question rising within her. Why hadn't that boy asked Temperance to marry him already? It seemed inevitable when you saw the two of them together. They were always discreet, never being demonstrative in public, though Ginny had caught them kissing a couple of times when they thought they were stealing a moment alone.

She and Bree had talked about it once or twice over the winter. What was Josh waiting for? Some men tended to take things like a woman's love for granted, but Ginny would be surprised if Josh did. He was too practical. Johnny had said once, *Never bank on tomorrow's sunshine. The weather might decide to rain.* Josh seemed to live by those words.

And yet, the girl was not wearing his ring.

It then occurred to Ginny what the reason might be. She had always been halfway good at looking at scattered pieces of a puzzle and figuring what the picture might be.

"Temperance," she said.

Temperance looked up. "Oh. Aunt Ginny. I didn't see you there."

"Where's Bree? I thought she was going to be helping you in the kitchen this morning."

Temperance shrugged. "I told her I didn't really need her, if that's all right with you, ma'am."

Ginny nodded. "I understand. She tends to get in the way when it comes to kitchen duties."

Temperance nodded with a smile. She hadn't wanted to say it so Ginny said it for her.

Temperance said, "She wanted to go riding this morning. She said there's nothing like riding a horse through a new-fallen snow. When she's out there on horseback, it's like she's doing what she was born to do."

Ginny smiled. "You have that look about you right now, yourself."

Temperance nodded, returning the smile. "It does feel like it. Running a household is something that seems to bring me contentment. But then, I've had a good teacher."

"Temperance, come with me a minute. There's

something I'd like to show you."

Ginny crossed the parlor to the doorway that led to her room. Temperance followed.

Ginny went to a little cedar box on the dresser and opened it. "This is where I keep my jewelry. Some of it I was given as a young woman, but many of the pieces are heirlooms."

She produced a small ring. It looked fragile, with just a hint of gold to the metal. The stone was small and red.

Ginny said, "The Brackston family first came to these shores in the years before the Revolution. My great-grandfather got his start working the docks in Boston when he was a young man, and eventually built a small shipping empire. His grandson, my father, went to San Francisco and did the same there. The woman my great-grandfather married was from Ireland. He met her when she got off the boat in Boston, and she was wearing this ring.

"The stone is a ruby. A little small, considering the money he would eventually make and the elaborate things he would buy her as the years went by. But it was the first ring she ever had. I am one of only two heirs. The other is the mother of Johnny's late wife."

Ginny handed the ring to Temperance.

Temperance said, "It's really quite beautiful."

"Try it on."

Temperance gave her a look that said, Do *I dare*? And then slipped it on her ring finger.

"It fits perfectly," Ginny said. She had thought it would because she had a good eye for such things.

Temperance held her hand out before her, getting the full appreciation of the ring on her hand.

Ginny said, "I want you to have it."

Temperance then gave her a look that was mixed with the wonder a woman seems to have in her eyes when she's given a piece of jewelry that just speaks to her, and the shock at owning something that is someone else's heirloom.

She said, "Oh, Aunt Ginny. I just can't. It wouldn't be right."

"It's right if I say it is. Child, you're a part of this family, now. The only heirs among your generation are Bree and the boys, and I just can't see one of the boys with a ring like this on their finger."

That got a little giggle. "But, wouldn't Bree..?"

"Bree's getting her share of jewelry. She already has some. But you're family now, too. It would mean a lot to me if you would accept this."

Temperance held her hand out in front of her again. "Thank you so very much. I feel like family now more than ever."

She gave Ginny a hug.

Ginny watched Temperance bound up the stairs to her room, to put the ring in a safe place. After all, she wouldn't want to risk harm befalling it while working in the kitchen.

A wheel had been set in motion, Ginny thought. Now to see what becomes of it.

9

Josh was finished with the porch, then began to clear off the steps. As he worked, Bree walked up from the barn, wading through the snow. He had seen her ride in earlier. She had taken one of the horses out for a romp in the new-fallen snow.

She was in a woolen coat and had a scarf tied up to her chin, and her hair was pulled back in a long dark tail. A wide-brimmed hat was pulled down over her head, and she was in men's levis, which she usually wore when she was riding. He figured she was probably wearing her new Colt under the coat.

She bounded past Josh and off to a snow drift beside the house. The wind had blown it to as much as four feet deep. She charged into the drift until the snow was to her hips. She was smiling wide.

"Oh, isn't it grand?" she said, and held her arms out and spun in a circle a couple of times.

Josh said, "It's grand if you don't have to shovel it."

"Oh, it's so beautiful. Magical."

He went back to clearing the steps. "You'd think you'd never seen snow before."

"Every snowfall is like the first."

Josh stood up from shoveling.

He said, "I was thinking about a ride into town, once I was done with this. Check on things. Make sure Hunter and Jack and the others are all right."

Not that Hunter and Jack and Franklin and all the others weren't capable. But sometimes if something had happened, like a roof caving in under the weight of snow, a little extra manpower was helpful. And town was only three miles away. It was shorter by the horse trail that came out behind Hunter's, but the snow tended to drift deep over that trail and he doubted the horses would be able to get through.

He said, "You want to come along?"

Bree said, "Are you going to wear that funny hat?"

"Hey. Leave the hat alone. It keeps the chill away from my ears."

Josh found Fat sitting in the bunkhouse playing

solitaire, looking like he was about out of his mind with boredom. Josh asked if he wanted to come along, and he jumped at the chance. Josh wasn't sure if it was solely to get away from the boredom, or a chance to ride with Bree.

Fat said, "You look mighty nice today, Miss Bree."

Bree looked at Josh, turning away from Fat as she did so, and rolled her eyes. "Thank you, Fat."

Josh said, "On the way into town, we should check in on the farmers. The Fords and the Brewsters and the Hardings."

Bree said, "I think Jack's probably got the Hardings checked in on, already."

Their horses charged through the snow with a friskiness and a joy that only a horse can manage in the snow. Pa had said they love the feel of the cold snow on their hooves.

The day was warming up a little as they rode. The sun was rising higher in the sky. Josh loosened the scarf from around his head and draped it around his shoulders.

Bree said, "I wish you'd lose that hat."

"Keeps my head warm. Pa has one, too."

"He doesn't wear it to town, though. The hat makes you look like Daniel Boone."

"Daniel Boone didn't wear one of these."

Bree said, "That's right. Pa said the Old Man knew Daniel Boone. Said he always wore a felt hat."

The Old Man. The term they usually used for the first John McCabe.

"But that proves my point," Bree said. "Even Daniel Boone wouldn't be caught in one of those hats."

They rode along a bit. Then Bree said, "So, Josh, when you gonna ask her?"

"Ask who what?"

"You know."

Josh looked at Fat. "Just what in the world is she talking about?"

Fat was grinning. He shrugged his shoulders but said nothing. When Bree was around, Fat tended to become so tongue-tied he was almost mute.

Josh looked to Bree. "What are you talking about?"

"I'm talking about you asking her. When are you

gonna do it?"

Josh was truly perplexed.

Bree said, "We've all been talking about it."

Josh said, "Talking about what?"

"For goodness sake. Is that hat squeezing your brains too tight?"

He shook his head, totally perplexed, and looked skyward like he was asking the Almighty for help.

Bree said, "For goodness sake. You and Temperance."

"Who's talking about us?"

"Everybody."

"Who's everybody?"

"Me and Aunt Ginny. Jack, Nina, Hunter, Mister Chen, Mary."

Mary was Henry and Lola Freeman's daughter, who was a year younger than Bree. Aunt Ginny hired her sometimes to help with the housework, and she and Bree were friends.

Josh looked at Fat. "I suppose you've been talking about us, too?"

Fat shook his head quickly. "No sir, not me."

"I'll bet." Josh looked back to Bree. "Besides, what is it about Temperance and me that's worth talking about?"

"Well," she said, "you have known each other for a while, now."

"What of it?"

"Well, when are you gonna ask her?"

Oh. Now Josh got it. "When am I gonna ask Temperance to marry me?"

"*Bingo.*" Bree almost sang the word.

He said, "All right. Not that it's any of your business, but I've thought about it. A lot. But the problem is, I don't have a ring. I want the best for her. She's had such a hard life until she came to live with us. I want to give her the very best. But where's a man going to find a ring out here? You know how ranch life is. We hardly ever have any hard cash on hand."

"Well, Franklin has a couple of rings in his store. He would probably let you have one on credit. Or you could maybe work out some sort of trade with him. And there's a small jewelry store down in Bozeman."

"No, I mean a *real* ring. A beautiful one. One that'll make her eyes sparkle."

"Josh," Bree said, "her eyes sparkle whenever she looks at you. You two bring out the best in each other. And I'm sure it's no easy thing bringing out the best in you."

She reached over and gave him a punch in the shoulder as she said it. Fat was laughing.

"So," Bree said, "what're you gonna do about it?"

"What I would like to do is not get pestered about it."

"But it's what I do best."

"Ain't that the truth."

They rode along. The pass named after Pa was wide, but the snow had piled deep and the horses had to prance a little to lift their hooves high enough to make their way through. A ridge rose tall on one side, and one slope that was grassy in the summer was now white with snow. Pines stood tall above the slope and along a stretch beside it, and between the pines, the ground was white.

As they rode along, the wind picked up high on one ridge and a shower of snow was lifted into the air and fell on them, covering their hats and shoulders. Bree's horse shook the snow from its head and mane.

The little town was almost buried. The snow had drifted high around Miss Alisha's establishment, and the only sign of life was smoke drifting from the chimney.

The snow was less deep in the area between Hunter's saloon and the hotel, the area that was the closest thing to a street this little town had.

Snow has a way of blowing away from some areas and then filling up others. One area that filled up was the front of Hunter's saloon. It had a drift rising almost to the roof. Hunter had shoveled out the door, but that was as far as he had gotten.

Bree, Josh and Fat tied their horses at the livery stable because Hunter's hitching rail was buried, and as they went into the saloon, there was a feeling of stepping into a deep cavern because of the high wall of snow on either side of them.

It was warm in the saloon. The stove was going, and Mister Chen was putting on a fresh pot of coffee. Hunter and

Jack were at a table. Franklin was with them.

Hunter said, "Chen just baked some muffins."

"Yum," Bree said.

They kicked off the snow from their boots and sat. Josh pulled off his cap, glancing at Bree once as he did so, and shook the snow from it.

Franklin said, resuming the conversation that had been in progress, "I might as well just close up and not bother to open till spring. There won't be enough business to buy a can of beans with until then."

Bree said, "Not until the wagon roads open up again."

The door opened and Henry Freeman stepped in. "Hey, Hunter. Got any hot coffee left?"

"You got the sleigh?" Josh asked.

"That I do."

A sleigh was not an inexpensive item to come by, but Henry's had been provided by everyone who lived within riding range of McCabe Gap. Including Zack Johnson, who lived down the stretch. Granny Tate was the only doctor this side of Bozeman, and it made sense for Henry to have a sleigh so he could get Granny out and about during the winter months.

He said, "I just dropped Granny off at Darby's. She's gonna visit with Jessica a little while."

Granny didn't see patients, she visited with them. Part of helping get a patient well again was learning what they were all about. Getting a feeling for the patient's life. An herb that worked wonders on one might not do as well on another. Granny had said that every patient's treatment was unique.

Henry shook off the cold and sat down at the table, and Hunter placed a tin cup of hot coffee in front of him.

"Much obliged," Henry said.

The door then opened again, and Frank Shapleigh came in. The hotel owner. He sat and Chen brought him over a cup of coffee.

Shapleigh said, "Well, I done it."

"Done what, Frank?" Hunter said.

Shapleigh hesitated a moment, like he didn't want to say what he was about to say. "I sold the hotel."

They all looked at him.

Josh said, "I didn't know it was up for sale."

"I didn't tell anyone. The buyer paid in cash for it. He didn't want me to say anything until he gave me the word. But I just couldn't keep it to myself any longer."

Jack said, "Is this what that business trip to Bozeman was all about, a couple of months ago?"

Frank nodded sheepishly. Apparently a little embarrassed at not saying anything sooner. But not too embarrassed to look at Hunter and say, "That coffee sure smells good."

Hunter brought him a cup.

It was Jack who said, "Who'd you find who would pay cash for it? I mean, it's a fine hotel, but out here in this remote area?"

"A man from St. Louis, by the name of Aloysius Randall."

Josh said, "That name sure is a mouthful."

"He came out on the stage, back in June. Just got off the stage and rented a room for the night. Said he was a land speculator. Checking out potential properties. I told him this area wasn't the best place for land speculators. The nearest incorporated town is Bozeman, and that's a fair ride down the trail. But then he wrote back in November. Said he wanted to buy the hotel. Offered a pretty penny for it, too. Wanted to meet me in Bozeman, as soon as the weather allowed. I rode to Bozeman and sent him a telegram. He caught the next stage. Got here really fast."

Bree said, "Why would you want to sell, Mister Shapleigh?"

"It's not that I was lookin' to sell, exactly. But the price he offered was dang good. More than I could turn away from. And these winters aren't getting any easier. And I got my wife to think of. With the money he's offering, we'll be able to move back east. Maybe St. Louis. Or even back to Cincinnati, where I'm from."

Franklin said, "What would you do there? Open another hotel?"

Shapleigh shrugged. "I might just retire early, considering how much money he's offering."

Jack shifted in his chair. "Maybe I'm just naturally suspicious, but did you ask why someone from all the way off in St. Louis would want a hotel way out here so badly?"

Shapleigh shook his head. "Nope. When someone offers you that much, you don't ask questions."

Jack glanced at Josh and Bree. Bree shook her head. This didn't sound right to her, either. She looked at Josh, and the look in his eye told her he was thinking in their direction.

Maybe she and her brothers were too suspicious. Maybe they had been shot at a few times too many. This is what Zack said was the reason for Pa being the way he was. The reason Pa slept with a gun within reach. The reason if the house creaked at night, Pa was instantly awake. But suspicion is the kind of thing that's hard to shake, once it rears its head.

They drank coffee and chatted. Josh about the herd and the condition they expected to find the range in come spring. Bree about a couple of new foals they were expecting in a few weeks. Henry about the long sleigh ride that was ahead of him—Tom Willbury's infant granddaughter was sick with some sort of fever, and Granny wanted to go out and check on her. Tom Willbury's ranch was easily a three-hour sleigh ride.

"You want Jack and me to come along with you?" Josh said. "That's a long ride in snow this deep."

"No, I don't think so. But thanks anyway. If you don't hear from us, just come lookin' in the spring."

The coffee was finished, and Henry left to go fetch Granny and be on his way to the Bar W. Bree wanted to check on Jessica, so Josh offered to walk with her up to Jessica's and Darby's cabin. Fat went along, too. Not that he had any special interest in Darby and Jessica—he hardly knew them. But he wanted to be where Bree was. Shapleigh returned to his hotel, and Franklin went back to his store to fret about the lack of business.

"You know what would really warm you up?" Hunter said to Jack. "Even more than the coffee?"

He had no idea.

Hunter said, "Chen, could you go get the surprise I got for Jack?"

Chen smiled. "Be right back."

Chen hurried off behind the bar and came back with a

bottle, and handed it to Jack. The label read, OLD TUB. Beneath the drawing of an old wooden tub were the words, KENTUCKY STRAIGHT BOURBON WHISKEY. In the finer print to the bottom of the label, JAMES B. BEAM DISTILLERY.

"Hunter," Jack said with wonder in his voice. "Where did you ever find this? This is some of the really good stuff."

"I ordered a case a while back. It arrived on Old Hank's last stage run, just before the snow."

Jack said with a little regret, "It's a little early in the day to be breaking this open, don't you think?"

Hunter shrugged with a smile. "It might be early here, but it's late somewhere."

"A man after my own heart." He pulled the cork on the bottle while Chen fetched some glasses.

Jack poured a couple of ounces for each of them. Jack knocked back a mouthful and shook his head. "Outstanding. I'm still in awe that you ordered this."

Hunter shrugged. "Gotta have the best for my customers."

"You've got to let me pay you for this."

"You know the rules."

Jack nodded. "You'll never take money from anyone in my family."

Chen said, a glass in his hand, "And with what you pay me, I couldn't pay for this, anyway."

Hunter chuckled. "This *is* your pay."

Jack said, "So, what do you think of Shapleigh selling his hotel?"

"Gonna miss him," Hunter said.

Chen was looking at Jack curiously. "What are you thinking?"

"How much would you say land is worth around here?"

The question was directed at both of them, but it was Hunter who shrugged. He said, "Haven't thought much about it. Can't be worth much, really."

"If you were to sell this place, what kind of price do you think it'd fetch?"

"This place?" Hunter glanced about him and scoffed. "It's home to me, but it ain't worth much. I make barely enough to cover the cost of staying in business. Half the time, when I buy something at Franklin's I have to do it on credit."

"That's my point. How much would you pay for Frank's hotel?"

"Well..." The wheels were turning in Hunter's mind. "The place isn't built all that well, really. Not compared with hotels you see in bigger towns, like Bozeman or Helena. It's a little rickety. But in a town like this, a building that's built entirely of wood is doing well. The first hotel he put up was really not much more than a tent. Wooden framework with canvas walls."

Jack glanced to Chen, then back to Hunter. "So, why would a gent from St. Louis want to spend enough money on it so Frank could retire? How old is Frank, anyway?"

Jack shrugged. "I'd say fifty-five. Maybe."

"Kind of young for a man to retire, unless he's gotten hold of a huge pile of money."

Chen said, "So, what are you saying?"

"Nothing really." Jack took a sip of bourbon. "Just kind of curious, that's all. Whenever someone pays a huge amount of money beyond market value for something, it makes me wonder what's going on."

Hunter grinned. "You have a suspicious mind. Anyone ever tell you that?"

"It comes with being a McCabe."

10

Come the third week of April, the weather began warming considerably. It was still cool enough that you didn't want to step outside for very long without a jacket, but the snow was melting and the streams were flowing strong. The waters of the small lake at the middle of the valley were high with spring runoff.

Some of the ridges still showed a little white, but the valley floor was now free of snow. The grass was brown in some places, but in others was showing touches of green. Fred had turned the remuda loose and they were frolicking in the open expanse of meadow that stretched from the McCabe house to the line of woods at the base of the nearest ridge to the south.

Josh leaned against one fence, watching the horses. One galloped toward another, and the two raised their fore hooves at each other playfully, then engaged in a game of chase, their manes flying wildly.

Fred walked over and leaned one elbow on the fence, watching the horses with a smile on his face. "It's a nice time of year."

Josh nodded. The night would be cold. They often were in the early spring. Probably dipping below freezing. The family would be burning a fire in the hearth tonight for warmth. And there might still be one last light snowfall ahead of them, but for the most part, winter was done.

Perched on Josh's head was a sombrero. It wasn't really a sombrero—a lot of cowhands used the term loosely. It was actually a wide-brimmed felt hat that had been peaked into four corners when he had first bought it, but now the crown was rounded and the brim growing a little floppy.

It was still early in the day. He had finished breakfast about half an hour ago, but was hankering for one more cup of coffee.

Josh said idly, "I've gotta ride out to the line cabin and check on things. See what the herd looks like. We should be starting spring roundup in a few weeks, depending on what I find out there. Prob'ly gonna bring Fat with me. I'll have to hire some men. Maybe a couple extra, because I doubt Pa and Dusty will be back in time."

But Josh wasn't in any mood to get moving. The sun felt warm on his shoulders, and the air was fresh and clean the way it is in spring. He thought he caught the smell of wildflowers. Fred was right. This was indeed a nice time of year.

There was also a hint of peach on the air. There were no peach trees in the valley, but sometimes he could swear there was a hint of it on the breeze.

Fred said, "The roof needs working on. Aunt Ginny was in the attic a week ago and said she noticed a wet spot on the ceiling. Some shingles might need replacing. I can do it, if you'd like. You bein' short-handed, and all."

"No, I can do it. If I sent our prized wrangler up there and he fell and broke his leg, I would never hear the end of it from Pa. You know how he feels about a good wrangler. And he's right."

Fred said, "But on a day like this, it's good to just stand in the sun and breathe the air for a while."

"You ain't whistling Dixie."

"Besides, it's still a little too cool to go climbing up there."

"Exactly. Especially since I hear a second cup of coffee calling to me. And Chen makes great coffee. And I haven't seen him or Hunter or Jack for a week."

Josh remained where he was for a moment longer, appreciating the taste of spring on the air.

He said, "You know what I'm going to do? I think I'm going to saddle a horse and ride into town. Check on things there before I climb up on that roof. And before I head out to the line cabin."

"Spoken like a ramrod," Fred said. "A true leader."

"Why, thank you."

Fred nodded with a smile. "Want some company?"

"I wouldn't say no."

There was a buckskin gelding that was one of Josh's preferred mounts. Second only to Rabbit. It was a cutting horse but the horse and Josh seemed to work well together. A rider wanted a horse that could intuitively anticipate what the rider wanted, and the horse could do it well.

Bree, with her impish humor, had taken to calling the animal Bucky, which was short for buckskin. So Josh said,

"I'd like Bucky, if you think he's ready to ride."

Fred nodded. "I'll drop a loop on him for you."

"I'll get the saddles."

Fred chose a sorrel for himself, and Josh went to the house to tell Ginny that he and Fred would be riding into town for a couple of hours.

They found Hunter, Franklin, Jack and Darby at a table. Jack and Darby normally had morning coffee at Hunter's, but Darby had begun staying home in the morning once Jessica got into her eighth month.

"Darby," Josh said. "What are you doing here?"

"Flossy Knight's with her. She told me to come down and have coffee with Jack and Hunter. She said it might be the last time for a little while."

Flossy had stayed in town after Jack and Darby and the others faced down Two-Finger Walker and his boys the previous summer. She now had a job waiting tables in the hotel's restaurant.

Hunter poured Josh and Fred a cup of coffee each, and they sat down.

"Anything new going on in town?" Josh asked.

He expected the answer to be *no*. The last time he had ridden into town for coffee and that question had been asked, Franklin had said, *Oh, the sun rose and set yesterday. Right on schedule. The wind blew a little.*

Not much happened beyond the usual in a town with a population of less than thirty. One of the things Josh liked about this little town.

But he didn't get the expected answer this time.

Hunter glanced at Jack and Darby, then all of them glanced at Franklin, and Franklin gave a look like he had just gotten a letter saying the Grim Reaper was going to come a-calling.

Hunter said, "Old Hank came through with the stage yesterday. Had some news."

Jack said, "Governor Potts has pardoned Victor Falcone."

"Victor Falcone?" Josh said. "I didn't even know he was still alive, from what Jessica and Flossy said about how Walker beat him up and set him off into the mountains with only a horse and the clothes on his back. And the condition he was in even before that. Just wait till Dusty hears."

"I don't know any of the details about it, but that's what Old Hank heard. It's in the newspaper out of Helena. On top of that, he was wanted for robberies and murder in Kansas and Texas, and in both cases, those charges have been rescinded."

"You mean he's not wanted in those states anymore?"

Jack shook his head. "Apparently not."

Franklin said, "He must have some powerful friends somewhere."

Josh drew a breath. He said, "Well, I don't really know what to think about that. I suppose it doesn't really affect any of us, though. As long as he stays away."

Jack said, "I can't imagine what reason he would have for coming here."

"Has Jessica been told? And Flossy?"

Jack nodded. "I told Darby, and he told them both."

Fred took a sip of coffee. "Anything else going on we should know about?"

Hunter said, "Frank Shapleigh's gone. He and his wife left on yesterday's stage. And on last week's stage, Aloysius Randall arrived."

"What do you think of him?"

Franklin looked from Hunter to Jack, and shook his head.

Josh said, "That bad?"

"It's just that he's going to take some getting used to, that's all."

The front door opened, and Jack glanced over. "Now's your chance to meet him."

A man stepped in. Maybe six feet tall. He had a square chin and a neatly trimmed mustache. A felt bowler was perched atop his head, and he removed it with a hint of dramatic flair and revealed a full hairline and hair that was swept back. He was in a dark gray jacket and a checkered vest and tie. In his hand was an ivory-tipped cane.

"Gentlemen," he said, with just a touch of aristocratic Boston in his voice.

Franklin and Jack nodded. Hunter said, "Mornin', Mister Randall."

"Now, Hunter, I've told you. Please call me Al. All of my friends do."

"Al," Hunter said, correcting himself.

Randall's eyes immediately fell on Josh and Fred. The only two in the room he hadn't yet met. He walked toward them, hand extended. "Aloysius Randall. Please call me Al."

Josh stood and shook his hand. Good firm grip. The man gave a wide smile that was all teeth, and there was a glint in his eye. Made you want to think he was truly grateful to meet you. Randall shook Fred's hand the same way.

Randall said, "Hunter, what do you charge for a morning coffee?"

Hunter shrugged. "It's on the house."

"Much obliged. Can't really turn much of a profit that way, though, can you?" The smile was still there.

Hunter said, "I'm not really open for business yet. I just put a pot of coffee on in the morning, and my neighbors show up. Kind of a community thing."

Randall nodded, "I do so love small towns. You just can't get this kind of fellowship and feeling of community in a larger city."

"Well, if you like small towns, you'll love it here."

Fred looked at Jack and said, "Fellowship?"

Jack said, "Folks sittin' around jawin'."

Fred nodded. Josh laughed.

If Randall had heard, he didn't indicate it. Josh had met men who seemed interested in only what they were saying, not what others were. Maybe Randall was that kind of man. And yet, something about him gave Josh the impression that he missed nothing.

Randall said, in response to what Hunter had said, "In the interest of community, I would love to join you."

Randall looked to Chen, who was behind the bar wiping the dust out of whiskey glasses. "Boy, pour me a cup."

Boy? Josh thought. He hated it when people called a black man or a Chinese man *boy*. One thing you learned real quick on the frontier was that race was irrelevant. Sure, in the bigger towns like St. Louis or San Francisco, the prejudices of civilization could be found. But in the more remote areas, you learned to evaluate a person based on things like courage, work ethic and such. When a blizzard was dropping four feet of snow on you, or your barn caught fire and you needed help putting up a new one, which continent a man's ancestors hailed from stopped seeming so important.

Besides, Chen was old enough to be Randall's father. Possibly his grandfather. And from what Josh had heard of Chen, he could probably put Randall down on the floor with one hand.

Chen ignored the comment, and fetched a tin cup and filled it with coffee and handed to Randall.

The man sat at the table, setting his bowler in front of him, and sipped coffee and listened to the conversation, sometimes joining in to ask questions. Such as, just who Granny Tate was. Jack explained and Randall seemed fascinated. He had never heard of a granny doctor before.

Everything the man did bore a hint of the theatrical, Josh thought.

Finally, Josh decided to ask the obvious question, the one that he figured was probably on everyone's mind. "So, Mister Randall..."

"Al," he said, humbly but with a hint of the theater. "Please, call me Al."

"Al. You seem like a refined city feller. What could there possibly be about a small town like this that would draw you here?"

Jack grinned.

Al said, "You do get right to the point, don't you?"

Al was giving a broad smile. Josh was not amused.

Josh said, "I'm not known for beating around the bush too much."

"Well, it is true I have lived most of my life in larger cities. Yes, I was born in Chicago. Most of my adult years were spent in St. Louis. A marriage that failed, alas, despite my best efforts. And that, gentlemen, is what brings me here. An attempt to start anew, in a simpler land. With simpler people."

Josh didn't like that term *simpler*. Sounded like an insult. If it looked like an insult and smelled like an insult, then it probably was an insult no matter how sugar-coated it was.

But it was Jack who said, "The people of this town and

these hills might be lacking somewhat in formal education, but I would hardly call them simple. In fact, they are some of the least simple people I have ever met."

"Oh," Randall said. "I really didn't mean it to come out that way."

Josh said, "And we're not all uneducated, backwoods bumpkins, either. Jack, here, has a bachelor's degree in biology and two years of medical school behind him."

Randall raised his brows, swinging his gaze over to Jack. "Really."

Jack said, "Our aunt has a classical education. Mister Chen is a Confucianist scholar." Jack didn't know if Chen really was, but what the heck. The man spoke like a scholar of many different things. Chen was smiling.

Jack continued, "Josh's and my sister Bree reads Tolstoy and Dickens for fun."

Randall's brows rose again. "You have a sister? A member of the fairer sex among your community?"

"Don't take her too lightly," Jack said.

Hunter stepped into the conversation. "She arrested one of the more notorious outlaws in the territory by herself last summer. Beat him to a pulp."

Randall was looking from Jack to Hunter to Josh. He wasn't sure if he was being put on.

Hunter said, "I didn't see it happen, but I saw the results. She's a McCabe, through and through."

Randall said, "I truly didn't mean any insult. I just meant that here, people aren't worried about all of the small and foolish things people in the city seem to bother themselves so much with. Here, it's all about survival. Simple, straightforward."

As he spoke, a man stepped in through the door. During the winter months, Hunter often kept the door shut. The batwing doors found on most saloons further south did little good in keeping the cold out.

The man had a long, dark beard. He wore a wide floppy hat that was covered with dust, and a flannel shirt and baggy trousers. His boots were flat-soled and laced up the front. Not the kind for riding, Josh noticed at a glance, but for working on your feet. That meant he was either a farmer or a gold prospector. And this man was no farmer.

Josh knew there were diggings a little south and west of town. A place called Williams Gulch. Gold had been found in Montana, which led to the towns of Helena and Virginia City springing up, and prospectors were digging through the hills trying to find the next mother lode.

"Open for business?" the man said.

Hunter shook his head. "Kind of early in the morning for whiskey."

"I was hopin' for coffee."

"What the heck." He glanced at Chen and nodded, and Chen went and got another tin cup.

Chen brought the coffee to him and the man stood at the bar and took a sip.

"New in town?" Hunter said.

The man shook his head. "Been workin' a small claim out at Williams Gulch. I haven't filed it officially, yet. Haven't seen enough color yet to bother."

Randall got to his feet and approached the man, offering his hand. "Aloysius Randall. Folks around here call me Al. I'm the new proprietor of the hotel. Soon to be renamed the Jubilee Hotel."

"Jubilee, huh?" Josh said, glancing to Jack. Jack shrugged, as if to say, *I have no idea.*

The man shook his hand. "Hayes," he said simply.

"Well, Mister Hayes, it's good to make your acquaintance."

Randall had just violated a piece of frontier etiquette, Josh thought. The prospector hadn't offered his name. As the newcomer to the group, it was his place to do so if he chose. But you didn't ask a man's name, and you didn't offer yours if the newcomer didn't offer his first.

Randall returned to his chair and said to Hayes, "So, you say you're not finding much color up there?"

The man called Hayes shrugged his shoulders. "A little. Not near as much as I was hopin' for. I'm headin' down to Bozeman now, to get it assayed. I was riding through town and I could smell the coffee."

"Well, it's on the house," Hunter said. "I'll never deny a man a cup of coffee on a chilly morning."

"Much obliged."

Hayes finished his coffee and left. He still had a lot of

miles to cover between McCabe Gap and Bozeman. Franklin drifted away, and Fred returned to the ranch. He had some work ahead of him. Josh said he would sit a spell and have a second cup of coffee before riding home. Randall told Josh how glad he was to meet him, then headed back to his hotel. The *Jubilee* Hotel. Josh still wasn't sure he knew what to make of the name.

After Randall was gone, Hunter said, "I miss Frank already."

Josh said, "He's a businessman, maybe. But he gives off the impression that he's running for office."

"No office here for him to run for."

"I still wonder what would bring a man like him all the way out here."

Jack said, "And I still have to wonder why he would be so willing to pay above market value to do so."

Hunter said, "He says he's here because of a divorce. Wants to start over. No better place to do it than out here in a place like this."

Josh nodded his head. "Maybe. But he's trying awful hard to sell himself."

"You boys sure are suspicious," Hunter said.

"Like I said before," Jack said, "it comes with the territory. Besides, I wear a badge. It's my job to be suspicious."

Chen normally preferred tea to coffee, but this morning he poured himself a cup from the kettle and joined them at the table.

He said, "Randall made a big show out of introducing himself to the prospector. Hayes."

Jack said, "He's very theatrical."

Chen looked at him. He did well with English but it was his second language, and sometimes he came upon a word that was new to him.

Jack said, "Like an actor. On a stage."

"Ah." Chen nodded. "Theatrical. Very good. Like in *theater*. Yes, he is *theatrical*. But he has met Hayes before. They already know each other."

Chen had all their attention now.

Chen said, "When Hayes walked in, his eyes went right to the table and held on Randall for a moment. And Randall looked at him for a moment before getting up and introducing himself. They know each other but were trying not to let us know this."

"Why Chen," Hunter said. "You're as suspicious as these two."

"Sometimes it pays to be."

Hunter said, "Sometime, you're going to have to tell me how a Confucianist scholar knows so much about fighting outlaws and things that aren't the way they seem."

Chen gave him a sidelong glance. "I never actually said I was a Confucianist scholar."

11

The second week of May, the snow was gone like it had never been there. The grass along the valley floor had dried out and was turning a bright green. Wildflowers were growing. *Life returns to the land,* Ginny thought as she stood on the porch looking off toward the distance. There were still patches of snow along the ridges, and one peak that was visible beyond the valley still showed white. But here in the valley, spring had taken a full grip.

She stepped down from the porch to the ground. Where the sod had been wet and soft when the snows had first started melting, it was now solid feeling. The day was warm and no shawl or jacket was needed. The sun was warm enough that if she was going to be outside long, she would have gotten a hat.

In the meadow out back, horses were frolicking. Fat Cole was up on the barn roof replacing some shingles, and the hammering rang out and echoed in the distance. Josh had ridden out to the herd and they didn't expect him back until tomorrow.

She took a deep breath of spring air. A beautiful time of year. Her favorite. And yet, why did she feel so melancholy?

Fred stepped out of the tack shed and called up to Fat. Ginny couldn't hear what he was saying. Fat called something back to him, then resumed hammering. Fred went back into the barn.

Ginny thought about a leisurely walk about the grounds. Then she decided against it, and climbed the steps back up to the porch. She hated indecision, and she hated it even more in herself.

She went back into the house. Bree was at the desk, a ledger sheet open and a pencil in her hand. It was unfashionable for a lady to be involved in the nuts and bolts of running a business, but Bree was good with numbers and Josh had said, *Hey, it's one thing I don't have to do.*

She looked up from the ledger. "Hi. Temperance kicked me out of the kitchen so I thought I'd make myself useful."

Ginny stepped into the kitchen doorway. Temperance

had bread going in the oven and was washing the breakfast dishes. A kettle of water was heating for tea, and she had a pot of trail coffee ready for the boys outside.

She said, "Aunt Ginny. There you are. I was thinking of maybe frying up some steak for dinner. But we're running low on lard so, as soon as the bread's finished, I thought I would take a ride into town to buy some from the Freemans."

"It looks like you have things well in hand."

"I guess so."

Ginny went back into the parlor and sat in her rocker. She realized she hadn't planned a meal in days. In fact...how long had it been? She and Temperance had worked together for Easter dinner. Nina and her family had come out, and Hunter and Fred and Mister Cole had joined them.

She thought about the rocker she was sitting in, and where it had been situated in her house in San Francisco. In the sunroom on the second floor, which overlooked the street below and the harbor beyond. Oh, how she used to love to sit and watch the harbor. The ships with their tall masts and full sails making their way in from the sea. On a spring day, she would open the windows and let the air in. She loved the salty tang of an ocean breeze.

She realized, fully realized for the first time, that she was truly missing San Francisco. She wanted to see the old family home again.

It amazed her that she hadn't really felt this way before. She had been away from the city for sixteen years, and was only now starting to miss it.

She thought about the possibility of the train building a line up this way. She had heard no specific plans for it, but she thought as soon as one was built, she would be taking a visit west.

Then the thought occurred to her—why wait? Weekly stagecoach runs from McCabe Gap to Bozeman had resumed now that the trails were clear. And there were a few stages weekly from Bozeman to Cheyenne. From there she could take a train to San Francisco.

Such a thing would have been out of the question not long ago. She was needed here. She was helping Johnny raise her niece's children. She had even come to think of them as her own.

But now the children were not children anymore. And Temperance was here, and she was showing more and more that she could run this household.

Ginny made the decision, then and there, as she sat in the rocker and stared at the dark, silent hearth. As Bree worked away at the ledger and Temperance was a flurry of activity in the kitchen. She was going to San Francisco for a visit.

She couldn't go until Johnny and Dusty returned. She had to know they were home safely. But then, once they were back from California, it would be her turn to go west and visit her old home. Reconnect with old friends. Breathe the ocean air again as it drifted its way in from the bay.

That night, over dinner, she decided it was time to make the announcement. Jack had come out from town to have dinner with the family. She would have liked to wait until the entire family was present, but the entire family was seldom all together in one place anymore.

Oh well, she thought. *No time like the present.*

Jack was talking at the moment about the previous Saturday night. Some cowhands had gotten a little too rowdy at Hunter's and Jack and Darby had locked them in the town's only jail cell until they sobered up.

Jack said, "One of them was Tom Willbury's son."

That got a chuckle from everyone.

"Oh, no," Bree said through a grin.

Willbury was an upright, stern, old-school type of man. Deeply religious and filled with righteous anger. Ginny doubted the man had tasted a sip of wine or beer ever in his life. Let alone allowed himself to actually smile.

She said, "I'm sure that boy got a talking-to when he got home."

Jack was grinning and nodded. "I'd sure like to be a fly on the wall and hear that one."

After the conversation seemed to fall into a short lull, the way it often does between topics, Ginny said, "I've made a decision. I wanted to tell you all about it."

Now there was silence, and all eyes were on her.

She said, "I've been thinking for a while that I might like to visit San Francisco again. It's been a long time since

I've seen my home. And I'm thinking this might be the summer to do it."

After dinner, Jack saddled up and headed back to town. Josh went out for a final walk about the grounds, making sure everything was secure. Fred was in the bunkhouse along with Fat and a man he had hired for spring roundup. They were engaged in a game of penny ante poker that they were taking very seriously.

All was quiet and dark in the barn and the tack room. Josh headed back toward the house, his pistol swinging loosely on his leg. He hadn't bothered to tie it down. He had left his hat in the house, and the evening breeze was cool on his head and ears.

The house stood before him, a dark mass with lighted windows. The smell of wood smoke drifted to him. A smell he always liked on a cool evening.

His eye caught motion on the front porch. Someone was there. He had been heading for the kitchen door, but instead swung toward the porch.

"Hello?" he said.

"It's me." It was Bree.

He climbed the steps. In the light from the windows, he could see she was standing with her arms folded tightly against the coolness of the evening. Her dark hair was tied up in a bun. She was in a skirt, and she wore the light jacket she often wore when she rode the ridges.

Josh said, "What are you doing out here in the dark?"

"Just thinking."

"About something in particular?"

"About Aunt Ginny going to San Francisco."

She was facing out toward the valley, even though you couldn't see far in this darkness. He faced the same direction, grasping a railing with both hands and leaning onto it.

He said, "Yeah, that was kind of unexpected, wasn't it? She's been living here all these years with us. It never occurred to me she might miss San Francisco. This valley, this is where we grew up. It's home to us. But she had lived a lot of years in 'Frisco before we all moved here."

"I have this bad feeling."

"A premonition? Not you too."

She shook her head and cracked a grin. "No. Nothing like that. Just what Pa would call a gut feeling, I guess."

"And what's your gut tell you?"

"That once she's gone, she might not be coming back."

PART FOUR

The Gold Rush

12

The following day, Ginny dug into a trunk in her room and found what she was looking for. Narrowly gauged white yarn and a thin crocheting needle. She then went to her rocker by the hearth and set to work on making a doily.

She had actually been quite good at this, at one time. She had learned from her grandmother, who was an artist at making doilies. Ginny had never progressed to that level, but she was a fair hand at it. Over the years, she had gotten little time to devote to this, but now she seemed to have time on her hands. Temperance was becoming increasingly more active in managing the household, and Ginny didn't feel it would be right to hold the girl back. But it left Ginny with little to do.

She wondered if one day this house would belong to Temperance and Josh. If Temperance would be the woman of the house, and they would be raising children here. Or if they would build their own house somewhere in the valley.

This brought her thoughts to Josh. There was something she needed to give him. An heirloom that she doubted he even knew about, but the time was now right for him to have.

She set her crocheting fixings on the coffee table and crossed the floor to the front door and stepped out onto the porch.

Some of the men were at the corral. Josh was with them, sitting on a fence rail. The stallion Fred had been working with earlier now had a saddle on its back, and Fred was riding it easily around the corral.

Mister Cole was not among them. Ginny saw him stepping out of the barn. He had a lariat coiled up and in one hand and was heading off toward the meadow out behind the house. Probably going to fetch himself a horse and go off and do whatever chore Josh had assigned him.

"Mister Cole!" Ginny called to him.

He ambled over with his long-legged gait. He somehow never seemed to be hurrying, even when he was.

He touched the brim of his hat with one hand. "Miss Brackston?"

"Could you go and tell Josh I would like to speak with him a moment?"

"Yes'm"

Mister Cole turned and began his amble toward the corral.

Ginny stood on the porch and waited. She watched as Josh hopped down from the fence and crossed the grassy expanse between the corral and the house, and climbed the steps to the porch.

His face was streaked with dust and sweat, and he was wearing leather chaps over his levis.

"Aunt Ginny," he said. "Is everything all right?"

"Yes. Come in the house, please."

He glanced down at his chaps and boots. Both were decorated with a layer of dust. "Well, I'm hardly fit to traipse through the house."

"Nonsense. Come with me."

He followed her across the parlor and to her bedroom.

"Shut the door," she said. "I don't want Temperance to hear."

He did as she said. His hat was now in one hand and he stood patiently. His aunt was a woman of mystery, but prodding her would not make her reveal her thoughts any sooner than she was ready to.

"I have something for you," she said, and slid open the top drawer of her dresser.

She removed a small box. It was a maroon color, but looked old. It might have been velvet, once.

She opened the box. He could see a tiny ring was in there.

"This belonged to my great-grandmother, on my father's side." She removed the ring from the box. A thin band and a setting that held a square-cut emerald, and what looked like little diamonds about the edges. "There was money in the family back then."

Josh wasn't surprised. It seemed like every generation of Brackstons managed to somehow find a way to make money.

She said, "This was her engagement ring. Given her by the man who would become my great-grandfather."

She held the ring out to him. "I want you to have this."

He blinked with surprise. "Me?"

"I understand you want to ask for Temperance's hand in marriage, but you are waiting until you can find a suitable ring."

"Bree talks a lot."

"Bree voiced her concerns, and she was right to. Temperance is a fine young woman, and for what it's worth, I totally approve of you bringing her into the family. She's practically a member of the family, already. Your mother was a good judge of character, and I think she would be pleased."

"You want me to offer her this ring?"

"If you are of a mind to. The ring will fit. I already made certain of it, without her being aware of it."

He took the ring in hands that she realized she wished she had asked him to wash before she brought him in here. Josh was one of these men who didn't wear work gloves. His hands were calloused and dirty.

He looked at the ring with wonder. "Do you think she'd say yes?"

Ginny shook her head and smiled. "Joshua, she would be a fool not to."

Temperance called from out in the house somewhere. "Aunt Ginny? Jack's here."

Ginny took the ring back and set it in the box, and then handed the box back to Josh. "Stuff this in your vest. Don't let her see it until the proper time."

He nodded with a smile. "Thank you."

He took her in a hug. Despite his sweaty and dusty shirt, she didn't balk.

They stepped into the kitchen as Jack was setting his hat on the back of a chair.

"Well," Ginny said with a smile. "Twice in two days."

Josh said, "You keep coming out here so often, I'm gonna put you to work."

Jack reached into his vest and pulled out an envelope. "A letter from Pa. The stage came in today. And I have lots of news." He looked at Josh. "News you're gonna want to hear."

A kettle was on the stove. Temperance said, "The coffee's fresh. Sit down and I'll pour you a cup."

Once the boys were seated and each with a tin cup of coffee in front of them, and Ginny and Bree with a cup of tea, Temperance poured herself some tea and joined them.

Jack said, "Old Hank has lots of news from Bozeman. News that's gonna affect us all."

"Hopefully good news," Josh said.

Jack shook his head. "Don't see how it's going to be."

Jack took a sip of coffee. "Remember that Hayes character? The prospector we met at Hunter's a month or two ago?"

Josh nodded. "Chen seemed to think he and Randall knew each other, even though they were working hard to convince us otherwise."

Ginny was listening with a feeling of dread. Josh had told her about Randall and Hayes.

"Well, Hayes has been working out at Williams Gulch. Turns out he's struck gold. Real gold. He showed up at the assayer's office with a few chunks of ore that had serious gold content."

"Ore?" Josh said. "The prospectors out there are only panning."

Jack nodded. "Well, apparently Hayes has been doing some digging. He rode into Bozeman a couple weeks ago with large chunks of ore, and they assayed out to have a lot of gold content. Enough to cause lots of attention."

"What kind of attention?"

"It made the news back east. Apparently in Chicago, and in Boston."

Josh looked from Bree to Ginny. He said, "You know what that could mean?"

"What?" Bree said.

Josh looked back at Jack.

Jack said, "Gold rush."

Bree said, "Would that be bad?"

Josh said, "It could mean people swarming here."

Ginny nodded.

"I wasn't much older than you," she looked at Bree, "when the gold rush of forty-nine happened. We were living in

San Francisco and Father had a successful shipping business. But it was a small, sleepy city, back then. Life had a slow, easy pace. It had an almost dreamlike quality, in some ways. We seemed so cut off from reality. I had family in Baltimore back then. On my mother's side. We visited once, and I was surprised at the faster pace of an eastern city. Hectic. Almost chaotic by comparison.

"But then gold was found in forty-eight, and the next spring saw covered wagons pouring in. Some of the wagon trains were almost a mile long. I had never seen such a thing. The city became a flurry of activity. The worst part of it all was the hydraulic mining. Blasting water at the hills to wash away the soil and expose the ore.

"Wealth was brought to the town. Father's shipping business grew faster than ever before. But even though a lot was gained, a lot was lost, too."

Bree was looking at her with horror. "Could that happen here?"

"I never would have thought so."

Jack said, "Old Hank did some prospecting once. He said he was about as surprised by the news as anyone. He said he has never seen anything about the hills around here that struck him as worthy of getting a prospector's attention."

Aunt Ginny took a sip of tea. "One thing that drew your father to this section of the country was its remoteness. I never thought a gold rush could happen here."

"It may not be so bad," Bree said. "Look at Helena. There was a gold rush there, but it wasn't so big. Not like in forty-nine. Maybe that's all that'll happen here."

"One can only hope."

Jack said, "There's more news. Old Hank knows a man at the claims office. He says that Aloysius Randall has laid a homestead claim for McCabe Gap."

Josh said, "The entire town?"

Jack nodded. "Six hundred and forty acres."

"How'd he get so much?" Bree said. "I thought the homestead act is supposed to allow for only a hundred and sixty acres."

"He applied using the ranching exemption."

Josh said, "He's no rancher. And besides, from what I've heard he has to irrigate every piece of it for the claim to stick."

"Or once he files for a claim, he can buy the claim at twenty-five dollars an acre."

"Twenty-five dollars. Why, that would be..." Josh looked up at the ceiling, doing the math.

Jack said, "Sixteen thousand dollars."

"That's a fair chunk of money. Do you think he has it?"

Jack nodded. "My gut says yes."

Ginny said, "So, he's essentially buying the town of McCabe Gap."

Jack nodded again. "That's what it appears like."

"So this Hayes fellow strikes gold, and then we find that Aloysius Randall has bought McCabe Gap." Ginny looked from Jack to Josh. "Do you think it's related?"

Jack said, "Hunter calls us suspicious. But we're just looking at things the way Pa taught us to."

Bree said, quoting Pa, "If something doesn't look right, assume it's not right until proven otherwise."

Ginny nodded. "Another saying he attributes to the Old Man."

Josh said, "What do you suppose the Old Man would have to say about all of this?"

Jack drew a breath, letting the question knock about in his head for a moment. "I think he would say not to ignore our suspicions, but try to get more facts."

Josh said, "I'm wondering about this gold strike in Williams Gulch, too."

"What are you thinking?"

"Maybe we should just take us a ride out there and have a look for ourselves."

"Boys," Ginny said. "I don't want you getting into trouble. Or starting trouble."

Josh put on his best look of innocence. "We're just going to have a look around. Nothing else. I promise."

Ginny gave a skeptical nod of her head. "Mm-hmm."

The letter from John was on the table in front of her. She tore open the envelope, and with the letter in one hand she brought her cup of tea to her lips with the other. Then she almost dropped the cup.

"Oh, my," she said.

Bree volunteered to go out and ask Fred to fetch a horse for Josh. Of course, Josh preferred Rabbit more than any other horse in the McCabe remuda. Even Bucky. When Josh and Jack stepped out of the house, they found Bree had asked Fred to get a horse for her, also. She had a Winchester tucked into her saddle boot, and had somehow managed to get upstairs to her room and grab her gunbelt without them being aware of it.

She stood by her horse, her hair that had been in a bun now falling in a long tail, and her wide-brimmed hat pulled down about her temples. She was still in the dark gray skirt she had been wearing, but she now had riding boots on and her gun was buckled in place.

"Just where do you think you're going?" Josh said.

"I'm going along."

Josh glanced at Jack.

Jack said, "Why not? I think she's won her right to stand beside us. She whomped White-Eye last summer, and was really helpful when Two-Finger Walker and his boys attacked the town."

She gave a smugly triumphant look at Josh.

Josh said, "All right. Let's mount up."

They took the horse trail that would bring them out behind Hunter's.

As they rode, Bree said, "What do you think of that letter? Pa being married? To some woman he didn't even know until he got there?"

Josh just shrugged his shoulders.

She said, "Don't you think it's kind of sudden?"

Jack said, "Pa never does anything impulsively."

"Well, it looks like he did this time."

Josh said, "I say we wait till he gets home, and then he can tell us about it."

"We all know Pa," Jack said. "I'm sure there's a lot more to it than the letter indicates."

Williams Gulch was the name for a section of the Earth that began as a gulch, but then opened up in a wide ravine. It was mostly gravel and scrub brush. In the spring, it was a small river bed, which made it ideal for panning. In the late summer, the river dried up, and prospectors sometimes scoured the stones and gravel for any specks of gold.

Not that gold hadn't been found here before. A few prospectors had found enough by panning in previous springs to buy supplies. But there had been no digging, as far as they knew.

The gulch was about four miles southwest of McCabe Gap. There was no road, but the few prospectors who worked the area had worn a small trail to town. Josh, Jack and Bree followed this trail, and when they topped one wall of the ravine, they saw what Josh had expected.

The water was about two feet high, which was right for this time of year. A month earlier, it would have been nearly four feet high.

One man was standing in the water, a pan in his hand. Thirty or so yards further upriver, another panner was there.

"No sign of any diggings," Josh said.

Jack sat in the saddle beside him. "There wouldn't be any down here. Any diggings would be up there."

Josh followed his gaze to a slope that began at the far wall of the ravine and rose to a pine covered ridge.

Bree said, "Why don't we just ask some questions?"

Josh said, "I suppose we could do that."

She started her horse down the wall of the ravine. She rode to the water's edge, and called out to a man standing in the water.

He wore levis, which were now wet from the knees down. He had a flannel shirt and a tattered vest. A wild, unkempt beard and an old bowler completed the picture.

"Excuse me," Bree said, and threw on her best smile.

The man looked up and did a double take. He probably hadn't been expecting a girl this far from town.

"We're looking for a Mister Hayes. We're friends of his."

The man said, "Hayes?"

"We're told he has a small claim up this way."

The man nodded. "Yeah. Bert Hayes. Up that-a-way."

He waved with a hand upriver.

She and her brothers followed the water upstream. They found a second man. He was taller, thinner, but otherwise looked a lot like the first one. Tattered clothes. A wild-looking beard. Bree thought these men probably looked older than they were. There was something about prospecting that apparently aged a man.

He said he knew Bert Hayes and the man had a claim a short way up the slope.

The slope he spoke of was a gradual rise, covered with pine.

Josh said, "We could ride through those woods all day and not come across his camp. That's a lot of woods. Probably five hundred acres."

Bree sighed and shook her head, feeling a little defeated. "He has to come down sometime, right? Maybe we should just ride across the base of the slope, cutting for sign."

Jack smiled. "I do believe our little sister has listened to Pa more than we realized."

They did as Bree suggested, and found an old trail. There were no tracks, as there had been some rain a couple of days before. But there was a trail worn into the earth.

"This is no game trail," Josh said. "This was made by a horse. And it's well worn. It's been used a lot."

They followed the trail up the slope.

After a short while, they came to a camp. A canvas tent was set up, and the remains of a campfire were in front of it. Behind the tent a trench had been dug.

There was no horse or mule picketed. The only activity in the camp was made by one tent flap, fluttering a bit in the breeze. The camp looked deserted.

Josh swung out of the saddle and reached into the blackened ash of the campfire.

He said, "It's cold. No one has been here in days."

They left the horses ground hitched and walked out behind the tent to have a look at the trench.

Josh said, "I don't know much about prospecting, but it looks to me like he dug a trench in the dirt. Nothing else."

The trench was three feet wide, and about ten feet long. Jack walked into it.

He said, "There's no outcropping of rock. Nothing to get ore from."

Josh said, "I wish Old Hank was here with us."

"I don't know much about prospecting, but it would seem that you have to dig it from rock. It's not going to be lying loose in the dirt."

"There was no ore here."

Bree said, "Then, where did he find it?"

Josh sighed bitterly. He hated a mystery. "That's a good question."

13

The first train of wagons arrived eleven days later. Jack had joined Darby and Charlie Franklin and Henry Freeman for coffee in the morning, and as Jack was stepping from the saloon, he saw the wagons approaching. The first building you passed on the trail that was called the McCabe Trail was the hotel, and the first wagon in the train was holding up there.

Twelve wagons in all. Four looked like freight wagons, and the rest were conestogas with white canvas stretched over wooden arches.

Aloysius Randall had a number of lots divided off and marked at the corners with wooden stakes. Essentially, he was building a town. The expanse of grass and dirt between Hunter's saloon and Jack's marshal's office had been sectioned off into three lots.

Jack said to Hunter, "I just had a thought. You did claim your land down at the land office in Bozeman, didn't you?"

Hunter was silent.

Jack said, "Hunter?"

He shrugged. "I always meant to. But I never saw the hurry. We're way out here in the middle of nowhere."

Jack said, "Randall has claimed six hundred and forty acres. It looks like he's dividing off lots to sell. I'm no lawyer, but I don't think he'd be able to sell it if he didn't have title to the land. That means he's paid the fee to buy it."

"And my saloon is right smack dab in the middle of it."

"Off to the side a little, I'd say. But essentially, yes. Your saloon sits on land now owned by Aloysius Randall."

Over the next two weeks, three more wagon trains pulled into McCabe Gap. A line of freight wagons came up, too, carrying various supplies but mostly milled lumber. Two-by-four frameworks were being set up on lots folks had purchased from Randall.

Randall had his men post a sign at the far edge of the first of two streets he was building, welcoming folks to the town. Except it didn't identify the town as McCabe Gap. The sign read WELCOME TO JUBILEE.

Jack saw the sign during his morning rounds. He went to the hotel and knocked on the door of Randall's office.

"Mister McCabe," Randall said, from where he sat behind a desk. "Come on in."

The desk was a roll top, standing against one corner. Randall was in an office chair with small wheels at the legs, and spectacles were perched on his nose. Without his hat, he struck Jack as having a long face.

Randall's jacket was off, and he wore arm garters. Randall's hairline was thick, but Jack noticed his hair was thinning at the top of his head.

Jack asked his question with one word. "Jubilee?"

Randall nodded with enthusiasm. "I had to come up with a name for my little town. How do you like it?"

"First of all, it already has a name. The place is called McCabe Gap. Second of all, it's not *your* town. There are a number of residents who live here. A community, as we talked about when you first moved in. The town belongs to the community."

"It was said that you attended medical school, is that right?"

Jack nodded.

"It wasn't law school. Otherwise, you wouldn't be asking that question. With the exception of the land I've already sold, I actually own every square inch of this little hamlet. Including, I might add, your quaint little marshal's office."

This hadn't occurred to Jack.

Randall continued, "But then again, it's not really a marshal's office, because you're not really an officer of the law. This is an unincorporated community. You have no official status at all. That badge you wear is little more than an empty disguise."

"It means something to the folks that live here."

Randall chuckled. "The folks who live here. Quaint indeed. You have to realize the population has almost tripled this week alone. Those *folks* you refer to are now an ever decreasing minority. But the unincorporated status won't last much longer. As soon as we have the necessary population, which should be soon, I'll be filing for incorporation with the Territory of Montana. Then we'll see about electing an actual lawman."

"There are people who live here. You can't just uproot their lives like this."

He smiled and held his hands out before him. "I already am."

Jack returned to his office, and stood on the small deck out front, letting that conversation play about in his head. He was thinking he would like a cup of coffee, but to brew up some coffee he would first have to fire up the wood stove, and the day was much too hot for that. Maybe a beer at Hunter's would hit the spot better, anyway. Or even better, a glass of that bourbon he had shipped in.

As he was thinking about this, he saw Bree riding along the newly forming street. She had left the house for a morning ride through the mountains, but her curiosity got the best of her and she wound up in town. She reined up in front of Jack.

"I've never seen anything like this here," she said.

Jack said, "I wouldn't have thought any of this was possible."

Darby was taking some time off. Jessica had given birth, and Darby was staying home with her. And the cabin he built was now also on Randall land.

Jack said, "I'm heading over to Hunter's for a drink. Want to come along?"

This surprised Bree. "For a drink?"

Jack shrugged. "How old are you?"

"I'll be eighteen in the fall."

"Aunt Ginny would kill me."

"Spoil sport."

Across the newly formed street, Aloysius Randall stepped out of his hotel. His hat was once again covering his thinning hair and his jacket was in place, and he was striding as with a purpose.

Two men were with him. They had shoulders that filled out their shirts, like men who used muscle for a living. One wore a dark cap with a short brim. Jack had seen some of the seamen out of Boston wear them. This man had a face that looked like it had taken punches before. He wore a pistol holstered to his belt. He didn't look at all like a gunman, but like a fighting man who might also know how to use a gun.

The other man looked more like a westerner. A hat with a wide brim, a vest over his shirt. He wore a gunbelt that looked like a military holster with the flap cut away. He also had a face that looked like it had taken some punishment.

"Here it comes," Jack said.

"What?" Bree asked.

"Wait here."

Jack stepped down and walked toward Hunter's.

Randall got there first. He and his two thugs stepped in, and Jack was right behind them.

Hunter was standing by the center of the room, the woodstove behind him.

He said to Randall, "I've been expecting a visit from you."

Randall nodded. "You're an astute man. By now, I'm sure you're aware that I own all of the land in this little community. Except for the lots I've sold in recent days."

Hunter glared at him from under thick brows. He looked like a grizzly who was growing annoyed.

He said, "Get to the point."

"This establishment of yours is in a prime area. Right at the corner of what I'm calling Randall Street and Main Street. Randall Street, of course, being the one you first encounter when coming in from Bozeman, and Main Street being the other one."

"So you want me off this land so you can sell it for top dollar."

"Not necessarily. Your saloon is well known for miles around here. It's a drawing card, to some extent. When one business succeeds in a town, it has a ripple effect. What I'm willing to do is sell you this lot for, say two dollars a square foot. That's not a bad price. I marked each lot off at one hundred square feet. So, for two thousand dollars, you can have the title to your saloon."

"Two thousand dollars? That's more than four times what a lot that size is worth."

Randall shook his head. "Value is in the eye of the purchaser. Price is set by the seller. In this case, me."

"I don't have that kind of money."

"Then I give you a week to vacate the premises so we can bring down this log-built eyesore of a structure. It's bringing down the real estate value."

"You're giving me a week to get out of my own saloon? What's to stop me from breaking your scrawny little neck like a stick?"

Both of Randall's thugs took a step toward Hunter.

Jack had come in behind them and stepped off to the side. Randall and his thugs had been focusing all of their attention on Hunter, so they weren't aware Jack was here until they heard the hammer of his pistol click back.

"Gentlemen," Jack said. "Back off."

Randall looked at him with a smile. Not a smile of amusement or warmth, but that of a triumphant player who knows he is fully in command of the game.

He said, "That badge means absolutely nothing. You have no real authority here."

"The badge doesn't, but this gun does."

"You'd shoot me down in cold blood?"

"I will if you don't leave. If Hunter tells you to leave and you don't, then no frontier court would convict me for putting a bullet in you. Especially with the two apes you brought in. I really doubt you hired them as business consultants."

The man in the sailor cap chuckled. "Business consultants."

Randall said, "Shut up." To Jack, he said, "Hunter hasn't told us to leave."

Hunter said, "Leave."

Jack said, "There you go."

The one with the sailor cap said, "I think we can take him, Boss."

Randall said, "Don't be foolish. You wouldn't survive against a McCabe. Especially with his gun already out."

The man blinked and audibly swallowed at the mention of the name, and took a step back.

"Now," Jack said. "I'm going to count to three."

Randall shook his head and rolled his eyes with disgust. The smile now gone. "No need to be so dramatic."

To his men, he said, "Let's get out of here."

Jack watched as Randall strode out the door and his two bruisers went with him. He then went to the doorway and made sure they were crossing the street. Pa had told him to always be careful that the enemy doesn't double back on you. Jack had studied history in school back east, an elective on his way to medical school, but when it came to battle strategy, he didn't think Napoleon had anything on Pa.

"They're gone," Jack said.

Hunter walked up behind him. "I think we've both made an enemy today."

Jack told the family about it over dinner that evening.

Josh said, "Randall is going to be trouble."

Jack nodded. "I think he confirmed that today. He already mentioned to me that he owns the land my office is on. I doubt he's going to wait much longer before approaching me about it."

Bree said, "Do you think he's going to try to sell you your office?"

Jack shook his head. "I think he's going to try to force me out."

Josh said, "It'll be a cold day in..." he glanced at Aunt Ginny and amended his words before they got out, "in you-know-where before a McCabe can be forced out of anywhere."

"Unfortunately, Josh, he has the clout of the law behind him. We were all blissfully insulated here for a long time. But now the law is here, and prowess with your fists or a gun will no longer be the deciding factor."

Josh didn't like the sound of that. He wanted to argue it. But he knew Jack was right. Josh's lip curled with the anger he was holding back. Temperance reached over and took his hand and gave him a look that said, *I love you, but calm yourself down.*

Jack was struck by just how much a woman could put into just her gaze.

Josh looked at her, and then chuckled in spite of himself. He looked at Jack and said, "Well, you spoke that like a true college boy."

"I am what I am."

"What say you get away from town for a while, and ride with me tomorrow? Get some real work in? Put some callouses on those schoolboy hands of yours? We're a man short at the moment, and we've got about a couple hundred head to move into the valley. The grass is green and they've just about grazed out the range they're on. The rest of the herd are going to be moved out to the northeast corner."

Jack said, "That might be a good idea. Watching what's happening to the little town is going to give me an ulcer. Besides, as Randall was so eager to remind me, I don't have any real authority in town, anyway."

14

    Jack hadn't done much cattle work in years. But it was the kind of skill you retained. Once he was in the saddle, with leather chaps strapped to his jeans and a lariat in his hands, everything fell into place.

    The last time he had done this was when he was fourteen years old, working alongside Pa. Josh had been there, too. And Zack Johnson. This was before Zack had started his own spread. It had been just the four of them, moving the herd from one range to another. But now it was Jack working alongside Josh and Fat, as well as a cowhand Josh had hired a couple of weeks earlier in town.

    The new cowhand's name was Kennedy. That's the only name he gave, and you didn't ask further. Josh said he had sized him up and thought he would be a good man. He wore a pistol high on his hip, which meant he was no gunfighter. But that was fine. What they needed at the moment was a cowhand, and Kennedy was showing he was all of that.

    He was mid-twenties and wore a wide-brimmed sombrero. His hat was actually a Mexican hat, so the word *sombrero* applied. He wore spurs with big rowels, which Jack knew was more common in the southwest than here in the north. Jack and Josh each wore spurs with smaller rowels.

    Kennedy wore his spurs wherever he went. When he pulled off his boots at night, the spurs stayed on his boots. Jack and Josh both took their spurs off. Pa had said once that there were times when a man needed to move silently, and the jingling of spurs can give you away. Even if they didn't jingle, they sometimes made the leather of your boot creak a little when you walked along. Pa always took off his spurs when he was done riding.

    To move a herd from one range to another, first you have to conduct a small round up. Cows tend to stray as they graze. A longhorn can run like a horse, so they tend to roam. The first day Jack and the others rounded up the ones who had roamed too far. Then it was a case of getting them moving.

    There was always one or two lead steers. Jack had no idea how the herd chose them, but once you got them moving, the rest of the herd tended to follow. It was this way over a long-distance trail drive, and it was this way when you were just moving the herd twenty miles from one range to another.

One steer decided he didn't want to move with the herd. Apparently feeling independent. Jack turned his horse and went charging after him, and he cut in front of the steer and turned it back toward the herd. Nothing like a good cutting horse. This one was a palomino Bree had named Pal.

Funny how you can be working and concentrating on the task at hand, but part of your mind could drift off toward other things. Part of Jack's mind was focused entirely on keeping the cows moving, and chasing after any who decided to stray. But the other part of Jack's mind, the part that wasn't on work, was thinking about Pa.

How they worshipped him. Jack and Josh. And even Bree, in her own way. How they tried so hard to be like him. Dusty didn't try, because essentially he *was* Pa. In all the ways that counted, at least. A younger version of him. But Jack, Josh and Bree. They were forever living in the great man's shadow.

But funny how distance can give you objectivity. While Josh and Bree had been living right here on the ranch, in the daily presence of the man, Jack had been away back east, attending school. And since he had been home, Pa had been gone. Off to California to visit Ma's grave. Jack had seen very little of him.

Years ago, when he had been Jack's age, Pa had found himself on the wrong side of the law. Jack didn't really know the whole story, but Pa's name had been on a reward poster for a while. As had Jack's uncles, Matt and Joe. But there was so much about Pa that Jack didn't know, and he didn't think Bree or Josh did, either.

When Pa went to bed at night, he kept his Colt within reach. When the house creaked at night, the way a house will, Pa was instantly awake with the gun in his hand, and wouldn't go back to sleep until he had walked the house and made sure the creaking sound was just that.

The man went everywhere with a pair of buckskin moccasin-style boots in his saddle bags. He also carried an extra gun in those saddle bags.

Jack's mind was brought back to the task at hand. The cattle. Another steer was trying to break away from the herd. It was too far away for Jack to pursue and he was going to call to Josh, but Josh saw it on his own. Jack saw Josh turn rabbit toward it and chase it down.

Jack's thoughts returned to Pa. Zack Johnson had said Pa had been shot at one time too many. That's why Pa was the way he was. But Jack wondered about that. He wondered just how many times Pa had been shot at. And how many times Pa had been forced to kill. It struck Jack as not normal to sleep with a gun within reach. It wasn't normal to wear your gun when you were just going out back to the outhouse. When Pa stood outside talking about cattle or horses or the various things a rancher talks about—range conditions, cattle prices—his gaze was often drifting about, from nearby trees where snipers might lie in wait, to the earth about his feet, searching for tracks of anyone or anything that might not belong.

Jack and Josh and the men slept in one of the line cabins that night. The McCabe ranch actually had three. Josh had brought a bottle of bourbon with him from Hunter's. Kennedy had begged off. Never touched the stuff, he had said. He rolled into his bunk and went to sleep. Jack, Josh and Fat passed the bottle back and forth, sitting by a small cast iron stove. It was still June, and the nights at this altitude could be cold.

Jack thought about mentioning his ruminations about Pa to Josh. But then he decided against it. Partly because Fat was sitting here. Family business shouldn't be discussed in the presence of outsiders. Fat was a good man and had been working at the ranch for a year or two. A friend and a good hand. But he wasn't family.

Another reason Jack didn't bring it up was because even though he and Josh were both living in the same shadow, it didn't affect them each the same. Josh idolized Pa. At times he maybe fought too hard to become his own man, but even then he wanted to be his own man in the way that Pa was. To Jack, however, living in Pa's shadow was becoming a burden. It had haunted him back at school, and even now it still did.

Jack didn't think Josh would fully understand this. So

instead he drank his bourbon and laughed along with Josh and Fat.

In the morning, with the sun barely peeking above the horizon, they were saddled and on the move. Jack's head was hurting a little from all of the bourbon the night before, but he had poured two cups of strong, black trail coffee down his gullet.

Josh and Jack left Fat and Kennedy at the line camp. Cows tended to wander a little when they were first introduced to a new range. Even though they had grazed here the summer before, cows tended to have short memories. Fat and Kennedy were to keep the cows from roaming too far. Josh would ride back out in a few days and check on them.

Josh was in a hurry to get back home. He wanted to spend the afternoon with Temperance.

As they rode, Josh said, "I'm going to ask her the question."

Jack's head was still hurting a little from the bourbon. What he was thinking about was the pot of trail coffee he hoped Aunt Ginny or Temperance had on the stove. It took him a moment to fully take in what Josh had said.

Jack said, "What question?"

"*The* question. I'm gonna ask her to marry me."

Jack looked at him with a big grin. "Why, Josh. Congratulations."

"Well, she hasn't said yes, yet."

"Is there any question?"

"Well, Pa said not to bank on tomorrow's sunshine when it might decide to rain. But I have to admit, I'm like a kid at Christmas. Full of anticipation, but scared to death."

"Josh." Jack shook his head. "She'll say yes."

"How can you know for sure?"

"Because I've seen the way she looks at you. She says yes every time she looks at you."

They arrived at the house by mid-morning, and Jack found a pot of coffee waiting for him. While he poured a cup and sat at the table to drink it down and let it work its coffee magic on his headache, Josh went about drawing a bath for himself.

While Jack sat indulging in his coffee, Temperance's

voice drifted in from the parlor. "But Josh, I can't just up and leave like that for the afternoon. I need to help Aunt Ginny with dinner. And there's a pig to slaughter. Fred's getting the smokehouse going, now."

Josh had just filled a bucket with hot water from the stove and was on his way upstairs. Jack heard him say, "It can wait."

"But..."

"Aunt Ginny can handle things. She may have to put Bree to work."

Jack smiled. Temperance had no idea of the wonder in store for her this afternoon. Jack had once seen a college classmate ask a girl to marry him. Jack had seen him open the ring box and ask the question, and watched the girl's eyes sparkle. Something about a man asking a girl to marry him. For the man, it could induce anxiety. Would she say yes or no? But for the girl, it could be the stuff of dreams.

Once Josh was done with the bath tub, Jack thought it might be a good idea. He heated some water and filled the tub.

When Josh and Temperance were leaving in the buggy, Jack sat and soaked for a while, a cup of coffee in hand. And then, freshly shaven and in clean clothes, it was time to return to town.

There was one section of woods that had always been special to Josh. When he needed to be alone, this was the place he went to. When he was missing Ma, he went here. He had taken Temperance to this place twice, and it was to this place he took her now.

To get to this little section of woods, you had to go down the horse trail that came out behind Hunter's. Most of the trail was too narrow and rugged for a buggy, but the first half mile or so was good enough for wagon wheels, and the first half mile was all he needed.

He then left the buggy and he and Temperance went in on foot. It wasn't a long distance. He had a picnic basket in one hand. He wore a white shirt and a black string tie. He had taken the time to wipe the dust from his riding boots and his gunbelt.

Temperance was in a blue checkered dress and her

hair was pulled back across the top but hanging freely down her back.

"I love this place," Temperance said. "It's so quiet and peaceful here."

Jack spread out a blanket on a section of grass that overlooked a small brook. Maples and birches were standing tall about the little expanse of grass, like silent sentinels. Behind them, a ridge rose high and was covered with a pine forest. The very ridge where Bree had found Nina the previous summer.

They sat on the blanket and Josh opened the basket. Aunt Ginny had made up some fried chicken parts for them and there was a glass tub of potato salad. And a bottle of white wine and two glasses.

Ginny knew what Josh's plan was for this afternoon, so she had looked into her wine collection and gave him a bottle of Riesling that was twenty years old.

He dropped his hat to the blanket, then used the corkscrew his aunt had provided and dug it into the cork and slid the cork out.

They enjoyed a glass of wine, laughing and chatting about the kind of things a young couple in love chats about. Nothing of any consequence. Pure small talk. And yet, when you're with someone you love, it's of the most consequence.

They ate, and then Josh got to his feet and began pacing off the section of grass.

"What are you doing?" Temperance said with a laugh, her glass once again filled with wine.

"Marking off our house. This will be the perfect place to build, don't you think?"

"Our house?"

Josh walked back to the blanket and knelt down in front of Temperance. He reached into his vest pocket and came out with the ring box.

"I've been waiting for the right moment," he said, and opened the box. "This was the ring worn by Aunt Ginny's great-grandmother, when she became engaged to be married. I would be honored, Temperance, if you would consent to be my wife."

She stared at the ring, tears in her eyes. The wine glass in her hand was now forgotten.

"Oh, Josh."

He took the ring from the box and held it out to her. She went to extend her left hand to him, and then remembered the glass and set it down. He then slid the ring onto her finger.

"A perfect fit," he said.

"Just like us. Yes. Yes, I'll marry you."

With the ring on her finger, she gave Josh a long kiss. And then they walked about the flat section of grass, deciding where the bedrooms would be. The kitchen. She wanted their bedroom and the front porch to both overlook the little brook. He would cut a trail in from the horse trail. A barn would be put up over toward the edge of the small clearing. A few trees might have to come down, but he would take as few as possible. He wanted to insert the house into this clearing without in any other way disturbing the tranquility of it all.

They stood, his arm over her shoulders and her head nestled on his shoulder, looking off at the brook. He wondered if anyone else in the world knew the happiness he did at this moment.

Jack decided on one more cup of coffee before he began the ride back to town. Aunt Ginny caught him in the kitchen and said, "Are you busy tomorrow?"

He shrugged. "Not especially, I suppose. Since I apparently no longer have a job."

"I need you to ride down to Bozeman for me. I have an errand that needs to be tended to. I would ask Fred to hitch up the buggy, but you would make better time on horseback without having to drag an old woman along."

She just realized she had referred to herself as an old woman, again.

He said, "I'm going to ride to town and check on things. After all, Hunter and Franklin and a few others hired me to be their marshal. I should make sure they're all right. And I'll check in on Darby and Jessica while I'm there. Then, I'll ride back out and spend the night here so I can get an early start tomorrow for Bozeman."

He rode along the horse trail and passed the buggy. It was empty and the horse was looking bored. Jack smiled. He figured Josh would take Temperance here. It had always been Josh's private place. Jack and Bree both knew about it, even though Josh wasn't aware that they knew.

The time was coming soon when Jack would need to make some decisions regarding his future with Nina. This would involve deciding where they were going to live, and what type of work he wanted to do.

Until recently, he had figured he would work as the marshal of McCabe Gap. They could have a small cabin nearby, like Darby and Jessica did. They could have a garden out back, and Jack could possibly work roundups for the ranch. He was one-sixth owner of the ranch, so when cattle were sold he automatically acquired one-sixth of the profits. But he felt better not just taking the money, but earning it.

Now, with the little unincorporated village of McCabe Gap being transformed into the town of Jubilee, soon to be incorporated, Jack's status of town marshal no longer existed. It never had existed officially, anyway.

So, now he had to decide what he was going to do for a living. Did he want to just work for Pa and Josh for a wage? Jack and Nina could build a house a short distance from the ranch so he could ride out to meet Pa and the men every morning.

There was also the option of farming, like Nina's family did. And the other families who had come west with them. The Brewsters and the Fords. Jack and Nina could build a small farm down toward the center of the valley. But he really couldn't see himself farming. He was too much of a cattleman to ever find peace working the land.

He followed the trail to where it came out behind Hunter's. His head was no longer hurting, but the thought of a bourbon was still unappetizing, so he rode past Hunter's and out to the newly forming Main Street of Jubilee, and to his office.

Except his office was no longer there. The entire lot was empty. It was like someone had somehow lifted the building and carried it off.

He sat in the saddle and stared at where his office had been. How does an entire building just disappear? He blinked his eyes a couple of times and looked again. Was he losing his mind?

He didn't even hear Hunter walking up behind him.

"It's gone," Hunter said. "Yesterday, Randall had some men come in and tear it down. They hauled off the lumber in buckboards. Hauled off the wood stove. I made a point to tell him the guns were given to you by Franklin, so he let me have them. They're back at the saloon."

"He just tore it down?"

Hunter nodded. "I wanted to stop him, but there wasn't anything I could do. He owns the land. Has clear title to it."

"Doesn't mean he has ownership of the building on it."

"He said it did."

"We'll see about that."

Jack turned his horse and covered the open expanse between where his office had been and the hotel. He swung his leg around the saddle but didn't take the time to step down. He jumped out of the saddle and landed on his feet, gave the rein one turn around the hitching rail and strode into the hotel.

He cut through the lobby, through a curtain and into a hallway, and to the office. Shapleigh's old office, which now belonged to Randall.

He stepped into the office without bothering to knock. Since Randall had totally demolished his building and hauled it away, Jack no longer felt obliged to knock on the door before barging in.

Randall was sitting at his desk, going over what looked like a ledger book. His hat and jacket were on a small stand in one corner, and spectacles were on his nose.

He looked up with surprise at the sudden intrusion. Then he said, "Mister McCabe. I should have been expecting you, I suppose."

Jack heard footsteps behind him, and looked over his shoulder to see one of Randall's thugs behind him. The nautical-looking one.

Jack said to Randall, "I was told you tore down the marshal's office yesterday."

"Yes. It's my lot, and I did with it what I chose to. That's prime commercial real estate, Mister McCabe. I need the lot empty if I hope to fetch a price for it. I already have a blacksmith interested. And the bank down in Bozeman is considering opening a branch up here."

"That building wasn't yours. It belonged to the people who built it. The people who made up the community of McCabe Gap."

"I beg to differ. Sue me if you want. But by the time the courts get around to hearing it, there will already be a new business on that site. And believe me, I have good lawyers."

"We had a nice little community here. Then you came into this area, from out of nowhere, and you started destroying everything. Why?"

Randall let out a long, weary sigh, then set his spectacles on the desk and rose out of the chair. "Mister McCabe, I am not destroying anything. I am building a town. I am taking what was in fact a little backwater community, and I'm bringing civilization to it. This is called *progress*. One can't stand in the way of progress. And why am I doing it? For profit, of course. There's money to be made here. Gold has been found. And gold isn't the only source of revenue in a gold strike. There is profit in the fact that the miners have to be serviced. They need supplies. They need lumber to build their homes with."

"Forcing out a good man like Hunter. How is that progress?"

Randall shrugged. "It's regrettable. But sometimes, if you're going to make money and be an agent for progress, you have to be willing to make some hard decisions."

"And you tore down the marshal's office when I was out of town because you knew you would never be able to do so if I was here. You're a coward, Randall. You hide behind the letter of the law."

"I *abide* by the law, McCabe. Everything I am doing is within the law."

"Well, there's no law here, now. Just you and me. Standing man-to-man. Are you up to that?"

"You forget Torgeson, standing behind you."

Jack made a sudden turn, pivoting on his right foot, and stepped toward the thug called Torgeson and delivered a hard right hook to the man's face.

While the man began to fall, Jack made a similar turn, back to Randall, and drove a right hook into him.

Randall's knees folded and he hit the ground barely a

moment after Torgeson did.

Randall took a moment to regain his bearings, then propped himself up on one elbow, a hand to the side of his face that had taken the punch.

He said, "I'll have you arrested for that, McCabe."

"Who's going to do the job? The only lawmen in town are myself and my deputy. But oh, that's right, we have no authority. You pointed that out yourself. By the time you get a territorial marshal in here, your bruised-up face will be healed."

Jack turned to walk away. Torgeson was propping himself up on one elbow and was preparing to try to rise to his feet. Jack pushed one foot into his chest and flattened him back down again, and then stepped over him and out the doorway.

Jack walked back to the now empty lot where the marshal's office had been. Darby came walking down the hill from his cabin. Jack noticed Darby wasn't wearing his badge.

Darby said, "I saw it happening yesterday, but didn't know what I could do about it. There were too many of 'em, and I couldn't go taking a chance on getting myself shot. I have a family, now."

"No," Jack said. "You did right."

"Randall is giving me the chance to buy the lot my cabin is on. Fifteen cents an acre. That's about what the going rate is back east. My cabin's not in a prime commercial real estate area. It's probably going to be housing, back there. My father has cut me off, but I still have a savings account with some money in it. I was smart enough when we were in school to take some of the money he was letting me have access to and start my own account."

"Maybe you should do that."

Darby shook his head. "But if I do, I'll feel like I'm somehow betraying you and Hunter."

"Nonsense." Jack put a hand on his friend's shoulder. "I don't think you have it in you to betray someone. You have to do what's right for Jessica and the baby."

"I've been thinking about maybe letting the cabin go and building in the valley. Taking up farming. I don't know anything about agriculture, but her father could show me."

"Either way, you have my full support."

Jack let his gaze settle back on the empty lot. "I suppose Randall is right. We never had any real authority here."

Darby said, "No, he's not right. Even if this little town wasn't incorporated, and the Territorial government didn't acknowledge us as real lawmen, we still represented the law. The spirit of the law is more than just something written down on paper. It's about right and wrong."

Jack pulled the badge from his shirt and was about to toss it onto the empty ground. But then he thought better of it.

He looked at Darby and said, "Maybe you're right."

"Besides," Darby said, "we did some good here. We saved the town from Two-Finger Walker and his men, last summer. If we hadn't been here to do what we did, a lot of people probably would have been killed. Hunter, Franklin, Shapleigh. Maybe the Freemans."

Jack slipped the badge into his shirt pocket and slapped Darby on the arm. "Come on. Let's go over to Hunter's. I'll buy you a drink."

Darby walked with Jack over to Hunter's and they stepped into the barroom. Chen was behind the bar, puttering about.

"Give us a bourbon," Darby said.

"Actually," Jack said, "maybe you should make mine a beer. Bourbon might be a little too strong for me today."

Chen said, "I'll make it a cold one."

He went to the root cellar and came back with a mug of cold beer for Jack, and then placed a glass in front of Darby and poured into it a shot of bourbon.

Jack said, "Here's to a good year behind us, and an uncertain future ahead of us."

Darby shook his head. "Here's to good friends."

Jack nodded. "Good friends."

He took a sip of the beer, and Darby knocked back a mouthful of whiskey.

Hunter stepped from the backroom. He said, "I thought I heard voices out here."

Jack said, "Come to wash down the dust."

Hunter walked up to the bar. "I noticed you boys ain't

wearing your badges."

Jack nodded. "I'm afraid those days are behind us."

"So, what're you boys going to do now?"

"I think this little area is going to see a war in the upcoming months. Maybe not a conventional war, but war nonetheless. And it could get ugly."

Jack took another sip of beer. He said, "Hunter, how would you like to hire a bodyguard? You might need one, because Randall is going to try to force you out. Whether it's by guns, fists, or trying to burn you out, it could get really bad."

"I don't have any money to pay you."

Jack said, "I'm not asking for money."

"Jack," Hunter shook his head with a silent chuckle. "I can't ask you to do that for free."

"It seems to me you never charge us for drinks when we're here. Or for food. From what I hear, a couple summers ago you were out there at the ranch, ready to defend it against Falcone and his men. And if I remember right, Pa and Josh helped you build this place. I don't recall any of it being done for money. We're family, Hunter."

Darby said, "You've just hired yourself two bodyguards."

Jack looked at him. "Darby, that might not be a good idea. You've got Jessica and the baby. You don't want any harm to come to them. You know how men like Randall operate. Nothing is beneath them."

"I certainly do know how they operate. I'm afraid my father is just like them. I'm moving Jessica and the baby out to her parents' farm this afternoon. Randall can do with the cabin what he wants. When the dust settles, then I think I'm going to take up farming."

"All right." Jack looked to Hunter. "You just hired yourself a couple of gunhawks."

15

The following morning, Jack made the ride down to Bozeman. He had with him an envelope that he was to deliver from Aunt Ginny to the bank manager. Jack didn't ask what it was about, and Aunt Ginny said nothing. He knew she wouldn't until she was ready. Such was her way. He had long ago accepted it.

The ride was long and gave him some time to think. To cool down a little, because he was still a little riled about Randall tearing down the marshal's office.

Jack understood the realities of the free market, and that this country was founded with the concept of entrepreneurism as a way of allowing a person to succeed. In the old country, if your father was a carpenter, then you were a carpenter. If he was a bricklayer, then that was what you were going to be. Making entrepreneurism part of the foundation of the country meant the sky was the proverbial limit for everyone.

And yet, there was such a thing as using the system to bully people, too. This was what Randall was doing, and Jack hated bullies.

He went to the bank. Not quite like the structures he was used to back in Boston. Brick buildings two or three floors high. This was a ramshackle one-floor building. One section of the roofline was noticeably lower than the other. The floor underfoot creaked when he walked.

There was a counter with three teller stations, though only one was open. Jack asked to see the manager, and he was ushered to a small office behind the counter. A roll-top desk took up clearly half the room.

Jack gave the man the envelope with Aunt Ginny's instructions in it, and when he returned, he gave Jack another envelope that was packed with what felt like wide paper strips. Cash, Jack figured. Aunt Ginny had made a withdrawal.

The man had a thick mustache that connected to thick sideburns, which offset a bald head.

He gave a grin, and said, "Tell Miss Brackston it's a pleasure doing business with her."

I'll bet it is, Jack thought. She was one of this bank's largest depositors.

It was evening when he got back to the ranch. He handed the envelope to his aunt, and this time he decided to press a little bit.

"So," he said, "can I ask what's going on?"

"Business," she said, and that was all.

The following morning, she had Fred hitch the buggy and drive her into town.

He sat in the wagon while she went into the hotel. A tall thin man with spectacles perched on his nose was standing at the front desk.

She had a hat pinned to her hair, and a drawstring purse in one hand.

"Miss Virginia Brackston, to see Mister Randall," she said.

"I'll see if he's in."

"Now," she said, fixing him with the Gaze.

He withered. Most people did. He said, "This way, please."

The man gave a knock on the door of Randall's office and said, "Miss Virginia Brackston to see you, sir."

He said, "Didn't I say I was busy?"

But she walked in, and said, "This won't take long."

She didn't wait for him to invite her to be seated. There was an upright chair by his desk, and she took it.

He sighed wearily. "All right. Miss Brackston, is it? What can I do for you?"

"I see my nephew left his calling card," she said.

His cheekbone had a bruise from where Jack's fist had connected. He said, "I should sue him for that."

"But you won't."

He looked at her curiously. "And why is that?"

"Because you're not foolish. You might be ruthless and something of a sneak, but you're not foolish."

"Are you threatening me?"

She grinned. "I don't think I need to."

He shook his head. "Is this what you've come here to do?"

"No. I've come to do business."

"And what kind of business might you be in?"

"At the moment, I'm in the business of buying saloons. I believe the price you commanded from Mister Hunter was two thousand dollars. Am I correct?"

He nodded cautiously. "That is what I said, yes."

She opened her purse and pulled out the envelope Jack had fetched for her in Bozeman yesterday. She handed it to him. "I believe you'll find the full amount there."

"You're buying Hunter's saloon?"

"I'm buying half interest."

"Does he know that, yet?"

"No, but he will."

He gave her a long look. "All right. Sold. The saloon is yours. Whether you want to let him have half interest or not. I'll make out the deed in your name."

"I'll expect it delivered to Mister Hunter tomorrow morning."

She rose to her feet. She didn't feel the need for niceties around this man.

"Good day," she said, and turned and strode for the door.

Fred was waiting for her in the buggy outside.

"Come on," she said. "We're going to Hunter's. I want to talk with him a moment, and I'm sure you could use a cold beer."

While Fred stood at the bar and enjoyed a mug of beer fresh from the root cellar, Ginny told Hunter that she had given Randall the two thousand dollars he had requested.

"Aunt Ginny," he said. "I'm much obliged. Really, I am. But I can't ask you to do that."

"Nonsense. You can consider me a silent partner. We'll split the profits."

"I hate to tell you, there really aren't any profits."

"Be that as it may. The saloon now belongs to the both of us."

And that was how Ginny got into the saloon business.

16

Jack stood in front of Hunter's saloon. A bench had been placed on the small boardwalk out front, and he had one foot up on the bench and was leaning his elbow on that knee.

It was a leisurely morning. Days had passed since the marshal's office had been torn down. Days since he had driven a fist into Aloysius Randall's face.

Violence is not the answer, Aunt Ginny had said more than once. Especially to Josh, but it applied to all of them. Jack had to admit, though, knocking down Randall had sure felt good.

A new building was going up on the lot that had once held his office. It was going to be home for the new town blacksmith. Looked like Henry Freeman was going to have some competition.

The Freeman house was actually a little further down the trail, between the newly forming town and the actual expanse between ridges that was called McCabe Gap. The McCabe family had already discussed this the evening before over dinner, and would still be taking their smithy business to Henry. Jack figured the Johnson ranch would too. But the new smithy would be getting a lot of business here in town.

The new smithy was a large man. Every bit as big as Hunter. He had arms that were swollen with muscle. He was also a black man. Probably a former slave, Jack figured. He answered to the name Miah Ricker. Jack had heard the man's wife call him *Nehemiah*. They had a son who was around Bree's age, and was called Abraham. After the president who had freed the slaves, Jack figured.

Aunt Ginny had said over dinner, "While we all harbor some ill feelings toward Aloysius Randall, it's very important that we not allow any of that to spill over to the new people in town. I've met Miah Ricker and his wife Ruth, and they're good people. Hard-working people. And I've met a woman who's setting up shop as a seamstress. Harriett Tucker. A widow woman. As nice as can be. I made a point to welcome them both to our community."

Aunt Ginny was right, he knew. It was all too easy to look with resentment on all of the new buildings going up.

But these folks were just trying to build homes in a new part of the frontier that looked promising. You couldn't blame them for that.

Jack was amazed at how fast the town was forming. Pa had told him about the two gold rushes of 1859. One was in Colorado, the other in Nevada. In both cases, the towns of Boulder and Virginia City went from nonexistence to small frontier cities over the course of one summer. Now he was seeing something very similar.

If Jack were to venture a guess as to the population of the town all of the newcomers knew as Jubilee, he would guess at probably somewhere between one hundred and two hundred. Williams Gulch was now a source of serious digging. He had taken a ride out a few days ago, and there were a dozen new claims being worked. Pickaxes breaking up bedrock and granite in an attempt to get to the mother lode they all seemed to think was there. In two cases, tunnels had been started. The miners were using timber brought in from Bozeman to shore them up.

Just south of town, near a spring run-off, four small farms had been started and crops put in. It was late in what was actually a very short growing season, and Jack questioned if they would have enough water for their crops come August. Time would tell, he supposed.

The town of Jubilee now had two distinct streets, forming an L shape. At the crook of the L were Hunter's saloon, at one side of the street, and the Jubilee Hotel at the other side. This sort of formed the town square.

Where the livery stable had been was now an empty lot. Randall was having granite slabs hauled in for the foundation of what he said would be the town hall. A new livery stable had gone up at the other side of Miah Ricker's blacksmith shop.

Jack could see the logic of this. It made sense to have the livery as close to the smithy as possible.

There were smaller streets out beyond the hotel, though those were mostly either empty lots or partially-finished houses. The cabin Darby had built was now gone like it had never been there, and a framework of two-by-fours was in its place.

Hunter strolled out and stood beside Jack.

Hunter said, "Enough to make you sick, isn't it?"

"I'm a little torn, I have to admit," Jack said.

"Torn? Over what?"

"Well, on one hand, I'm seeing potential profit here. Jobs are being created, and that's always a good thing. And these folks are going to need beef, and our ranch is the closest. Our ranch headquarters is only three miles away. On the other hand, I'm seeing our way of life yanked away from us, without any of us having so much as a say-so."

Hunter nodded. "I know one thing. I owe a lot to Aunt Ginny."

"We all do, one way or another."

"I'll never be able to pay her back."

"You might in profits. If this town keeps growing the way it is, your saloon might start showing some."

Hunter shrugged.

Jack said, "One thing bothers me, though."

"Only one? In all of this, only one?"

"Well, a lot of things, I suppose. But one thing stands out. And you're gonna call me suspicious, I suppose. But I have to wonder—I took a ride out to Williams Gulch a couple days ago. They're all digging out there like groundhogs. But none have found any ore at all. The only color anyone's finding is from panning, and then not much. Josh and Bree and I went out there a few weeks ago looking for the Hayes claim. All we found was a ditch someone had dug. No ore of any kind."

"What're you saying?"

"Not anything, I suppose. Just that somehow something feels wrong. Just being suspicious."

Hunter nodded. "You keep on being suspicious."

This was when the hotel door opened and Aloysius Randall stepped out. He was now in a tan jacket and matching trousers, and a matching hat that was flat-brimmed and flat-crowned. A string tie.

He strode across the street, followed by his two thugs.

Jack didn't bother with a greeting. No *good morning*, or *how're you doing this fine day?*

What Jack said was, "Your bruised-up face is looking better. Not that it was much to look at before."

The nautical-looking guy had caught Jack's fist in a

worse way. It had cracked the bridge of his nose and blackened his eye. The eye now was fully healed, but there was still a purple bruise on his nose.

He said to Jack, "I owe you. Don't forget that."

Jack said casually, "Anytime you feel you're up to collecting, come see me. But keep in mind, you'll just get more of what you got."

The man took a step forward, but Randall placed a hand on his chest. "Not now, Torgeson."

"Sit, boy," Jack said. "Heel."

Randall ignored him, and said, "I came to inform you both of something. I have applied with the Territorial Governor for a town charter."

"That process takes a while," Jack said.

Randall shook his head with a smirk of smugness. "Not in this case. I know people. It's being expedited. I expect the charter within the week."

Hunter said, "And how does any of this involve Jack or me?"

"It affects you, Mister Hunter. I'm forming a town council so we can begin making decisions regarding the town as soon as the charter is granted. Whether I like it or not, you are one of the most prominent businessmen in town, and have a right to be on the council. One of the first things we're going to be doing is drawing up town ordinances and procedures. One of them will be the election of a town marshal."

Hunter slapped Jack on the shoulder. "There you go. You'll have your old job back."

Randall said, "Not necessarily. You must realize, most of the people in this town, probably ninety percent, weren't here during your unofficial tenure as marshal. You might have worn a badge, but you were in effect a glorified vigilante. There's no guarantee you'll win the election."

"Depends on who he's running against," Hunter said.

"He'll be running against a man whose name is well known. In fact, almost legendary. A man who the council will be appointing as acting marshal until the election. Of course, the council will have to vote on it, but I have no doubt the motion will pass. After all, you'll be out-voted."

Jack said, "Who is this legendary figure?"

The sound of hoofs tapping on gravel was coming from up the street. The street that was now being called Randall Street. A rider was approaching, keeping his horse to a brisk walk.

Randall said, "Why, here he comes now."

The man wore a black jacket and trousers, a checkered vest and a string tie. A revolver was riding low on his right leg and tied down. A black handlebar mustache decorated his face.

"It was Victor Falcone," Jack said, telling the family about it over dinner. "Big as life, riding right down the street like he owned it."

Josh had speared a chunk of steak with his fork, but now the fork was hanging a foot or so from his mouth. "Are you serious?"

Jack nodded.

Josh said, "Randall intends to have *him* appointed as acting marshal?"

Jack nodded again.

"Son-of-a-bitch."

Aunt Ginny didn't try to correct him.

Josh said, "How can they allow him to wear a badge? He's a murderer. A thief. He belongs in jail."

"Not anymore," Ginny said quietly. All eyes turned toward her. "He's been pardoned of all of his crimes. Remember?"

Josh said, "And I'd like to know how that worked. He never actually stood trial for anything, did he?"

Ginny said, "I don't think so."

"How can you be pardoned for something you were never actually convicted of?"

"Clearly, there is more going on behind closed doors than we're aware of."

"Well, I intend to find out." Josh stuffed the piece of steak into his mouth and began chewing with a vengeance.

"How?" Ginny said. "How are you going to find out? Are you going to ride to the Territorial Governor's office and barge in and demand information?"

Jack grinned and said, "I'd like to see that."

"Yes, there are some underhanded things going on.

But unfortunately, we are on the periphery of it. We are on the outside looking in."

Josh swallowed the steak. "Are you saying there's nothing we can do?"

"I'm saying we'll have to play within the law. Frontier justice is no longer going to apply in this proverbial neck of the woods. I plan to take Hunter's place on that town council. I am, after all, half owner of his saloon. This makes me a prominent businesswoman in town. From there, maybe I'll be able to have some feel of what's going on. Maybe talk to the other council members. Charlie Franklin is bound to be on the council, too."

Bree said, "What do you think's going to happen when Pa and Dusty get home and find out Victor Falcone is in town?"

Ginny raised her eyebrows. "That is a situation that could turn explosive very quickly."

Josh said, "When that happens, you'll see frontier justice may not be as dead as you think."

The next morning, Bree stood outside the house with her pistol in one hand. On the fence railing in front of her were some empty cans. She squeezed off one shot and a can flew away. She cocked the gun and fired again, but the second shot was a clean miss.

Jack was standing beside her and back a ways. Josh was standing to her other side.

Josh said, "Don't try to aim. Just point and fire. It's an instinctive thing. Just let the bullet find the target."

"Now you sound like Mister Chen," Bree said.

Jack said, "And squeeze the trigger. Don't jerk it, just do a controlled squeeze. Hold the gun good and steady."

She cocked the gun and fired. One can spun and then fell from the fence. She had caught the side of it, at least. She cocked and fired again, and another can flew away.

"Direct hit," she said. "It's so much different than shooting a rifle, though."

Josh said, "Like night and day."

Fat drifted over. He had a grin on his face.

"What're you smiling about?" Josh said.

Bree looked at him, and he immediately lowered his

gaze and kicked at the dirt with his boot. He said, "Nothin', really."

"Come on," Josh said. "Let's hear it."

"Well, it's great that Miss Bree is learnin' to shoot, I guess. But with a twenty-two? Could a twenty-two really stop a man?"

Josh looked at the fence and said, "Bree, do you think you can hit that fence post?"

She brought her arm out to full extension, hauled the hammer back and fired.

"Come on," Josh said, and walked up to the fence. They all followed.

Josh said, "See where the bullet hit?"

Fat bent over a bit and squinted at the fence post. A hole as big around as a pencil had been drilled into it. The bullet was fully buried in the wood.

He said, "Yeah."

"Imagine if that was a man's skull. You don't think that would stop a man?"

Bree was smiling smugly.

Jack said, "I still can't believe Randall invited Victor Falcone to town. And wants him to be the marshal. I mean, of all people, *Vic Falcone*."

Josh nodded. "I've gotta wonder what's gonna happen when Pa and Dusty get home."

Bree said, "I can't believe Pa's married. I wonder what his wife's like."

Fat said, "Looks like you'll be able to find out soon."

They looked at him. Fat was looking down toward the wooden bridge. Just beyond it were three covered wagons making their way along the valley floor.

"Looks like your Pa has come home," Fat said.

PART FIVE

The Homecoming

17

Jessica stared in wonder at the house, as the wagon brought her toward it.

She said, "Oh, Johnny. It's everything you said it was."

Johnny was sitting on the seat with the reins in his hands. Cora was sitting between Johnny and Jessica.

Jessica said, "Look, Cora. This is our new home. Isn't it beautiful?"

Cora nodded silently.

Jessica said, "Are you scared?"

Cora nodded again.

"Oh, honey. You don't have to be."

Johnny said, "Everyone's gonna love you. I promise."

"I have to admit, though, I know how she feels. This is a lot to spring on everyone."

Johnny said, "It'll be all right. Everyone's gonna love you, too."

She looked at him with a smile. "Promise?"

He returned the smile. "Promise."

But he was thinking that it was indeed a lot to spring on everyone with very little preparation.

"Look," Jessica said.

Johnny followed her gaze to the four out behind the house. Looked like target practice had been in progress. That's where you usually stood to shoot cans off of the fence rail.

Jessica said, "The girl has to be Bree. The one with the long blonde hair has to be Josh. And that makes the other one Jack."

Johnny nodded. "You know the cast of characters."

"You've talked so much about them. But who's the tall one?"

"That would be Fat Cole. One of the men who works for us."

Johnny brought the wagon up to the corral and pulled the team to a halt.

"Pa!" Bree called, running toward him.

She had holstered her revolver and it was flapping against her hip as she ran. He climbed down from the seat and she threw her arms around him.

"You're finally home," she said.

He glanced down at her holster. "Looks like some things have changed since I was last home."

Jack said, "A lot of things have changed. Did you go through town?"

Johnny nodded. "That we did. I presume you have a lot to tell me."

"We do indeed." Jack extended his hand. "Welcome home, sir."

"It's good to be home."

Josh extended his hand and Johnny grasped it.

"Good to have you back," Josh said.

"I trust the ranch is in good shape?"

Jack said, "You left it in good hands."

Johnny reached up to take Jessica's hand as she climbed down.

"Everyone," Johnny said, "allow me to introduce my wife. Jessica."

Bree was smiling as wide as it was possible to smile. She said, "It's so good to meet you."

"Likewise," Jessica said. "I've heard so much about you."

"And this," Johnny said, reaching up to the seat and taking Cora under the arms and lifting her down, "is your new little sister Cora."

Bree knelt down to look her eye-to-eye. "Hi, Cora. Welcome to the family. I'm Bree."

Cora said, "Are you really my sister?"

Bree nodded. "Sure am. And these two apes behind me are your brothers."

Cora knitted her brow. "They're monkeys?"

Everyone laughed.

Bree said, "Sometimes they act like it."

Matt and Peddie walked up, along with Tom and Lettie and Mercy. Old Ches was with them, too, and Danny.

Johnny made the introductions all around.

"Uncle Matt," Josh said. "I've heard a lot about you."

Matt said the thing people usually said in such situations. "Nothing bad, I hope." And they laughed.

"Hey," Bree said. "Where's Dusty? And Zack? And your letter said Uncle Joe was with you."

Johnny said, "They're all right. We have a long story to tell."

The wagons were unloaded. A trunk filled with Jessica's belongings was hauled up to Johnny's room. Another trunk was hauled up to the guest room, which was going to become Cora's.

Matt and Peddie would be staying at the ranch for a few days while they decided what they were going to do. While they were still on the trail, Matt had asked Peddie to be his wife, and Tom had agreed to perform the ceremony. The question then was where they were going to live.

There were also the legal matters to work out about cattle ownership. Jessica and Matt were co-owners of the two hundred plus head they had brought with them. Since Montana was a communal-property territory, Johnny automatically owned half of Jessica's share. Jessica also owned half of Johnny's share in the McCabe Ranch.

"This is going to be all too confusing," Johnny said to Matt. "Why don't we just form something called the McCabe Cattle Company, and we'll all just be co-owners."

"Well," Matt said. "I'm grateful for the offer, but you have over two thousand head. I'll be co-owner of a lot more than I would have been. I'm not sure I earned it."

"True, you'll be co-owner of a lot larger herd, but you'll own a smaller share. It'll all even out in the end, more or less."

Matt nodded. "Why not? I've been involved in too many complex business deals over the years. Let's keep this as simple as we can."

"We're all equal co-owners then. You, Peddie, Jessica, the boys, Bree, Aunt Ginny and myself. We each own one-ninth."

"What about Cora?"

"That's right. One-tenth. We're all one-tenth owners."

They shook hands. It was all the binding this contract would need.

A small table was kept in a shed outside for times when there were too many guests for the kitchen table. This was such a time. Josh and Jack hauled the table in and dusted it off.

They all talked over lunch. There was so much to tell.

Johnny told of his ride to California. Of meandering through the Rockies. Of visiting Lura's grave, and of the family now living at the old ranch.

He told about his adventures in California, and how he had met Jessica and Cora. Matt filled in with pieces of the story.

They told about Sam Middleton, and where Dusty and the others had gone.

Ginny gave Johnny a look that was filled with concern. "They're going to try to break a man out of a Mexican prison?"

Matt said, "They won't just try. They're gonna do it."

Josh wasn't happy. He looked at Jack. "They should have let us ride with them."

Jack said, "They can't have more than a few hours' head start on us. If we start now, we should be able to catch up with them in a day or two."

Johnny held up a hand. "Now hold on, you two."

"Pa," Josh said. "They're gonna need us."

"Hold on, and we'll talk about it."

Josh was angry. He wanted to get out of the chair and run upstairs and pack his saddlebags, and go outside and saddle up Rabbit and catch up with Dusty and the others. Jack was more calm. He was not as quick to anger as Josh. But he was having similar thoughts.

Johnny could see it in their eyes. He said, "We'll talk later."

They both nodded and remained in their chairs. Reluctantly.

That evening, once Cora was in bed and asleep, Johnny felt it was time for a talk with Josh and Jack. Aunt Ginny said they had stepped outside, so Johnny went out and found them milling about by the barn. Jack was leaning his shoulders against the barn wall, and Josh was pacing about restlessly. Johnny had a good idea what they were talking about, so he decided not to segue into it gracefully but to jump right in.

He said, "Listen, you two. I want you to know something. There are a couple of reasons Dusty didn't wait for the both of you. One of them is the simple fact that neither of you has any experience with this sort of thing."

"Pa," Josh said. "I stood by you defending this place when Falcone and his men attacked."

Jack spoke more quietly, but still with feeling. "And I've been in more than one gunfight. I defended the town last summer."

Johnny said, "Yes you did. Both of you are good men, and I'm proud of you. But neither of you has the experience to do something like break a man out of a Mexican prison. Dusty has. So has Zack, and so has your Uncle Joe. Matt couldn't have gone along. He's a good man, but he would have been in the way. I was going to go, but they convinced me I was needed here. Jessica and Cora needed me, as well as all of you."

Josh shook his head. He looked like he was going to say something, but then he didn't. He just shook his head again and went back to pacing.

Johnny decided to say it for him. "Look, Dusty did some talking to me. It was a long ride up here from California. Longer than I had expected it to be, even. We had a lot of time to talk. He talked to me about what it's like to be my son."

"What does he know?" Josh said. "I don't mean it in a bad way, but he didn't grow up here. He doesn't know."

"He's seen the both of you. And Bree. He's seen what it's like. There's something I want you both to know. I don't want you to be like me. I want you both to be your own men. The fact that you couldn't go along to break Sam out of prison, well, that's a good thing. The skills you have to learn—the things you have to learn to do those things. Those are things I want you boys spared from. You don't know what it does to a man, inside."

Josh said, "Dusty is like you."

Jack spoke. "It doesn't seem to be bothering him any."

Johnny said, "That's because he's young. He hasn't been riding that trail very long. Once he's back, I hope to get him away from that sort of life, before it starts eating away at him."

Josh said, "I don't see it eating away at you all that much."

Johnny was silent a moment, letting the words settle in. Then he said, "Then maybe you haven't been looking all that close."

Josh and Jack both looked at him.

Johnny said, "Look at me. I can't sleep without a gun within reach. When I come down for coffee in the morning, I have a gun tied down to my leg. Even now, standing out here talking to you boys, I'm listening. Listening for any sound that shouldn't be out there. The crack of a twig. The sound of a horse out there in the night."

He looked down at his gun, and his hand that was brushing the pistol's grip and the trigger guard. "Look at me. I'm ready to pull iron at the moment something is not as it should be. It's almost impossible to get the jump on me, because I've seen the results of a man getting taken by surprise. I've killed more men than I can count. So has Zack and your Uncle Joe. And Dusty's on the way to that. But he won't be if I can help it."

Johnny realized he was shaking a little. This was a subject he didn't talk about much. He drew a breath to steady himself. "It's you boys that have kept me sane over the years, you know that? And Bree, and now Dusty. Even your aunt plays her part, though I'd never admit that to her."

Josh and Jack both gave a silent chuckle at that.

Johnny continued. "And now Jessica brings a joy to my life that I haven't known since your Ma. And Cora plays her part. If not for all of you, I'd have probably drowned myself in a bottle of whiskey long ago. You boys aren't qualified to ride along with Dusty and Zack and Joe. And I thank God for that."

They were silent for a moment. Crickets were chirping out there in the darkness. From somewhere off in the night, a whippoorwill called.

Josh said, "You really pulled a surprise on us, you know? Suddenly you're married."

"It kind of surprised me, too," Johnny said. "When I met Jessica, our feelings for each other just sort of bloomed out of nowhere, and it happened really fast. But I suppose the situation we were in caused that."

Jack said, "Little Cora sure is a peach. I think we're going to like having a little sister around."

Johnny paced a moment. He drew in a breath of night air. He had stopped shaking. He dug into his vest pocket for his pipe. At first he was hesitant at the thought of lighting it, because any sniper hiding off in the trees would be able to see his location when he struck the match. But normal people struck matches and lighted pipes and weren't always bracing themselves for a bullet. He forced himself to relax, and he struck the match and lit the pipe. No bullet came for him. There were no snipers out there in the dark. He shook the match out and let it drop to the wet grass.

He said, "So, what do you boys think? Do you like Jessica?"

Josh nodded. "She's really easy to like. And watching you both together, it's like you were born to be at each other's side."

Johnny heard the kitchen door open. He forced his hand away from his gun. He so wanted not to be reaching for it at the slightest sound, anymore. He so wanted not to be instantly awake at night and ready for battle if the house creaked, or the wind rattled a window.

He then did something which he doubted the boys even noticed, but it was a major thing for him. He shifted his pipe to his right hand, rather than hold the pipe in his left so his right would be ready to go for his gun if need be.

Johnny saw someone walking toward the barn from the house. Then he heard Bree's voice. "I thought I'd find you boys out here."

Jack said. "We're just talking."

Johnny took a draw of sweet tasting smoke from his pipe. "I was just asking them what they thought of Jessica and Cora."

"Oh, Pa. They're both just so great. You couldn't have picked a better woman. It's like you two were just made for each other."

"Didn't I just say that?" Josh said.

Jack said, "I think you did."

Josh said to Bree, "Weren't you the one who was so

concerned about all of this?"

"That was until I met Jessica. She's great."

"I want all three of you to know," Johnny said, "that she'll never replace your mother. That's not my intention."

Bree wrapped an arm around her father for a hug, and rested a head on his shoulder. "Oh, Pa. We know you loved Ma. You always will. But I don't think she'd want you to be alone. And Jessica is great. And now I have a little sister. I'm not the baby of the family anymore."

Josh said, "So, there's no longer an excuse for you to act so spoiled."

"Spoiled? Me?"

Jack interrupted their bantering before it moved too far along. "Pa, you said there were a couple of reasons you didn't want Josh and me riding along to Mexico."

Johnny nodded. "That's right. The second reason is right in town. This Aloysius Randall—I haven't met him, but intend to take care of that in the next few days. And Vic Falcone is in town and potentially wearing a badge. We could have serious trouble on the horizon, and I want you two here with me. I want you to know, there's no one I would want more at my side than you two."

"What about me?" Bree said.

"Young lady, Dusty told me about your part in helping defend the town, last summer. You were on a rooftop with a rifle? And you beat up an outlaw?"

"I'd better be getting inside," she said. "I told Aunt Ginny I wouldn't be long."

18

While the boys were outside, Ginny and Jessica sat in the living room. A fire was crackling away gently. Ginny had a glass of sauvignon blanc. It had been bottled in 1832, and she had been saving it for a special occasion. She figured this evening qualified. She was pleased to find that Jessica had a taste for fine wines, too.

Bree had gone out to check on the boys, and Temperance had fallen asleep on the sofa. Cora was snuggled into her new bed upstairs.

Ginny was in her rocker, and Jessica was in Johnny's chair. She had curled her legs up under her.

"This is such a comfortable chair," she said.

"Then I know you and John were meant for each other," Ginny said. "Until now, he's the only one I've ever known who found that chair comfortable. Sometimes when he's gone, one of the boys will sit in it and endure it, because they want so badly to be like him."

"This is such a lovely home you've all built for yourselves here."

"Well," Ginny nodded and raised her brows. "John gets most of the credit. He did the building."

"Yes, but you did the furnishing. This wouldn't be a home without you. Your touch. I want you to know I don't want to change that. This is still your household."

Ginny was silent a moment. She stared at the glass in her hand, noticing the sort of golden reflection of the fire in the wine.

She said, "No, Jessica. This has to be your household."

Jessica was about to protest, but Ginny cut her off. "It's only right. I was needed for a time. After Lura died, this family needed me. A foundation for a family is the mother and father, and one half of that foundation had been ripped away from these children. So I stepped in, and I helped John raise my niece and nephews. I only wish we had known about Dusty. John would have gone for him and brought him home."

Jessica said, "He told me about all of that. I don't believe he'd ever knowingly leave a child of his behind."

"And that goes for your child, too. Cora might be

yours, but I know that man and he will now consider her to be his, too."

Jessica nodded with a smile. "He said a couple of times that family isn't made so much by blood as it is by love."

"That's Johnny." Ginny took a sip of her wine.

"But what will you do? I mean, this has been your household for so long."

Ginny nodded thoughtfully. "It has been. But the time has come to pass the torch. It now has to become your household."

"But what about you?"

Ginny smiled. "I'll be all right, child. I've been thinking for a while that it's time I returned to San Francisco. Visit old friends. Maybe I'll stay awhile and open the old house up. My only concern was for this household. How would it fare while I was gone? Temperance does a fine job, but she and Josh are going to be building their own home soon. Now I know the household will be in good hands."

"You know so little about me."

Ginny looked at her with a deep smile. "I know much about you. I saw the look in Johnny's eyes when he introduced you. I see the smile he has now. Did you know he never really smiled after Lura died? Oh, he would grin. He would laugh. He and I have this little game of one-upsmanship. You'll see that. This game has induced a good belly laugh out of him more than once. But he never really smiled. Not like he does with you. He smiles from within. You see it in his eyes. He hasn't smiled that way since Lura.

"So you see, I know all I need to know about you. He is a very good man, one of the best I have ever met. Not that I'd ever admit that to him. And since you're so right for him, you must be a good woman."

Jessica leaned over and reached from Johnny's chair to the rocker to place one hand on Ginny's arm. "I see why you are so easy to love. He said you were, but now I see it."

Ginny gave her a questioning look. "He said that?"

Jessica nodded. "Don't worry. I won't tell him you know."

Johnny eventually came in from outside. Jack and

Josh bedded down in the bunkhouse so Matt and Peddie could have their room. Tom and Lettie set up a tent outside. Bree went to her room, and Temperance to hers.

Jessica changed into her nightgown, and climbed into bed with Johnny.

A straight back chair was beside the bed. Its sole purpose was to be where he placed his gun at night, so it would be within reach. He draped the gunbelt over the chair and then drew the gun to place it on the chair.

But then he stopped, holding the gun in his hand. He looked at the chair. Maybe he should just put the gun back in its holster, and place the gunbelt over on the dresser. He thought about it. After all, he had held his pipe in his right hand as he talked to the boys, and found it created no anxiety. Ever since his years with the Texas Rangers he had held everything in his left. His pipe, a coffee cup. He had done this so his gun hand would be free.

Could he do this? Could he sleep without a gun within reach?

No, he thought. He had made a little progress tonight. A little progress toward becoming more like the Johnny he had once been. The Johnny who had grown up in a farmhouse back east. The Johnny who didn't jump every time a stick cracked out in the woods or a door shut, or a floorboard creaked. But he needed to take this slowly.

He placed the gun on the chair, and then rested back on the pillow.

He said, "Been so long since I slept in a bed, it might take some time to get used to again."

Jessica nestled her head on his shoulder. "This place is so wonderful. So strong. Just like you."

He loved the warm feeling of having her next to him. The scent of her hair. Her breath on his neck as her head rested on his shoulder.

He said, "I'm not really all that strong."

"Oh yes you are, Johnny. More so than you realize."

"So, what do you think of Ginny?"

"We did some talking while you and the boys were outside. She's really a remarkable woman."

Johnny nodded. "Not that I'd ever admit that to her."

Jessica giggled. "When did you both start this little

contest of yours?"

"When I first met her. What seems like a lifetime ago. She has this way of glaring that just makes a man's knees want to buckle and his spine turn to jelly. Many a man has wilted under that gaze. Zack can't take it. But I can. For some reason, everything she dished out I just gave right back to her. And we became..." he hesitated, trying to find the words. "We became whatever it is we are, I guess."

"You became family."

Johnny nodded. "I guess that's it. We became family."

19

They all settled into a gentle, daily rhythm.

Johnny and Josh would tend to matters of the ranch. This meant sometimes riding out to spend a night or two at a line shack. When one range became grazed out, the cattle on that range had to be moved to another one. One night, a lightning strike that wasn't accompanied by rain got a grassfire going, and six hundred head stampeded. Johnny and Josh were gone for four days getting them rounded up. Fat and Kennedy went with them, along with a couple of other men Josh had hired before Johnny came home.

Josh had been running the ranch while Johnny was gone. Rather than retake the reins of the ranch, Johnny decided to take a step back and let Josh continue to run things. This seemed to be the boost that Josh's confidence needed. If a cowhand rode up to the ranch and asked for a job, Johnny said, "See my son, Josh. He does the hiring."

Often Johnny went along to work alongside Josh, and occasionally Josh asked his advice, but he made sure it was Josh who made any final decisions.

One of the cowhands Josh hired was Danny McCabe. Danny had grown up on Matt's ranch and knew how to do pretty much everything a cowhand did. But he had very little experience at any of it. The first few nights, Danny collapsed on his bunk, every joint in his body aching. But after a time, he was able to keep up and he quickly grew into a fine cowhand.

One afternoon, Danny and Kennedy rode in, covered with dust. Danny sat his horse as well as Kennedy, and looking at them, you wouldn't know Danny had grown up as a rich kid. You would have thought Danny had been cowpunching for years.

Matt and Peddie were at the house. Matt was standing with Johnny by the corral, watching Danny and Kennedy ride in.

Johnny said to Matt, "He's a good boy, Danny is."

Matt said, "That he is. I wish Hiram could have turned out like this. But I try to focus on what I have, not what I've lost."

"That's the way Pa taught us."

Jack spent most days in town at Hunters. Darby was often there with him. At first they were there to make sure Randall or the men working for him didn't try something underhanded. After all, if the saloon just went up in flames one night, a major obstacle in Randall's way would be eliminated. But more and more, Jack and Darby found themselves taking part in the saloon. Helping Hunter with his bookkeeping. Overseeing Aunt Ginny's investment.

For years, Hunter saw serious business only once a month, when the ranches in the area paid their cowhands. Now he was seeing business all week long. Miners drifted in after a hard day at the diggings. The stage came through town three times a week now, and the customers usually made their way to Hunter's because Chen was a good cook. Hunter now had ledger sheets that had numbers on them.

Jessica settled into learning the ways of the household. Temperance was her teacher as much as Ginny. Just how the boys liked things cooked. Johnny liked his steaks rare, and so did Josh. Bree liked to have her steak cooked a little more. Jack preferred his well-done.

Jessica was used to making strong coffee, but the boys actually liked theirs with the coffee grounds floating on top.

"Just the thought of it makes me go pale," Ginny said. "But that's the way they like it."

Ginny introduced her to the Freeman family. Ginny said, "We buy our lard from them, and their daughter comes out to help with the housecleaning sometimes."

They also introduced her to Granny Tate. The little old woman who was a former slave, and who had been doing the doctoring in these parts for the past few years.

Jessica had never heard the term *granny doctor* before.

Granny Tate said, "It's somethin' we used to say back where we're from. Back east, before the war."

Ginny had heard second-hand that a doctor was setting up shop in town, but she said she fully intended to take her ills to Granny Tate.

Ginny said, "A granny doctor cures people naturally, using herbs and roots and such. Granny looks at the woods and sees a great natural pharmacy. Her way, the old way, is to help the body heal itself. It's the better way. I've become convinced of that."

The days blended into weeks. Johnny ventured into town a few times, but always coming out of the woods behind Hunter's and never venturing any further than Hunter's. He had considered confronting Falcone, but then decided against it, considering what a confrontation with this man would probably lead to. As he had moved through life he had left a trail of bodies behind, and could no longer count the number of men he had killed. He didn't want to add another to it. Not even a man like Falcone.

Falcone decided to take care of the problem himself, though. One morning, almost a month after Johnny had come home, Falcone rode out to the ranch.

Johnny stood on the porch with a cup of coffee in his hand. He was making sure to hold it in his right hand, so he had no free hand to grab his gun with. It was morning, and he was enjoying the clean mountain air. Here in the valley, summer days tended to turn off hot, but today the breeze was coming down from the ridges to the northwest and the air was cool and refreshing, and with a touch of balsam.

Johnny saw the rider coming, taking the long way in from town. Maybe the rider didn't know about the horse trail behind Hunter's. At first Johnny didn't know who it was. The man wore a wide-brimmed black hat and a black jacket. He rode like he had ridden before. Johnny could tell by the way the man sat in the saddle that he was wearing a gun. You don't sit the same on the back of a horse when you have a gun at your side.

Then it occurred to Johnny who this might be. *No,* he thought. *He wouldn't have the brass to ride out here.*

And yet, Johnny couldn't figure who else it might be.

The man drew closer, crossing the wooden bridge. The iron-shod hooves of his horse clattered on the wooden boards. Johnny shifted his coffee to his left hand.

Then he thought maybe this situation warranted a little extra caution. He set the coffee on the rail of the porch, then drew his gun and checked the loads. Five cartridges, right where they should be. He reached to his belt and pulled a sixth one and thumbed it into the empty chamber, then slid the gun back into the holster. But he slid it in loosely, so it would come free easily.

He did a quick mental inventory. Josh was out back

with Fred, working with the remuda. Fred liked to walk among the horses, seeing how each horse was. Jack was in town, at Hunter's. Jessica and Ginny and Temperance were in the house. Bree was...where was Bree?

The rider was now past the bridge and approaching the house. It was indeed Victor Falcone.

Johnny stepped back into the house and called out, "Jess? Ginny? Temperance?"

It was Temperance who answered, stepping out of the kitchen. "Yes, Pa?"

"Where is everyone?"

"Aunt Ginny and Jess are upstairs, changing the bed linens. Cora's with them. Why?"

"Stay inside. Tell them all to stay inside."

She could see the serious look in Johnny's eyes and hear it in his voice. "Yes, Pa."

Johnny stepped back out, and the rider reined up.

"Morning," Falcone said.

Johnny reached for his coffee cup—with his left. He said, "Nice morning for a ride."

Falcone nodded. "Mind if I step down?"

"I'd take it as a kindness if you didn't."

Falcone nodded with acquiescence. "I deserve that."

"That, and a whole lot more."

Falcone looked over one shoulder, past the long expanse of green grass that stretched to the edge of the pine forest at the foot of a ridge.

He said, "That's where we charged the house from. Right there. Rode right up here."

"That you did."

"Except we didn't know you had split your forces into two halves. Had one half in the house and the other one waiting down by that little clump of trees, over there."

"Short-sightedness on your part. You attack this house, you gotta expect I'm gonna come at you with everything I have. And everything I have is quite a lot."

Falcone nodded. "I learned that the hard way."

"One of your men put two bullets in me."

"I see he didn't do a very good job."

"What brings you out here?" Johnny took a sip of coffee.

From above came the sound of a rifle's lever action being worked. A round being chambered.

Johnny said, "I'd be very careful how you answer that question."

Falcone looked up at the ridge of the roof, and then raised his hands away from his body.

Johnny called out, "That you up there, Josh?"

"Yeah, Pa. I saw him riding up and grabbed a rifle and climbed up here."

Josh had been positioned in the same place the night Falcone and his men attacked. Johnny wondered if Falcone would appreciate the irony of the situation.

Bree stepped from around the back side of the porch, her pistol drawn and aimed at Falcone. She hauled back the hammer and said, "And Josh ain't alone."

Falcone looked at her and couldn't suppress a grin. "Even your daughter has a gun?"

She said, "Don't take me lightly, Falcone. You reach for that gun, and I'll put one right between your eyes."

Johnny took another sip of his coffee. "She's a McCabe. You'd better take that seriously."

Falcone said to Johnny, "I just rode out to tell you I don't want any trouble. I wanted to make sure you felt the same."

Johnny noticed Falcone was wearing a tin star. Ginny had told him how she had gone to the town council meeting and lobbied strongly against Falcone being given the job of acting marshal. Charlie Franklin had been there. But there had been people she didn't know. The new owner of the livery in town. Miah Ricker, the blacksmith. The owners of two new saloons in town. The owner of an assaying office that was still in the process of being built. Frank Stillman, the new doctor. Miah Ricker had voted with her, and Ginny had been able to convince three of the others, but the remaining four had all voted in favor of Falcone, after hearing a rousing speech by Randall. Ginny had to admit, Randall had charisma and could make people want to listen to him. Since there was a four to four tie, Randall as chair was able to cast the deciding vote, and that was how Victor Falcone became their new acting marshal.

Johnny said, "I never wanted trouble. That night, two

years ago, if you had just rode on, there would have been no trouble. But you brought it to my doorstep. Threatened the women in my life, put two bullets in me, and put two of my sons in danger."

Falcone nodded. He looked Johnny in the eye and said, "I was a different man, then."

"Are we to believe you've changed all that much?"

Falcone said, "Don't you believe in second chances?"

Johnny nodded. "Sometimes."

"Maybe I just believe that fate has handed me a second chance, and I intend to take it."

"Maybe. But maybe it would be best if you don't ride out here again. Your jurisdiction ends at the town line, which is almost three miles from here."

He nodded his head. "I'm fine with that. But I want you all to know, I'm issuing an order that no guns are to be worn in town. I see a man wearing a gun, I lock him up. Fair warning, that's all."

"Is that what you came to say?"

Falcone nodded. "That, and I don't want trouble. I'm not asking you to forgive me. I'm just saying I don't want any more shooting matches."

"Falcone, I'd like to believe a man can change. But that doesn't necessarily mean you have. Maybe it'd be best if you turned your horse around and rode out of here."

Bree said, "While you can."

Falcone let out a weary sigh. "Well, if that's the way it's going to be."

Johnny said, "Did you really think it'd be any different? Don't forget, you're the one who attacked this ranch."

Falcone gave Johnny a long look, like there was something he was going to say but then decided against it. He turned his horse and started back toward the wooden bridge.

Bree walked around to the front of the porch, sliding her gun back into the holster.

She said, "That man is going to be trouble."

Johnny nodded. "He usually seems to be."

A few nights later, Jack and Johnny found themselves

on the front porch enjoying the cool, nighttime air. The day had been hot, but now a refreshing breeze was working its way down from the ridges and across the valley toward them.

Jack said, "There's a smell of rain on the air."

Johnny nodded his head. "The breeze has changed direction. Coming from the northwest. I think it's gonna bring rain."

Johnny had a glass of scotch in one hand, and Jack a glass of bourbon. They had been sitting about the parlor with Aunt Ginny and everyone else. Then Ginny bid everyone a fond goodnight and headed for her room. Jessica went upstairs to put Cora to bed, and thought she might climb into bed herself. Bree had headed to bed. Josh and Temperance made a discrete exit and Johnny didn't know where they were. Probably out back somewhere being romantic, he figured.

This left him and Jack, and they decided to step out to the porch to get some of the cooler night air.

Johnny knew that Two-Finger Walker and White Eye and a few additional gunfighters had attacked the town the summer before, and Jack and some others had stood against them. Dusty had told him about it. What he didn't know were the details. So as they sat enjoying the breeze and their whiskey, Jack told him step-by-step the details of the fight.

When he was finished, he said, "Is that how you would have handled it?"

Johnny was quiet a moment. He had been waiting for a moment to say what he was about to say. Sometimes the weightier things have to be said at the right time, or they wouldn't be effective.

He said, "It doesn't matter how I would have handled it. What matters is the way you handled it. And the way you handled it worked."

He took a sip of his whiskey.

He then said, "Dusty said something on the ride north. Something about casting shadows, and how you and Josh and Bree found my shadow hard to step out of."

Jack was silent. Johnny didn't know if he was embarrassed, or angry that Dusty had told him this. Jack might have felt that what he had discussed with Dusty was in confidence. But Johnny decided to press on.

"I'm just a man, Jack. I'm good at some things, not so good at others. Turns out the things I'm good at are the things that people want to talk about afterward. And you know how things are when people talk. People take a thing and expand on it until it's larger than life. That's how legends are formed. It's never about what a man does, it's about how folks talk of it afterward. How they stretch it to be something larger than life."

Jack said, "You really did take down ten Comanches with ten shots, while they were galloping right at you."

Johnny nodded his head thoughtfully. "Yes. I did do that. I've always been blessed with the ability to hold my gun steady when I'm being shot at. Most men find their gun shakes a little and their knees get a little weak. But for me, I find this strange sense of calmness seems to come on me. A blessing or a curse. I'm not sure, really. But there are things you can do that I can't."

"Name one thing I can do and you can't that's worth anything."

"Medical school. You went and did something I could never do."

"You have the ability to stay calm when bullets are flying at you. That's led to not only staying alive as long as you have, but you've picked up tactical military knowledge along the way. You saved everyone a couple summers ago when Falcone and his men attacked. And it's benefited you since then, in California. And in the years before that."

"Your medical school training saved the leg of Harland Carter. Without that, he'd be hopping around on crutches now. If it had been me or Dusty wearing the badge last summer, and you hadn't been here, Carter would have lost his leg."

This gave Jack something to think about. He sat silently as he let all of this toss about in his head.

Johnny said, "We all cast our own shadow, Jack. I have mine, but you have yours. It's easy to get lost in another man's shadow and forget about your own. It's easy to forget that your shadow is every bit as big as anyone else's. Even mine."

Jack gave him a long look. He was silent for a few moments more, then said, "Thank you. I feel like a weight has been lifted from my shoulders."

"A weight you shouldn't have had to carry at all. Somehow I hadn't been aware. For that, I apologize."

"No need to."

"Yes there is. Never think you're too big to apologize. And never be so filled with pride that you can't admit it when you're wrong. The path to being right is to realize when you're wrong, and don't be afraid to admit it. After all, everyone around you will see when you're wrong. You can't fool them just by not admitting it.

"I have tried to be a good father to you, Bree and Josh. All the years you were growing up."

"And you were."

"Maybe. But no matter how good a father you try to be, there's always gonna be something you miss. Part of being human, I guess."

"All right, then," Jack said. "Apology accepted."

They then sat and sipped at their whiskey and enjoyed the cool night breeze with the hint of balsam and the smell of rain, and listened to the crickets chirping from the grass all around the house. And they each sat comfortably in their own shadows.

20

San Francisco

Hezekiah Aikens was awakened by the feeling of something cold touching the side of his face. First one eye opened and then the other. His head was buried into a feather pillow and a sheet and blanket were pulled up to his chest. It was still dark, so he knew it was not yet morning.

He couldn't imagine what had awakened him. Something had touched his face. He reached up to brush it away. Nothing was there so he figured he must be dreaming. But then it touched him again.

He opened his eyes and in the dim lighting that slipped in from outside, from the moonlight and the gas-lit streetlights, he could see a man standing there.

"Wakey, wakey," the man said. "We have some business to tend to."

Aikens knew that voice. The man's face was lost in shadows, but Aikens could see he was wearing a buckskin shirt. Then he realized where he recognized the voice from. That little canyon north of here, up near Greenville. Johnny McCabe's son.

"What do you want?" Aikens said.

"Just some information."

"You can put the gun away." Aikens sat up in bed. "Since you've woken me up, maybe we should go put some coffee on. The missus has gone east to visit a sister in Missouri. I'll put the coffee on myself.

Aikens climbed out of bed and pulled a robe on over his night shirt, and the man with the gun followed him into the kitchen.

Aikens turned a lamp up and he found two others there. Joe McCabe and Zack Johnson. He had forgotten the McCabe boy's name. All three looked like they had been on the trail for some time. Joe McCabe had a full beard. He had back in Greenville, too. But the other two had whiskers starting to grow wild along their jaws, like they hadn't had a shave in a while, and all were covered with trail dust.

That was when he remembered the McCabe boy's

name. He said, "Dusty, isn't it?"

Dusty nodded.

"You won't need that gun."

"Well," Zack said. "Breaking into a man's home isn't exactly legal."

Aikens shook his head. "I figure this must be about Sam Middleton."

Zack nodded.

"I was kinda hoping you boys would pay me a visit."

They waited while Aikens made the coffee. There had already been a low burning fire in the stove because the night was a little chilly. Aikens added a couple chunks of firewood and soon the fire was blazing and the water was heating.

Zack sat, resting his elbows on the table. He looked worn out. Dusty was also tired. It had been a long ride from Montana. They had been pushing, covering as much distance as possible. But after so many hours in the saddle, Dusty didn't want the feeling of a hard chair beneath his backside.

Joe was on his feet, pacing. Aikens kept glancing at him a little nervously. Dusty had to admit, there was something a little dark and ominous about his uncle Joe, sometimes. When Joe paced, and sometimes when he just walked across the room or rode along on a horse, he reminded Dusty a little of a wildcat stalking its prey.

There was no conversation while the water heated. Dusty, Joe and Zack were tired. And the task before them was weighing heavily on them. It felt to Dusty like preparing to go into battle. A couple summers before, when he had first gone to Montana and they had been preparing for Falcone and his raiders to strike the ranch, it had felt like this.

Dusty decided to sit, after all. Zack had folded his arms on the table and was resting his head. Dusty thought he might be nodding off a little.

Soon the coffee was ready and Zack was instantly awake as Aikens placed a cup on the table in front of him. He didn't wake up startled, like most folks would. He just opened his eyes and sat up and reached for his coffee. Dusty had seen Pa wake up like this a number of times. He supposed men like Pa and Zack never slept very deeply.

Dusty decided to take the lead, and get right to the point. "We've come for Sam. We know he was going to be turned over to the Mexican consulate. We need to know where he is, now. If he's stood trial. If he was found guilty, where he has been sent."

Aikens pulled out a kitchen chair and dropped into it.

He said wearily, "I have only hearsay. After I delivered him to the consulate, my authority in the case ended."

"Well," Zack said, "let's have the hearsay."

Aikens looked at him gravely, then back to Dusty. "From what I hear, there wasn't any trial. He was just sent directly to a prison."

"Which one?" Joe said.

"El Rosario. Ever hear of it?"

"I've heard the name," Dusty said. "I've heard it's not a place you want to be sent to. A place they send criminals who they don't want dead yet, but who they don't want surfacing anytime soon. And when you go in, you don't come out. Some call it the Black Pit."

Joe stepped forward. "I've heard it might not even be real. No one even knows where it is."

Aikens nodded wearily. "It's real. And I know where it is. Or, at least, the general location. I've never been there. It's in the Mexican state of Nueva Leona."

Joe said, "Nueva Leona is just south of the border. South of Texas."

"There's a small town there called El Rosario. The prison doesn't even have an official name, as far as I know. It's supposedly near that small town, so it's called sometimes by that name. Or the Black Pit. Or just the Pit. There's no record of its existence, at least none that I've seen. It's something the Mexican government doesn't want our government to officially know about. It's said there's more than one American being held there."

Zack said, "I've been to Nueva Leona more than once. I rode with the Texas Rangers back in the fifties. We ran reconnaissance down there more than once. Unofficially, of course."

Aikens said, "Which means you chased Mexican raiders across the border and wreaked havoc on them."

Zack nodded. "Unofficially."

"Amazing how much happens that's unofficial, isn't it?"

Joe took a sip of the coffee. "Why would they have a place like that, where they might be holding Americans illegally, so close to the border?"

Aikens shrugged. "Hiding in plain sight?"

"I don't mean to be overly suspicious," Dusty said. "But the man who raised me taught me to always be cautious."

"You want to know why I'm telling you all of this." It was a statement more than a question.

Dusty nodded.

Aikens said, "I'm a U.S. Deputy Marshal. I'm sworn to uphold the law. And one time, I was young law officer with a hot temper. I took it as a personal offense that I couldn't find Addison Travis. The man you know as Sam Middleton. You see, I was trying to build a reputation as one who always got his man. But the one time I got close enough to him, he put a bullet in my leg, and even to this day I can't go far without a cane."

He took a sip of coffee. "But the years went by, and time has a way of mellowing out your fire. My obsession for capturing Travis sort of died. Really, it was pride only that made me so obsessed about it. In reality, he never actually committed a crime on American soil. The killing he talked about wasn't even intentional. It was just two young fools, liquored up and swinging fists at each other. If it had happened in this country, the most he would have gotten would be some sort of manslaughter, and that would have been only if his lawyer was a complete idiot.

"As a lawman, you're not supposed to make judgments. But as a human being, how can you not? Travis didn't have a price on his head because of what he did, but because of who it was done to. The son of a high-ranking general who was in tight with Juan Alvarez, the Mexican president at the time. There was no due process. He never stood trial."

Aikens took a long sip of coffee. "That's about all the help I can give you boys. I hope you can find the place, and if he's still alive, get him out of there. You can raid my cupboards for supplies, if you want. I have a sack of coffee in there, and some cans of beans. Help yourself. But ride, and ride careful. Because you'll be getting on the bad side of two governments.

    Joe went to a cupboard door and pulled it open. Four cans of beans. He pulled off his hat and turned it upright and loaded the cans into his hat. He then found a ten pound bag of coffee and lifted it off the shelf.

    "We're much obliged," Zack said. "Not only for the supplies, but the information."

    Dusty said, "I guess we ride for Texas, next."

    "Don't tell me that," Aikens said, shaking his head. "Because if you boys wind up with your names on reward posters, I might be the one assigned to go after you. And I sure don't want to find you. Especially since I believe what you're doing is the right thing."

21

Aloysius Randall was sitting in the lounge of his hotel. It wasn't a very big lounge, not for a man who was used to the more lavish lounges in places like St. Louis and Chicago. But it would do for the moment. He found it much preferable to the rustic environment of Hunter's, with its walls made of logs. Not that he was welcome at Hunter's, anymore.

He sat at a corner table with a glass of whiskey in front of him. The lounge was empty, except for a bartender who milled about behind the bar. The hour was late and the man wanted to go home, and was going to do so as soon as Randall left.

Vic Falcone stepped in. He looked so much different than he had in that saloon in Wichita so many months ago. His jaw was now shaved and his mustache neatly trimmed. He wore a black jacket and matching trousers and a checkered vest. His gun was tied down at his side. And a tin star was pinned to his lapel. What delicious irony, Randall thought.

"Why Vic," Randall said. "What brings you here at this late hour?"

Randall wasn't drunk, but he was feeling his whiskey.

Falcone said, "Just wanted a word, that's all."

"Why then, pull up a chair. Share a drink with me."

Falcone pulled up the chair, but he said, "I don't drink anymore. You know that."

Randall shrugged. "One can hope."

"I have already had enough whiskey to last two lifetimes. Look where it got me."

Randall was quickly becoming bored. "What can I do for you, Vic?"

"I was just wondering. I have been watching this town grow like a fire out of control. You must have over three hundred people here, now. And more coming in every day, following the trail up from Cheyenne. But for what?"

"I guess I don't follow your question. Maybe it's the whiskey." He chuckled, as though he found it funny.

Falcone looked over to the bartender. There were things he didn't want to say in front of anyone but the boss man.

Randall called out to the bartender. "Simmons! You can go home now. I'll lock up when I leave."

"Thank you, Mister Randall," he said, and he was out the door.

Falcone said to Randall, "This whole town is being built on the premises of a gold rush."

Randall nodded, with the exaggerated motion of a man who has had one drink too many. "Indeed. Quite right."

"But eventually, the fact that there is no gold is bound to become evident. These people might be uneducated, but they are not stupid. What happens when they realize the very gold strike that was the catalyst for the building of this town wasn't real? There is no actual gold strike."

Randall was smiling. "You are an educated man, indeed. I so love the way you use words."

Falcone said, "You won't love it around here when everyone realizes you faked a gold rush."

"By the time they realize that, I will be long gone. I'll have sold all the lots up and down the street, and I'll have sold the Jubilee Hotel, and then I'll be long gone. I'll have my profit. I'll have made many times what I invested in this piece of land."

"And you don't look back."

"No, sir. Not at all."

"What about the hard-working people who are investing everything they have to come here? People hoping to start a business, or to find work? They'll lose everything. This place will turn into a ghost town."

Randall gave a silent laugh and held his hands up as if to say, *what are you going to do?* What he said was, "It's not my problem."

"Not your problem? You'll be the cause of it all."

"You're an educated man, Falcone. You must be aware of the expression *caveat emptor*."

Falcone said, "May the buyer beware."

"Exactly. It's the free market, my friend."

"As I understand things, the free market only works when it's a *fair* market. There's nothing fair about this situation. None of these people know the game is stacked against them."

Randall's smile was gone. "That's because they didn't

research the situation properly. They left their lives behind and invested their life's savings on coming here because of what? Word-of-mouth? An article in a newspaper? For me to give up everything I had and start a new life somewhere else, I would first research the situation carefully. These folks jumped without any research at all. They get what they deserve. And me, I'll be sipping twenty-dollar-a-bottle champagne in Chicago. And you can be right there with me. I need a man like you in my employ. With your abilities."

Falcone shook his head. "No. I think this is the end of the line."

Randall was clearly becoming angry now. "I picked you up practically out of the gutter. You, who had raided ranches and farms and towns. Who had held up stagecoaches and robbed banks. Who had probably shot down in cold blood more people than he could ever count. I pulled political strings to get the charges against you dropped. And now you're suddenly developing a conscience?"

Falcone didn't know what to say. Before could think much further, Hayes came running in.

"Mister Randall! Mister Randall!"

Randall said with undisguised impatience. "I'm right here, Hayes. What could possibly be the matter?"

Hayes looked at him wide-eyed. "It's gold, Mister Randall. Real gold."

"What do you mean, *real* gold? There's no real gold between here and Helena."

"Yessir, there is. Two of the miners out at Williams Gulch. They been digging out beyond there, at the base of the ridge. They found it, sir. They brought some ore to the assayer's office. The assayer just told them. It's real gold, all right. The assayer said it's not the best strike he's ever seen. Not as rich as in Colorado, and not nearly what they found in Nevada. But it's good. A mining engineer from California is in town, and he's offering them a price for their claim."

Randall grinned and looked at Falcone. "A gold strike. How about that? Can you believe the luck?"

Falcone said, "So now you have a legitimate gold strike to build your town on."

Randall lifted his glass in a salute to himself. "You should stop trying to develop a conscience and let yourself appreciate life a little."

Randall knocked back a belt of whiskey. "Life has a lot to offer. You just have to reach out and take it. And don't feel guilty about it, because if you don't take it then someone else will."

22

They had set up camp not far from Johnny's ranch house, but off enough so they wouldn't feel in the way. Matt and Peddie, and Tom and Lettie.

Matt and Peddie weren't there a lot. Much of the time they were off looking for a place to build a small house. And there were times Matt was with the herd, checking on the cows with the Swan brand, seeing how they were fattening up after the drive from California. While he was doing this, Peddie would be at the ranch house, visiting with Jessica.

They all joined Johnny and his family for evening meals at the ranch, but often Tom and Lettie and their daughter Mercy ate breakfast at their little camp.

One morning, after coffee and some fried eggs and bacon, Lettie found Tom standing looking off toward the valley. His tin cup was in one hand, filled with coffee. With the other hand, he was rubbing the back of his neck. His gun was at his side.

He had taken to wearing a gun while they were still in Calfornia. On their ride north, his Uncle Johnny had shown him how to use it, and now he was wearing it slung low and tied down.

Lettie said, "Is everything all right?"

He looked over his shoulder toward her. "I don't know."

"Tom, I haven't said anything, but I lay awake some nights, thinking about it."

She walked up beside him. He put an arm over her shoulder.

"There's nothing wrong between us," he said.

She shook her head. "But when two people are married, they become as one. You've said that sort of thing more than once, when you were preaching or talking about marriage. So when something bothers one of us, it's a problem for both of us."

When she said the word *preaching*, he turned his gaze away.

He said, "I guess I'm just not so sure anymore."

"Sure about us?"

He looked at her with a smile. "Oh, I'm very sure about

us. I'm just not so sure about me."

"You're a good man, Tom."

He shrugged. "Maybe. I don't know."

"What happened? There was a time you were so confident."

"Seems like so long ago. Like another lifetime, almost. Almost like I was another man."

"Do you remember when it changed?"

He went silent, and looked off toward the valley.

She said, "Well, I do. It was when that marshal and his deputy forced their way into our house, back in Greenville. Your Uncle Johnny saved us by shooting that man."

He nodded. "Maybe that was when it all started. I've just seen and even done a lot of things that have…"

He went silent again.

She said, "Things that have what?"

He said, "Things that have left me questioning my faith."

He turned his gaze from the valley back to her. "I'm a preacher. It's what I do. Pa, he's a rancher. Danny's working for him. Or for Uncle Johnny." He shook his head. "I'm still not entirely clear on who owns which cows."

She shook her head with a grin.

He said, "But Pa and Danny are ranchers. So is Uncle Johnny and his sons. It's clear what they are. But me, I'm not a rancher. I thought about maybe building a house for us here in the valley and maybe I could farm. There are three farms down toward the center of the valley. I've seen them. We could build a house down there and I could try my hand at it. But I'm not a farmer either. There's only one job for me."

She said, "You're a minister."

"And yet, how can I preach the message I was preaching? How can I do that when I've seen so much killing? When I've done some of it myself?"

She wanted to give him the answer he needed. But she didn't have it. She wanted to tell him everything would be all right, but she had to admit to herself she wasn't sure it would be.

He said, "I suppose I could just preach the old message anyway. More than one minister does that. They don't really believe it themselves, but folks want to hear it. Like their sermon is a product and they're delivering it to their customers. But to me, preaching was always much more than that. It was about sharing what I believed with others, and helping them find their way. How can I do that when I can't even find my own way?"

She looked up into his eyes. "Have you prayed about it?"

He nodded. "I tried to. But I feel so dirty when I pray. Like I'm not even worthy anymore."

She was silent a moment. She looked off toward the center of the valley herself, as though the answers would somehow be in the gentle, low grassy hills that covered the valley floor, or the pine-covered ridges that rose beyond them.

She found herself saying, "I was talking to Aunt Ginny and Jessica a couple of days ago. Aunt Ginny mentioned the preacher in town had left a few months ago. A few times a minister from Bozeman has come up, and one time a minister from Helena came out. But most of the time the services are conducted by the lay people. They sing hymns and read scripture."

"It's a Baptist church. I'm a Methodist minister."

"Well, I know. But it's a church. And they're in need of a preacher."

He said nothing more, and they stood in silence for a while.

Then he said, "The one thing I am still sure of is you."

She said, "You can always be sure of that."

23

Falcone had decided not to resign his position as marshal. There was real gold here, now. Even if Randall sold out and moved on, the town would survive, and they needed a marshal.

Falcone had decided he was going to stay, even when Randall left.

He walked along the street. He was doing his rounds. Walking about the town and making the presence of the law known. But in reality, he was walking because he needed to walk.

The job of being marshal was a dull one. He didn't know how the McCabe boy had tolerated it. Forms to fill out. Money that needed to be requisitioned. He wanted to hire a deputy but he needed to get the Town Council to cough up the money. At the rate this little town was growing, soon upholding the law would be more than one man could handle. Especially on the first Saturday night after payday. It seemed every cowhand within riding distance came to town and lost his mind on that night.

Even the McCabe boy had had a deputy. As Falcone understood it, there had been no pay. But meals were provided by the hotel when Frank Shapleigh had owned it, or by Hunter. Guns and ammunition and even clothing were provided by Charlie Franklin.

But the way things were now, if Falcone wanted a box of cartridges for his pistol, he had to fill out a form and submit it to the Town Council, and they would take it up at their next meeting.

And so he walked.

But the frustrations of the job weren't the real reasons he was walking.

He passed the blacksmith shop. Miah Ricker was out there, using a pair of tongs to hold a horseshoe in place on his anvil, and he brought a hammer down onto it. Shaping it. The ringing sound chimed out to the town and the hills beyond.

"Morning, Ricker," Falcone said.

Miah looked up and nodded. "Marshal."

Falcone continued on. Hunter's was on the left. It was

morning and the coffee smelled good, but Falcone knew he wasn't welcome there. Charlie Franklin usually took morning coffee at Hunter's, and Henry Freeman often did. The McCabes sometimes rode in to join them. Even Alisha Summers. Sometimes other local business owners were there. Morning coffee at Hunter's was something of a ritual for many of them.

But not for Vic Falcone. He doubted he would ever be welcome there. He couldn't really blame them.

To his right and across the street was the Jubilee Hotel.

He had to wonder at the name *Jubilee* for a town. The name had come from Aloysius Randall. Falcone thought it was a screwy name. The obvious choice for the name of this town was McCabe Town. Or maybe just McCabe.

Just before the hotel was Franklin's general store. Charlie had just pained a new sign. It read FRANKLIN'S EMPORIUM. Vic supposed Charlie felt his store needed a bigger name for a bigger town.

The street formed an L here, and Falcone followed it along the bend and up and past what had become the town square, and onto what was now called Randall Street.

He went past where the old livery had been. An assayer had set up shop there. And beyond was a seamstress's shop. And beyond there, a church.

The church was the only building on Randall Street that had been here before the gold strike. It also served as a school during the winter. The walls were made of upright planks. The roof was peaked, though the ridgeline was not as straight as it should have been. The building was made out of whatever lumber the locals could find. There was a steeple, but it looked to Falcone like it leaned a few inches to the left.

The minister had moved on a few months ago, but the locals continued to hold services, anyway. He supposed if you wanted something bad enough, you found a way to make it happen.

A horse was tied outside. Someone was in there. He supposed since he was the marshal, he should check it out.

There were three steps that separated the floor of the church from God's earth. Falcone climbed the steps and found the door unlocked.

The sanctuary was small. There were a few rows of wooden pews on one side of an aisle, and more pews on the other. At the far end of the small room stood a wooden lectern.

In the center of the room, a man was standing. He was facing the lectern, so his back was to Falcone. The man wore a white shirt with suspenders over his shoulders, and tied down low on his right side was a gun. He wore it like he knew how to use it. His hat was off, and held in his hands.

Falcone said, "Excuse me. Do you have business here?"

The man turned. He was young, maybe mid-twenties. Maybe younger. Hard to tell.

He said, "Marshal. No, I don't suppose I have any business here. I did at one time. At one time, a place like this was almost home to me. But I suppose now I have no right to be here."

Falcone found this man puzzling, but in an intriguing way. He decided to play along and keep him talking.

He said, "The minister rode out, long before I came to town. I have no idea where he went. The locals are looking for another one to take his place."

The man nodded his head. "So I've heard. I sometimes think I might offer my services to them. But then I realize just how hypocritical that would be."

Falcone was now truly puzzled. His face must have shown it, because the man smiled and walked toward him and held out his hand.

"I'm a minister," the man said. "Or I used to be, at least."

They shook hands.

The man said, "Tom McCabe."

Falcone nodded. "One of the McCabes. I should have guessed by the way you wear your gun. Seems like, around here, if you wear your gun like you know how to use it, odds are that you're a McCabe."

The man snorted a chuckle. "I suppose so."

"You're a minister?"

McCabe nodded. "Used to be. I was a Methodist minister, back in California."

One thing about Vic Falcone—he was a student of

human nature. Always had been. He found it fascinating. He had thought about mentioning to this man that guns weren't allowed to be worn in town, but decided against it. He wanted to keep this man talking.

He said, "Just how do you go about being a former minister? Every minister I've known seems to be in it for life."

McCabe nodded with a small grin. "So I thought I would be. But I've seen things. Done things. I'm now no longer worthy."

"Do I dare ask?"

Tom shrugged. "Why not? I killed a man. In fact, I killed more than one. Back in California. Men had attacked our camp, and I killed them."

Falcone's turn to shrug. "That would be self-defense, wouldn't you say?"

"But I didn't mind it when it happened. In fact, I think I liked it. Something came alive inside me when it was happening. Some sort of rush. Some sort of fire. I found myself caught up in the moment."

"It happens. I've been in battle. Something happens to you. Makes you into some sort of animal. If it didn't, then you wouldn't come out alive."

Tom nodded. "Perhaps so. But there was a time before that, when a man was aiming a gun at my daughter. If not for my uncle Johnny, horrible things would have happened. Johnny made an impossible shot, killing the man."

Falcone said, "Sounds like Johnny McCabe."

"But I found myself wishing I could have done that. Killed that man. I started resenting myself for not being able to do it."

Tom then said, "I don't know why I'm telling you all of this. You're a total stranger. None of this is your business."

"It's not like I have anywhere else to be." Falcone said. "Sometimes it's easier to talk to a total stranger."

"Sometimes."

Tom drew a breath, and turned back to what he had been looking at before the marshal had come in. The empty pulpit.

Tom said, "Then to top it all off, before we left California, I threatened to kill my brother."

"Did you mean it?"

Tom nodded. "Yeah. I meant it."

"Did your brother deserve it?"

"I can rationalize all sorts of reasons to say no. Jesus taught us to turn the other cheek. Violence is never the answer. But, yes. I had reason. He had threatened my family. He was the reason those men attacked our camp. They worked for him. Ultimately, everything that had happened, from the men threatening my daughter and wife to the attack on the camp, had been because of him and my mother. Now my mother's dead, so the responsibility falls to him. I wanted it all to stop, so I told him that if he didn't leave me and mine alone, I'd put a bullet in him."

Falcone rubbed his chin thoughtfully. "And now you're having trouble reconciling all of that with your Christian beliefs."

"Uncle Johnny told me he believes the teachings of the Bible are a guideline. That often we are faced with two choices and both are wrong, and we have to use the teachings of the Bible as a guideline and take the choice that is the least wrong."

Falcone nodded. "I'd say that makes sense."

"Except that I wasn't horrified when I killed those men. And when I threatened to kill my brother, I fully meant it. I should have felt remorse and regret. I should have been awash with it. But I wasn't."

"That's because he was a threat to you and yours."

Tom turned away from the pulpit to look at him again. He said, "That's not reason enough."

"Sometimes that's all the reason there is, preacher. You hold yourself to too high a standard. You reacted like any man defending his wife and child. You're human."

"I'm a sinner."

"Same thing."

Tom felt as though he had been punched in the face. He found himself taking a step backward.

He said, "You're right. I've been preaching that message for years, but maybe now I'm only really hearing it for the first time. God forgives."

"There you go," Falcone said.

Falcone started toward the door. "Nice talking with you, preacher. Try going easier on yourself."

"Thank you, Marshal."

Falcone waved a hand in the air, as if to say, *think nothing of it.*

Tom said, "I wonder if maybe you should be preaching from the pulpit, not wearing a gun."

Falcone was at the doorway, but he spun on his heel to look at Tom again.

He said, "There's no forgiveness for me, preacher. Not after all I've done."

Tom walked toward him. "What have you done? Yes, I've heard people talking. You were an outlaw of sorts before all the charges were dropped, and then you became a lawman."

"I was more than just an outlaw of sorts. I was a killer. I burned farms and shot people down in cold blood, during the war. We were guerilla raiders, fighting for the South. We justified all of it as being simply acts of war. But it was still killing."

"Did you like it? Like I did, when I was caught in the heat of battle?"

Falcone nodded. "At the time. When it was happening. But then afterward, the guilt would set in. And I would numb that guilt with whiskey. After the war, we continued doing the only thing we knew how to do. Rob and kill."

"Now, that can't be the only thing you know how to do. You're an educated man. I can tell by the way you speak."

"A long time ago, in another life, I was a school teacher. I'm a graduate of West Point, did you know that?"

Tom shook his head.

Falcone said, "But somehow, after all we did during the war, all of the atrocities we committed, we couldn't just go back to normal life. Not with all of that death hanging on us. So we continued. But we didn't actually shoot anyone down in cold blood anymore. Sam wouldn't allow it anymore."

"Sam?"

"Our leader. Sam Patterson."

Tom nodded with sudden recognition. "You rode with Sam Patterson. Now I know who you are. I knew your name from somewhere but didn't make the connection."

"I was his right-hand-man toward the end of it. Then, one day, Sam just rode out. He said it was the end of the trail for him, and he put me in charge of the men and he just rode out. I haven't heard from him since. And the men he left me in charge of were rough men. It took a lot to keep them in line. Cutthroats. Men with names like Kiowa Haynes. You ever hear of him?"

Tom shook his head. "Can't say that I have."

"Well, if you were a lawman you probably would have. He wanted to kill just because he liked it. Being their leader was a volatile situation. Keeping them in line was growing more and more impossible. It was made even more so because I was losing myself in whiskey. The more I drank to numb the guilt, the more I lost myself. And the more of myself I lost, the more I drank.

"I couldn't tell you how many men I killed during the war, preacher. But I hear their screams when I sleep at night. I hear them more vividly now because I left whiskey behind a few months ago. And we killed some men during robberies, after the war. It was self-defense, because they were shooting at us, but they wouldn't have been shooting at us if we hadn't been trying to rob them in the first place. We had shootouts with posses more than once. We killed some of them, too. We shot some men when we attacked your uncle's ranch a couple of years ago."

Tom was now putting things together in his mind. Connecting the proverbial dots. "You were that outlaw gang."

Falcone nodded.

"My uncle told us about it, but didn't mention names."

"It was us."

"And you don't think you deserve forgiveness?"

"Do you?"

Tom said, "I think we all do. I suppose I had forgotten that, but you just reminded me. What you said applies to you too."

"Well, preacher, maybe I don't want forgiveness. Maybe I feel I deserve to burn."

Falcone turned and walked out.

24

  The last week of June melted into the first week of July, and brought with it the Fourth of July celebration.
  The Fourth of July was a holiday the folks of McCabe Gap had celebrated every year, ever since the little community of McCabe Gap began forming. Cowhands came in from all of the ranches, and prospectors and even some trappers came down from the hills. Some folks from as far away as Bozeman were known to wander up and take part in the festivities.
  It was a day that saw Hunter up to his neck in business. The barroom floor was often standing-room-only. He always stocked up for the celebration, which often began the day before the Fourth and continued into the day after. The last thing you wanted was to run out of stock with a room full of loud, rowdy customers wanting more beer or whiskey.
  The other business in town that went into full operation was Miss Alisha's. She had said once that the Third through the Fifth were her busiest days of the year.
  Things were different this year. The little community of McCabe Gap had been swallowed up by the boomtown that was known as Jubilee. It was now official—the territorial government had approved the town charter.
  But even still, Ginny saw no need for a local tradition to be abandoned just because the town was growing, so she brought it up at a Town Council meeting the third week of June. Charlie Franklin, of course, knew all about the local area's celebration of the Fourth. The porch roof over the front door of his store had caught fire one year, a story that was still talked about.
  A drunken cowboy had thrown a bottle of whiskey into the air and a cowboy buddy of his drew his gun to shoot it. He managed to do so, and the whiskey from the broken bottle splashed onto the tiles of the porch roof. The bullet ricocheted off something, the way bullets sometimes do, and a spark was somehow created, and the whiskey soaking into the tiles caught fire. Eight or ten cowhands climbed the roof and beat at it with their hats or stamped at it with their boots until it was out. Then they all had a laugh over it and went to

Hunter's for another drink.

Franklin hadn't found it all that funny. At least, at first. But now that the incident had faded into memory, even he cracked a grin when it was brought up.

The other Town Council members agreed the tradition should be kept up. Even Aloysius Randall thought it was a great idea.

Plans went into motion. Hunter's and the other two saloons in town would be fully stocked. So would the lounge of the Jubilee Hotel. The town square, the place where Main Street and Randall Street connected and formed a right angle, would be the center of activities. This meant most of the action would be happening between Hunter's and the hotel.

Randall placed a rush order at a small print shop in Bozeman, and the week before the Fourth he had small fliers nailed up throughout both Jubilee and Bozeman. He even sent some by stage to Helena, and asked a friend at the bank there to make sure they got around.

When the Third hit—the fliers specified it was a three-day celebration—people began to drift into town. Mostly cowhands from the surrounding ranches. Josh gave Fat and Kennedy the day off so they could get into town and get an early start at burning away their month's wages on three days of fun.

Fred wasn't told he could have the day off, because his tenure at the ranch had earned him the right to take a day off when he decided to. He just made sure Johnny or one of the boys knew so someone else could take over wrangler or hostler duties for the day. But he chose to stay at the ranch for the Third. He had business to attend to. One horse Kennedy had been riding the day before had thrown a shoe, and Fred was going to tend to the smithy duties himself. They had an anvil there and a small, portable forge. No need to bother Henry Freeman for just one shoe.

Another horse had stepped into a small hole and went down, sending Josh rolling in the grass. Josh came out of it with a banged up shoulder, and now the knee he had hurt falling off the roof a couple summers ago in the shoot-out with Falcone and his boys was bothering him again. The horse had come out of it with a sprained foreleg. Fred wanted to tend to the horse a little more before he went into town. He would ride in on the Fourth, when he hitched up the buggy to drive Aunt Ginny in.

The Fourth was going to be the central day of activity. There would be a horse race. A ring was set up in town for a boxing match. There was talk of getting Jack in the ring, with the man Jack had flattened in Randall's office. Torgeson, his name was. The fight was being billed as a grudge match and the winner would take fifty dollars, even though Jack hadn't actually agreed to the fight yet.

A dance was planned for the evening, and then after that would be a fireworks display. Randall had the fireworks shipped up from Cheyenne.

Jack thought about all of this on the afternoon of the Third, as he stood outside Hunter's. Hunter stood with him, and Miss Alisha had wandered down from her establishment.

She was about Aunt Ginny's age, and wore a little too much makeup, trying to hide deep lines in her face that came from hard living.

In the street, cowhands kicked their horses into a full gallop. They had pistols in their hands and were firing into the air and crying out as they rode. Jack thought one of them rode for Zack Johnson, and two of them from the Willbury ranch.

"It's gonna really heat up around here tonight," Hunter said. "We already got a dozen men inside, pouring down whiskey. Two card games have started up."

Alisha nodded. She looked out at the wooden buildings that made up the new Main Street.

Hunter said, "I have to admit, it's gonna be good for business."

"That it will. But that doesn't mean I have to like it."

Hunter grinned. "You're just mad because Randall won't let you sit on the Town Council."

She said, "He doesn't consider my business legitimate. I'll tell you one thing, though. He told me he owned the land my establishment is on, and I had a week to vacate. I asked him what he would say if I paid the same rate he offered you. He said that would be fine. I don't think he really expected me to have the money. I dug into my purse and pulled out two thousand dollars and handed it to him. He was staring at me wide-eyed. He hadn't expected that."

She chuckled and said, "Whorin' is one business that ain't run on credit."

Jack grinned. He would have to quote her on that, someday.

The following afternoon, the town was filled. The population had exceeded four hundred, and Ginny thought every one of them must be in the town square. There were also people up from Bozeman and even a few in from Helena. Ginny took a chair on the open boardwalk-like deck in front of Hunter's. Hunter stood beside her. Bree was there, too, standing and looking like she wanted to jump into the crowd and be a part of it all. But she held back, trying to act the part of a lady. Ginny let her be a wildcat most of the time, but when they were at events like this, she insisted Bree at least pretend to be a lady. But it was like trying to hold back the tide.

"Oh, Aunt Ginny. This is all so unbelievable. I don't think I've ever seen so many people all in one place. I would love to enter that horse race. Ride Rabbit. I bet there's no one who could beat me."

"Bree," Ginny said. "It's not always about *beating* men in a horse race. Sometimes you just need to stand still and let one catch you."

"But I don't want to be caught."

Hunter said, "What type of boy would it take to drop a loop on you, Bree?"

Ginny rolled her eyes at the cowboy metaphor.

Bree said, "I don't know. I suppose it would take a boy who could keep up with me. One who could fight alongside me. A boy I could build a life with, out here in these mountains."

Ginny gave a sigh of resignation. "You are indeed your father's daughter."

Jack and Nina wandered over.

Bree said, "Isn't this all so fantastic?"

Jack said, "If you had told me last winter that by July this would be turning into a boomtown, I never would have believed it."

"Nina," Ginny said, "I wanted to tell you that you look very nice."

"Why, thank you."

Nina was smiling wide, and her hand was in Jack's.

Ginny said, "Where are your parents?"

"Oh, they'll be in. You know Pa. He's not one for crowds. He'll warm up to the idea of coming in, but he'll have to do it in his time."

Falcone was pushing through the crowd and working his way toward them.

"McCabe," he said. "Any chance of me hiring you on as a temporary deputy?"

"Not a chance."

"It's going to be potentially wild tonight. I could use a man with me. A man who knows the area and what to expect."

"A man like you wearing a badge is a travesty, Falcone. A travesty I won't be a part of."

Falcone gave him a long look. To Jack's surprise, he didn't see the anger he would have expected from a man like Falcone trying to pass himself off as respectable. What he saw was sadness.

Falcone didn't even say anything about the fact that Jack was wearing a gun. Maybe it was because all of the cowboys hooting and shooting their way up and down Main Street were wearing guns. The ban on guns was going to be a hard law to enforce.

Falcone turned and walked away.

Nina said, "He was the one who kidnapped me from our camp last summer. I can't believe he has the nerve to even show his face around here."

She turned away. Her lower lip was quivering. She said, "Jack, I want to go home."

Bree said, "Nina, if you go home now, then you've let him win. You can't let a rodent like Falcone have this much power over you. Stand tall and proud and face the storm, and let them know you can't be beat."

Nina looked at her, then she drew a breath and said, "You're right. I'm here to celebrate the Fourth. I'm not going to let him drive me away."

Ginny gave her niece a long look, but this time it was

filled with pride.

She said, "You truly are your father's daughter."

Jack said, "Are you looking forward to the dance tonight?"

Bree shrugged. "I suppose."

"A dance should be an exciting time for a young woman. A chance to maybe meet a new beau."

Bree said, "I know all the boys around here. I don't really think any of them are beau material."

Jack flashed a grin at Hunter and said, "What about Fat?"

Bree shook her head and rolled her eyes. "Please."

"Well, Bree, he's a good man. And you know he likes you."

Hunter had to turn away and hold back a laugh.

Bree gave Jack a stern glance. "Don't start."

Jack laughed, and Hunter joined him.

"All right," Bree said. "He's a good enough boy. Yes. It's just that he's all thumbs."

Jack said, "Out on the range, he's one of the better hands with a rope, and he rides a horse like he's born to it. The spring roundup would have gone a lot harder without him. He's really a top hand. He's just all thumbs around you. And you know why?" He looked at Hunter.

Hunter said, "He likes her."

"Boy, I'll say he does."

They began laughing again. Even Aunt Ginny was grinning. Bree folded her arms and looked away.

She said, "I really don't like being the subject of your ridicule."

"Oh, it's not you," Jack said.

"No," Hunter chimed in. "We're just laughing at the situation."

Fat wandered over. "Hello, everyone."

"Hi, Fat," Jack said.

Ginny said, "Hello, Mister Cole."

Fat glanced at his shoes, then at Bree, then at his shoes again and then back at Bree. "Are you having a good time, Miss Bree?"

She rolled her eyes with a little impatience. "Yes, Fat. I'm having a good time."

To Jack, he said, "So, are you going to fight that man of Randall's?"

"I haven't really decided yet."

Nina said, "I really hope you don't. It all seems so barbaric."

Hunter said, "Well I hope you do. I've already put twenty dollars on you."

Jack looked at him with disbelief. "Twenty dollars? Where did you get that kind of money?"

"We had a good night last night. I bet the entire till on you."

Jack shook his head with defeat. "Hunter. I haven't even said I was going to fight."

"Well, now you have to," Bree said. "Everyone wants you to put Randall in his place."

Ginny said, "Jack, you don't have to do anything you don't want to."

After a time, Aloysius Randall made his way through the crowd toward Hunter's. One of his men was with him. Not Torgeson.

He was smiling broadly. "Miss Brackston. Hunter. I have to say, this is a grand day, indeed. My hotel has no vacancies, even at the increased holiday rate. I had five cowhands sleeping on the floor of the bar last night, and even they paid the usual price for a hotel room."

He held his hands out, as though it was raining manna from heaven.

He said, "Success is in the air. Can't you just feel it?"

Hunter said, "Is there something you want with us?"

"Hunter. Can't we lay aside the rivalry for at least this one day, and all simply allow ourselves the chance to revel in the success?"

His eyes fell on Bree. He said, "And who do we have here?"

Jack said, "My sister, Bree."

He removed his hat entirely. "Aloysius Randall, at your service."

She was not impressed. "I know who you are."

"I hope you will allow me the pleasure of a dance, this evening."

"You know what they say. Hope in one hand, and..."

Ginny cut her off. "Bree!"

"Well, that's what they say."

Jack was fully laughing.

Bree took a step toward Fat, who was still standing about. She slipped an arm into his. She said, "I've promised all of my dances to Mister Cole, here."

Fat beamed with a sudden smile, and his face began to redden. "You have?"

Randall said, "Well then, some other time."

Falcone was walking up to him. "Mister Randall, may I have a word?"

"Just a moment." Randall looked at Jack. "I actually came over here to make sure you're fighting tonight. I have wagered a hundred on your opponent. The odds are, of course, in your favor."

Jack said, "And I'm sure you rigged the odds."

Randall gave a look of surprised innocence that wasn't very convincing. "Who, me?"

"Well I'm not fighting, so just forget it."

"But the ring is already built. There is a lot of money being wagered. Potentially thousands of dollars."

"Not interested."

"What can I do to make it worth your while?"

"Jack," Nina said. "Let's take a walk."

Randall said, "I mean it. We need you to fight. Name your price."

Jack glanced at Hunter, then back to Randall. "Seriously? Name my price."

"Yes. Absolutely."

"Let Alisha Summers join the Town Council."

Ginny turned to Jack, her mouth falling open. "Jackson!"

"Aunt Ginny, she's a businesswoman."

"She most certainly is not."

"Didn't you and Pa teach us not to judge others? That we each walk our own path?"

Johnny and Jessica had been in the crowd and were strolling over. Cora was riding on Johnny's shoulders. He had caught the last part of the conversation and was grinning.

He said, "That is what we taught them all, Ginny."

She scowled at him. "Oh, you think this is funny."

Randall thrust a hand at Johnny. "The legendary Johnny McCabe. I am truly honored. My name is Aloysius Randall."

Johnny shook the man's hand.

Jack said to Randall, "I guess you didn't mean what you said. You're not a man of your word."

Nina gave Jack's arm a tug. "Come on, Jack. Let's walk. This isn't funny."

But he stood his ground and kept his gaze on Randall. "I knocked your henchman Torgeson flat with one punch. And I can do it again."

Hunter said, "What did you set the odds at?"

Randall said, "Five to one."

Hunter was caught between an open guffawing laugh and a look of disbelief. "Five to one? Jack, I'm going to bet against you, too."

Jack gave him a look that said he didn't think it was funny. Nina gave Jack's arm another tug.

Cora said, "Daddy, what's so funny?"

"What's it going to be, Randall?" Jack said. "Is the chairman of the Town Council not a man of his word?"

He gave a huffing sigh. "All right. If you win, Alisha Summers is on the Council."

Jack shook his head. "She's on the council if I fight. If I win, and I'm going to, then you make your money."

Randall nodded his head reluctantly. "Done."

Randall then looked at Bree and removed his hat again. "Until next time, Miss McCabe."

And he turned and strode away. He said, "Come on, Higgins."

The bodyguard who had accompanied him followed him away.

Bree said, "Why do I feel like I need a good scrubbing?"

Ginny looked at her niece and said, "Men like Randall have a way of making you feel that way."

Falcone hurried and caught up with him. Falcone said, "Mister Randall, what are you doing? Talking with the McCabe girl like that."

"Mind your own business," Randall said. "And mind your tongue."

"You might think it's harmless fun, but you don't know those people."

"Don't you have some laws to enforce?"

Falcone grabbed him by the arm and spun him around. "Listen to me. I've tangled with the McCabes. Three times. Every time, I wound up not just defeated, but soundly. The fact that I'm still alive, I attribute to their mercy."

Randall shook his arm free. "You don't know who you're dealing with when you deal with me. You're afraid of the wrong people, Falcone."

Randall turned away and pushed his way through the crowd.

The thug who had been with Randall said to Falcone, "We have trouble."

Falcone looked at him, not sure what to say or to ask.

The man said, "He can't keep his eyes off the young girls. Girls half his age. And he won't take no for an answer. He's gotten into trouble before with it. In Chicago. He was able to buy himself out of the trouble there. He's had questionable dealings with girls in St. Louis, too."

"I didn't know that."

"There's a good thing going here. The money's rolling in. Real gold has been found, so now there's no need for him to sell everything and be gone. But if he keeps chasing after that girl, he'll end it for all of us."

"If he keeps pursuing that girl, he'll wind up dead. And it won't matter who's wearing this badge."

Torgeson was in the ring. His shirt was gone, and shoulders that were rounded with muscle and a stomach that was like a washboard were now visible. He danced back and forth, bouncing from one foot to the other, jabbing outward with his fists. He was ready for a fight, and clearly knew what he was doing.

Nina said, "I don't know about this, Jack."

Josh slapped Jack on the back. "It's all right. You can handle this jasper. I'll be up there in your corner."

Men in the crowd, to either side of Jack and behind, began calling out to him. "You can handle him, Jack!" And, "Get in there and fight!"

Johnny said, "You don't have to do this, Jack."

Jessica was with Cora back at Hunter's. This was not the kind of thing she or Johnny wanted Cora seeing. Ginny was with them, but Bree and Temperance were here with Pa and the boys.

Bree said, "Do you really think you can handle him, Jack?"

"Of course he can," Josh said, and gave Jack a push toward the ring.

Jack climbed up and into the ring. Josh was with him. Jack began unbuttoning his shirt and handed it to Josh. He then pulled off his undershirt. Jack was also tightly muscled, but he stood a couple of inches shorter than Torgeson and his frame was not as stocky.

But Nina liked what she saw. She said, "Oh, my."

Bree gave her a grin.

Josh said, "All right. Get in there. Just remember everything Pa taught us about boxing. And all that stuff Chen has been teaching about evading a punch and footwork and all of that."

Jack nodded.

Charlie Franklin was to be the referee. He stepped into the ring and the crowd broke into cheers. He raised a hand to the crowd, and the cheering grew louder. *Half the people here are sloshed,* Jack thought.

"All right, gentlemen," he called out to the fighters.

"Step to the center of the ring."

They did.

Charlie said, "Gentlemen, you will observe the Queensberry rules. No eye-gouging. No hitting below the belt. No kicking or wrestling. Got it?"

Both fighters nodded.

"Now shake hands and at the sound of the bell, come out fightin'."

Jack held out his hand. Torgeson just stood a moment, staring at Jack with hatred in his eyes. He grabbed Jack's hand for a moment, and then turned and headed back to his own corner.

Jack went to his. Josh was there, just outside the ropes.

Josh said, "He's bigger'n you are, so you have to use mobility. Dance around. Let him wear himself out."

Jack said, "I know how to fight him."

The bell rang.

Nina called out, "Be careful, Jack!"

Jack heard Bree's voice. "Knock the daylights out of him!"

Jack walked toward the center of the ring. Torgeson came out, fists held high. Jack kept his arms down, hands at his side, though the right was held in a fist.

Torgeson squared off, as though he was waiting for an attack. Jack's attack never came.

"Put your fists up!" someone in the crowd called out.

Torgeson swung a right hook that would have knocked Jack unconscious. Except Jack ducked and then sprang up, driving a right cross at Torgeson and putting his body behind it. Torgeson's feet flew out from under him and he landed hard on the floor of the ring.

The whole maneuver had been just like Chen had taught him. Bait, evade and then counter-strike. The right cross he had learned from Pa.

Franklin knelt by Torgeson. He then said to Jack, "Back to your corner."

Jack walked back to the corner with a grin.

Franklin began counting. "One...two...three..."

The crowd waited to see if Franklin would get to ten, or if Torgeson would be able to get back to his feet.

A fiddle was being sawed away on, a guitar was being strummed ferociously, and magical fingers were twinkling away at a banjo. The crowd was whooping and hollering. In the center, two gold miners were doing something that was somewhere between clogging and an Irish dance. They were too filled with whiskey to care.

The crowd clapped and encouraged them on. Jack smiled, his hand in Nina's. Bree was clapping and bouncing to the rhythm.

Off to one side of the crowd, Randall's hands were in the air.

"Two thousand dollars!" he called out.

This was the amount of money he won when Torgeson failed to rise during the count. In fact, Torgeson hadn't even opened his eyes. He had been hauled off to the new town doctor on a stretcher.

The dance was done, and the crowd applauded and men whistled and let out high pitched whooping sounds.

The fiddler, the guitar player and the banjo player conferred briefly, then began a waltz.

"Would you care to dance?" Jack said to Nina.

"I would love to, kind sir."

Jack could dance. This was one thing Aunt Ginny had made sure he knew how to do before he was sent back east to school. Nina could dance, too. His left hand took her right and they fell into motion together.

She said, "Are you sure your hand doesn't hurt?"

He nodded. "It's something Chen showed me. A trick, really. He calls it hitting with a soft fist. How he knows all this stuff is beyond me."

"Randall is sure happy. You won him a lot of money."

"And I got Miss Alisha on the Town Council."

"Aunt Ginny is not too pleased about that."

Jack chuckled. "When she calms down, she'll see the whole picture."

Nina pulled back a little so she could see his eyes. "The whole picture?"

"According to Aunt Ginny, Randall made the Town Council's rules a little too complicated. Since he's the chair, he can vote only in a stalemate. The Council has eight members, not counting him. My aunt and Charlie Franklin make two. Then there's Miah Ricker, the new blacksmith in town, and Doctor Stillman. And the owners of the two new saloons, and the assayer. The saloon owners and the assayer are in Randall's pocket. Mister Ricker is neutral, but I believe him to be a good man. He'll listen to reason. The doctor, too."

She gave a smile of sudden understanding. "With Miss Alisha there, then there's potentially a five-to-four majority against Randall."

Jack nodded. "As long as Mister Ricker and the doctor go along with Aunt Ginny, Franklin and Miss Alisha. And since there's an odd number, there can't be a stalemate, which means I've essentially taken away Randall's vote, too. It's not a fool-proof plan, but it should make it easier to keep him in check."

"My goodness, Jack." She moved in close to him again as they danced. "I didn't know you could be so devious"

"Civilization has come to McCabe Gap, whether any of us like it or not. And now we have to play by civilized rules. Unfortunately, deviousness and trickery are part of it."

"I wonder if Randall has figured it out yet?"

Jack looked over to where Randall stood at the edge of the crowd. Randall threw his hat in the air, then he brought a mug of beer to his mouth and began chugging.

Jack said, "I don't think so. He's too busy celebrating all the money he won. But come morning, once he sobers up and his head stops hurting, he'll figure it out."

The next song was a Virginia reel. Bree accepted Fat's invitation to dance. To her surprise, despite how clumsy he generally seemed, he was at home on a dance floor.

The band went into a square dance. Charlie Franklin was a fair hand at square dance calling, so he joined the band for this one.

Bree decided to take a break and went to the punch bowl. She took the glass dipper and sunk it down into the bowl. Before she could bring it out, a hand landed on hers.

She looked up and into the eyes of Aloysius Randall.

He said, "This type of dance isn't anything that appeals to me, either."

She said nothing.

He said, "Let's take a walk, and talk a little."

She said, "Move that hand if you don't want it broken."

He grinned. "I like a girl who has a little spirit."

Fat was beside her. He seemed to come out of nowhere.

He said, "He botherin' you, Miss Bree?"

Before she could answer, Higgins was there and stepped between Fat and Bree.

He said to Fat, "Move along, boy. This ain't none of your concern."

Josh and Jack had seen what was happening and came over.

Josh said, "Maybe not, but it's our concern."

He was flanking Randall, and Jack was facing Higgins. Both Josh and Jack were wearing their guns.

"Back away," Randall said.

"No," Jack said. "You back away. You and your man. If you don't, there's gonna be bloodshed."

"You wouldn't dare."

Josh said, his gaze deadly serious, "You don't know who you're dealing with. Back away."

Randall glanced about the crowd quickly. Probably looking for Pa, Jack figured. Pa had taken Jessica and Cora back to the ranch. A little girl needed to be in bed by now. But Jack figured he and Josh could handle this situation.

Jack noticed Vic Falcone standing not far away. Standing and watching.

Randall said to him, "Well? Are you gonna just stand there?"

Falcone shrugged. "Has a crime been committed?"

Randall's lip quivered with fury. But he apparently decided he needed to pick his battles, and this was not one of them.

He said to Higgins, "Come on."

And the two of them started away. The crowd parted for Randall like the Red Sea parting for Moses.

Higgins tossed one glance at Falcone as he walked by. It was quick and it was subtle, but Jack caught it.

Josh said to Bree, "Are you all right?"

Bree said, "I want to go home."

Josh nodded. "Come on. I'll take you."

Ginny sat with Granny Tate at the far side of the town square. She missed the entire confrontation with Randall because there were just too many people pressed in and about. Some were dancing, some were standing and jabbering. Some were just listening to the music.

Lanterns were hung overhead. Smoke from a barbecue pit drifted by, and she thought the smell was heavenly.

As she looked about, she noticed a girl not much older than Bree standing at the edge of the crowd. The girl was holding a bundle that looked like it might be a baby. Something about the girl struck Ginny as lonely and maybe a little sad. Something about the way she stood. Her shoulders, her posture.

Ginny said to Granny, "I'll be right back."

Ginny walked over to her.

"Good evening," Ginny said. "You're new in town, aren't you?"

"Yes'm," the girl said.

"Well, allow me to welcome you. I'm Virginia Brackston, of the McCabe Ranch, just outside of town."

The girl nodded and smiled. She couldn't shake hands because both hands were holding the baby.

"Mahalia Gideon," she said.

"So, what brings you to our fair little but growing town?"

"My husband wants to prospect. He said a place like this, where the gold isn't all dug out yet, might be the place to go."

Mahalia, Ginny thought. *Where have I heard that name before?*

A little warning flare was going off in the back of Ginny's mind. She had heard the name recently. But where?

Ginny knew how her own mind worked. She would keep the girl talking for a while until she figured out whatever it was the part of her that John called her *gut* was trying to tell her.

Ginny said, "So, where are you and your husband from?"

"Well, originally I'm from back east. He is, too. But of late, we're from Oregon."

Oregon, Ginny thought. Mahalia. She remembered Dusty mentioning a girl by that name that he had met in Nevada. He and Josh had gone to Oregon and looked for her. They had spent three months there, the previous winter. They hadn't found her, which was no real surprise. Oregon was a big state and they had no idea where she might have been.

There was no reason to believe this was the same girl. But the name was right. The age was about right. The location had been right. Mahalia—the girl he called *Haley*.

Ginny said, "Do you know what? My nephew knew a girl by the name of Mahalia who had moved to Oregon."

"Really?" the girl said. "What a coincidence."

Ginny didn't believe in coincidence.

Ginny said, as innocently as she could, "Yes. His name's Dusty."

The girl's eyes widened and her mouth fell open.

She said, "Dusty? Is he maybe about twenty? Wears a gun like he knows how to use it?"

Ginny nodded. "He's talked about you."

The girl's face came alive. The sadness Ginny had thought she saw was gone. "Dusty's here? I figured he must have forgotten all about me by now."

Ginny shook her head. "Child, he hasn't forgotten you."

"Is he here?"

"Not at the moment. He's away on business."

The girl's sudden elation deflated. "It's probably for the best. I'm married now."

Ginny said, "Where is your husband?"

"Back at the hotel. I wanted to see some of the goin's-on. He wouldn't like it if I was gone long."

"He didn't want to come down himself?"

She shook her head quickly. "He doesn't go for dancin', and the like. He says it's sinful."

Before Ginny could say anything, the girl said, "I'd best be getting back."

She started away, but after a few steps, she turned back to Ginny and said, "When you see Dusty, maybe you shouldn't tell him about me. It'd be for the best."

Ginny nodded. The girl turned and scurried away,

cutting through the crowd and working her way back toward the hotel.

Ginny became aware of a presence beside her. Granny Tate, shuffling along on aged feet and using a cane to steady herself, had come up beside her.

Granny said, "You know that girl?"

Ginny shook her head. "No. Not really. Dusty does, though. He knows her from before he moved here."

"That girl's afraid."

Ginny nodded.

Granny said, "There's different kinds of fear. I could see in her eyes she has the kind of fear that's because of a man."

Ginny said, "Suddenly, I'm not in a mood for festivities."

PART SIX

El Rosario

26

 The church was old, with adobe walls that were cracked here and there. The air inside had the scents of dust and old wood, but at least it was cool. A refreshing change from the oven-like heat outside.
 Dusty sat in a wooden pew, his hat dangling along his back from a chinstrap. He had discarded his buckskin shirt for a pull-over shirt of white linen, which was better designed for the hot Mexican weather. His buckskin shirt was folded up in his bedroll, and his horse was waiting for him at a hitching rail outside.
 At the front of the church was an altar, elevated by a couple of steps. There was a wooden cross and a wooden carving depicting the crucifixion. It had been painted once in natural colors. Flesh tones and with brown hair, and red blood dripping from the nails in the hands. But this carving was probably as old as the church, Dusty figured. The paint was chipping away in places.
 This church was in Nueva Leone, in a small town twenty miles south of the border. Dusty was here for information. The thinking he and Zack and Joe were subscribing to was that they had to be in the general vicinity of the prison. But since there was little public knowledge of the place, and Americans were being held there illegally, they didn't expect to find any signs posted that would lead the way. But Dusty had an idea, and he had to execute it here.
 A couple of people were in the church. Off to Dusty's right and ahead a couple of rows was a woman. Graying hair and a matronly shape. She was kneeling and working at a line of beads she clutched in one hand. A young woman was in the front pew directly ahead of Dusty, and she was also kneeling.
 Dusty knew little of the Catholic church and its ways, so he just sat quietly, head bowed. But his eyes were open and he was glancing about, making certain he took in everyone in the room. Every movement.

A man walked in wearing a heavy looking brown robe and a thick belt tied about his waist. Must be the priest, Dusty thought. Or the brother, or whatever. He knelt at the altar and mumbled something and then rose to his feet and stepped off to a side room.

After a while, the young woman ahead of him rose to her feet and stepped out into the aisle. She couldn't have been much older than Dusty. Her hair was jet black and her skin a silky looking olive, and she wore a white peasant blouse that was falling off the shoulder.

She struck Dusty as jarringly attractive, but he forced his eyes downward as she walked past. He was here for information, not to draw attention to himself.

Dusty waited. Partly out of respect for the fact that he was in a church, and partly because, again, he didn't want to attract attention to himself. But he wasn't good at sitting still for too long, and it was hard not to fidget.

When it came to God and such, he wasn't sure what he believed. He knew Pa blended Shoshone beliefs with the teachings of Jesus to form a sort of seamless blend. He knew Aunt Ginny believed in Jesus but she didn't subscribe to any particular doctrine. She attended the church in McCabe Gap every so often, and was sure the more devoted church-goers thought she was something of a heathen, which made him grin. But he didn't really know where he stood on such matters.

He waited, and eventually the matronly woman was finished with her bead-driven prayer, or whatever it was she was doing, and then rose to her feet. She stepped out into the aisle, knelt toward the altar and solemnly crossed herself with her right hand, then with but a glance to Dusty she headed down the aisle and out the door.

Dusty waited some more. Eventually the man in the brown robe came back and went to the altar.

He knelt and crossed himself, but then before he could move further, Dusty was behind him.

"Excuse me, Padre," Dusty said. He sure hoped the Padre could speak English. Dusty's Spanish was really limited.

The man turned to face Dusty. He was maybe sixty, with silver hair and a hawkish nose. He said in a gently rolling Spanish accent, "What can I do for you, my son?"

"I need information."

The Padre nodded gravely.

Dusty had gunfighter written all over him, and he also was dusty and his linen shirt was streaked with sweat. He knew if he sat in a bath for a little while there would be a half inch of gravel and silt at the bottom of the tub. His face was covered with what was now easily two months' worth of whiskers. He looked more like an outlaw on the run than a man who had sought out the church for confession.

Dusty said, "I'm looking for a place called El Rosario."

The Padre's eyes widened.

He asked, "What do you need with such a place?"

Dusty decided on the spot to just say it outright. Be honest with the Padre.

He said, "A friend of mine is in there. I plan to bust him out."

The Padre glanced nervously toward the front door, over beyond the pews at the opposite end of the room.

He said, "Not in here. Follow me."

The priest led Dusty to a room out back. A kitchen that was built before the invention of the iron stove. A hearth as tall as Dusty covered half of one wall, and there was a long wooden table.

The priest didn't sit, and didn't offer Dusty a chair. Dusty figured the Padre didn't want him here any longer than he had to be.

The Padre said, "No one has ever escaped from El Rosario."

"There's a first time for everything."

"Many men go in. None ever come out. Everyone who goes in there eventually dies there. And they don't die easily."

"But it seems to me the guards and the warden are probably good Catholic men, or at least they want folks to think so. And good Catholic men aren't going to turn away a Padre going in there to pray for the inmates' souls."

The priest nodded. "Indeed. I know the way. I say nothing to anyone, though."

"I need you to say something to me. Draw me a map, at least."

"Trying to do this will get you killed."

"I'm not alone. There are two others waiting for me outside of town."

The Padre nodded. "I see. There is nothing I can say to talk you out of this?"

Dusty shook his head.

The Padre got a sheet of paper and a pencil that had been sharpened down to about two inches in length.

"We are here," the Padre said, drawing an X on the paper.

He then drew a wavy line that meandered its way along the paper, explaining that there was a set of low, arid ridges and then a small stream and a grove of trees, and then a dry arid stretch, and there was the prison."

"Where do they get their water?"

"The prison is built over a natural spring. The water is not good, but it is wet."

"Do you know all of the prisoners there?"

He shook his head. "I see most of them, and I know some of the names. It is not a large place, for a prison."

"Do you know the name Addison Travis? Or Sam Middleton?"

He shook his head. "Regrettably, no. But there is more than one gringo there."

"This man is maybe fifty, maybe a little older. A little taller than I am. Rugged build. Hair that's turning gray. He had a mustache, the last I saw of him. He speaks very well. Almost like an actor, or a politician."

The Padre's eyes lighted up with recognition. "I believe I might know the man. He has been there a few months. I saw him last Saturday, when I paid the prisoners a visit."

"He's still alive, then."

The Padre nodded. "As of last Saturday, yes."

"What can you tell me about the prison?"

"It is only one floor high, with adobe walls and a flat roof. It was at one time a hacienda to a ranchero, and it has since been added onto. Much of the building is a large, narrow hallway with cells at either side. It houses maybe thirty prisoners at the most."

"Do you know which cell he's in?"

The Padre nodded. "As of the last time I saw him, he was in the fourth cell on the left from the door facing the front of the building."

"Thanks," Dusty said. "I'll be on my way, now. If anyone asks, you never talked to me."

"You can believe that. I don't need the wrath of the government descending on me. The all-powerful Presidente Diaz. But I tell you what I know because I don't believe in the keeping of men in prison when there has been no trial. Many of those men are political prisoners who have done nothing wrong at all. I do not believe in dictatorships, and that is what we have now in Mexico. I love my country, Senor, don't get me wrong. I just think my country deserves much better than what Diaz offers."

Dusty didn't know about politics. What he did know was that he had to get moving.

He said, "Thanks, Padre."

The kitchen had a door, and from there he stepped out into the harsh, Mexican sun.

He pulled his hat back up and onto his head to shade his eyes, and walked around the building to his horse.

A man was walking alongside a cart that was pulled by a donkey, and as he walked he tossed a glance at Dusty. A couple of children running in the street were stopping to look at him, too. Apparently they didn't see a gringo too often in this little town, Dusty thought. Or at least one looking like a refugee gunfighter.

One other man stopped to look. On the boardwalk across the street. A soldier, in the uniform of the Mexican Army. Not good, Dusty thought.

He gave the man only a passing glance, trying not to look nervous or like he had any reason not to want to be noticed. He snatched the rein from the hitching rail and leisurely stepped up and into the saddle and turned his horse away down the street.

27

    The building was long and low, just like the Padre had said, and the adobe walls gleamed in the moonlight.

    There was a low oak out beyond the prison grounds, and they waited beneath it. Dusty and Joe, kneeling in the grass. The moon was bright enough to cast some shade, and they were hidden in the shade of the oak. Zack was with the horses a little ways back.

    "I can see the door toward the center of the building," Dusty said. "And windows. They don't look like anything but dark squares from here. Counting the windows going from that door out to the left, then Sam should be in the cell belonging to that fourth window."

    "Four guards outside," Joe said. "I count four of them, with rifles. Two moving clockwise and two in the other direction. They're circling the prison, cutting a perimeter."

    Dusty nodded.

    Joe said, "They seem to be crossing past each other. Once in front of the prison, and once in the back. If I'm counting right, then a pair of guards crosses the front of the prison every ten minutes."

    "There don't seem to be any guards on the roof. There's probably not enough visibility to make it worthwhile to put a guard up there."

    "They're doing it just the way I would. Guards on the ground. They probably got some inside, too. I'd have one or two by the door, and at least two others roaming about the place."

    "Considering the reputation of this place, I expected more."

    Joe said, "The location of the place ain't known by many. Their biggest concern is probably keeping prisoners from escaping, not keeping people from trying to break in."

    "Ten minutes, huh?"

    Joe nodded.

    "Isn't much time to do what we have to do," Dusty said. "How far do you think it is between here and the prison wall?"

    Joe shrugged. "Five hundred feet, maybe."

    Dusty nodded. "All right. After the next pair of guards

passes, I'm gonna make my way to the side of the building. Window number four. Between the two of us, I can probably move the fastest."

"You just be careful. One slip-up and the whole thing's lost. Keep in mind, one shot gets fired, you'll probably have a dozen armed men charging out of there."

"I don't see any other way to find out if Sam is in the room the Padre thinks he is. Or if he's even still alive. We can sit out here and watch the building for days. But watching ain't gonna tell us much."

Joe said, "All right. But if you get seen, then the whole thing's off. Even if we get away without getting shot, we'll never get close enough to this place again."

"This whole thing's a risky proposition. We knew that from the start. And we knew we might not succeed. But for Sam's sake, we have to try."

"So, let's say you get all the way up to the outer wall of the building. Then what?"

Dusty said, "I go to the window and call his name, I guess. I'll make sure he's there, then check out the condition of that window. See what it consists of. Iron bars, probably."

"Then you'll have to wait until the next guard crossing, and get back out here."

They each had pulled off their riding boots and replaced them with deerskin moccasin-style boots. Joe always carried a pair with him, and Dusty had started doing so. Something he had learned from Pa.

They waited. Two guards came into view right on schedule. Dusty and Joe were silent in the shade of the tree as the guards walked past, coming within fifty feet at one point.

Dusty could make out wide-brimmed hats, and each man was carrying a rifle or a shotgun. Hard to tell which in the moonlight. One man had a bandolier over one shoulder and across his chest.

They were talking lightly. One laughed at something the other said. They weren't really paying attention, because this was El Rosario. Very few knew the location, and for those who did, the reputation was daunting.

After the guards had moved on, Dusty began toward the building at a light run. He crouched as he moved. The moonlight gave him a reasonably good view of the terrain ahead of him, but he failed to see a sudden drop of about a foot, and he pitched forward and somersaulted to a stop. He laid there a moment in the grass and sage, deciding he wasn't seriously hurt, then pushed to his feet and continued.

He made it to the wall and crouched beneath window number four. He looked out at the land in front of the prison. In the moonlight, he could see a scattering of short oaks, including the one where Joe waited. There was a lot of open country beyond them. No guards were in sight, yet.

He tried to guess how many minutes had passed. He had been running at maybe half speed, and the distance was five hundred feet. There was also the time lost when he fell down. He estimated two minutes. He decided to play it safe and say five minutes, meaning he didn't have long before the next pair of guards came into view.

He stood up by the window. The sill was high, maybe six feet off the ground. He called out in as loud a whisper as he could, what Jack would probably call a stage whisper, "Sam!"

There was no response. He called out again, and he waited. He hoped Sam was in there. If not, then the longer he waited here, the greater the chance of being caught. And being thrown into this place as a political prisoner wasn't how he wanted to spend the rest of his days.

Addison Travis lay stretched out on the old mattress that had served as his bed for the past few months. Old, torn ticking. Bed bugs. Dark stains—he didn't want to guess what they were. Probably blood.

The floor of the cell was made of granite slabs chiseled off reasonably flat, and the floor was covered with straw. At the other side of the cell was another mattress, and that was where his cellmate was. Addison had heard the guards call him Pedro. Addison didn't know if this was actually his name, because his cellmate had actually said nothing in the five months Addison had been here. The man just sat with his arms folded over his knees and rocked and stared. At night he crawled over to his mattress and stretched out on it.

Near the door was a bucket partially filled with stale, muddy water. Addison and Pedro got one bucket to share every day. That was their drinking water. Once a day they each got a pail of some sort of slop. Yellowish sticky muck. Sometimes carrots were in it. Sometimes there were dead flies. This was their food.

At the corner of the cell was a gap between the granite flooring and the wall. This served as their outhouse. Addison had never seen his cellmate use this little hole in the floor. Judging from the smell of the man, he simply did his business where he sat. Addison could easily see how a man could lose his mind here.

Addison had been out of the cell only three times in the five months he had been here. These were for beatings. He had been tied to a chair and a man drove fists into him. Simply for the sake of doing so. They weren't trying to force a confession out of him or get any sort of information. They were simply beating on a prisoner for the sadistic fun of it.

Toward the center of the facility was a timber in the ceiling, and driven into the timber were two iron hoops. Once they had tied Addison's wrists to those hoops and taken a bullwhip to him. They had left his shirt on him, so now the back of his shirt was in shreds and soaked with dried blood.

It's all for Peddie, he told himself. Peddie and the others. Johnny McCabe and his group. He liked to think of Peddie as being safe, in a warm bed and under a dry roof. She had seemed rather taken with McCabe's brother Matt, and Matt had seemed so with her. Perhaps they were married. Perhaps there was a child on the way. Perhaps they would find the happiness that had been denied him over the years. A wife. Children. A home.

He realized he heard a whispering sound. His name. Well, not his name, really, but the name he had used for so many years, before he turned himself in. *Sam.*

He thought he was dreaming at first, but then he realized he was awake. Someone was outside his window whispering his name.

He got to his feet. He was a little wobbly at first because the slop he was fed was hardly nutrition. He supposed he was slowly starving to death.

He took a couple teetering steps toward the window, and called back in a loud whisper, "Is someone there?"

"It's Dusty McCabe. We're here to get you out."

Dusty McCabe. No kidding. Johnny McCabe and his people really took the cake. They had come all this way to try to rescue him.

"You can't," he said. "There are more than a dozen guards here. Storming this place would be like storming the bastille."

Dusty hesitated a moment. Then he said, "We ain't gonna storm nothing. This window's comin' out and you're gonna crawl out and we're gonna run like we've never run before."

"Just like that?"

"Give us a few minutes. We're gonna get you out of here."

"You're going to get yourself killed."

"That would have already happened last winter if you hadn't shown up when you did. Besides, from what we've seen they have only four guards outside, patrolling in pairs."

"They can have men on the roof really fast. Men with rifles."

"You leave it to us. We're not gonna leave you in here."

Addison had to ask. "Where's Peddie? Is she all right?"

"We can't talk now. I've gotta run. I'll be back in a few minutes."

Dusty waited until the second pair of guards had passed before he returned to the oak tree.

He said to Joe, "The bars are iron, and they're in a steel frame inside the window. The framework is rusty and kind of crumbly in places. I think if we got a horse and tied it to the frame and gave it a pull, the frame would either come apart or come loose."

Joe stared at Dusty a minute in disbelief. "And how do you expect to do that? It'll be impossible to get a horse up to that wall without being seen. Or heard."

"What we need is a distraction."

Dusty glanced about. The prison was out in the open for a reason. If a prisoner somehow managed to get outside, there was a lot of open country he had to run across before he got to the trees. The guards could easily pick him off from the roof.

The only thing between here and the prison wall was

five hundred feet of grass and sage. To the sides, there looked to be more than a thousand feet until the nearest tree.

Grass and sage, he thought. They needed a distraction. He stood up for a moment.

Joe said, "What're you doing?"

"Trying to figure which way the wind is blowing."

"From the southwest."

Dusty looked at him with a little surprise.

Joe said, "I always check which way the wind is blowing."

Dusty knelt back down and ran his fingers through some strands of grass at his feet. "This grass is really dry."

Joe nodded.

Dusty said, "Got a match?"

Zack waited with Dusty while Joe headed off toward the southwest, and disappeared into the night. Zack had brought the horses up and they were now picketed a little bit behind the oak tree.

Dusty glanced overhead, at the moon. He said, "Must be about two in the morning. Once we get Sam out of there, we're only gonna have a few hours before daylight."

"This plan of yours," Zack said, looking off toward the southwest. There was no sign at all of Joe. It was like he had been swallowed up by the night. "You're just like your father. You're good at what he calls tactical thinking. What I call it is the ability to make war with the best of them. It's a little scary sometimes, you know that?"

Dusty grinned. "Just like my father. That has a good sound."

"Your Pa's a good man. One of the best I've ever known. You can do a lot worse than to be like him."

They waited. Then Dusty saw it. From off in the darkness to the southwest of the prison, where the tree line was at least a thousand feet from the building, there was a quick spark. Like a lightning bug. It was there, then it wasn't.

"You see that?" Dusty said.

Zack nodded. "It's Joe."

Within minutes, there was the orange glow of a small fire. Looked at first like a small campfire in the distance, but it was growing fast. Spreading. Growing taller.

"Get the horses," Dusty said. "We'll have to be moving any minute now."

One pair of guards was rounding the corner of the building. One of them gave out a call. "*Fuego!*"

Dusty's Spanish wasn't good, but he knew enough to know what that meant. Fire!

The call was given out a few more times. Then a bell from somewhere within the prison began sounding. Men were rushing out toward the fire, which now had grown to a line of flames standing maybe five feet high. The breeze was not strong, but it was enough to start the grassfire advancing toward the prison at the pace of a man walking.

"Now," Zack said.

Dusty grabbed the rein of one horse. A coil of rope was slung across the saddle horn.

He said to Zack, "You stay with the other horses. I've got this."

"You sure?"

"Yes. If any of those horses run off, then we'll be in trouble."

Dusty took the horse by the reins, and started toward the building.

As Dusty led the horse across the grassy expanse toward window number four, he saw another orange glow from out behind the prison. Looked like Joe had maybe started a second fire.

There were shouts and the sounds of men running. But Dusty was approaching the prison from the north side, and the building hid him from view of the men dealing with the fire.

Dusty called out. He didn't keep his voice to a whisper this time. "Sam!"

Sam was at the window. "What's going on?"

"A fire started out back. Accidental-like, of course."

Dusty was tying the rope to the bars as he spoke.

Sam said, "What're you doing?"

"Think you can climb out this window?"

"Dusty, you're going to get yourself killed."

"Sooner or later. Bound to."

The rope was secure, and Dusty grabbed the horse by the reins and began leading him away.

He said, "Pull, boy. Pull."

The horse pulled.

Sam said, "Dusty, this is foolhardiness. Get away from here while you can."

The rusted steel window frame began to creak. Adobe crumbled around it. Then a section of the wall cracked and the window frame came free and landed in the grass.

Dusty ran back to the window. "Come on! Let's go!"

Sam got his shoulders and torso into the window frame, but he was too weakened. The beatings. The lack of proper food.

Dusty grabbed him by both shoulders and pulled, and Sam came out and Dusty fell back and did a backward somersault on the grass.

He scrambled to his feet. Sam was still down, on his hands and knees.

"Can you run?" Dusty said.

Sam said, "I don't know."

He tried to get to his feet but fell back to one knee. Apparently he couldn't, Dusty decided. He helped Sam to his feet and then with one arm around his back for support, got him to the horse, half-dragging him along.

Sam got one foot into a stirrup, and Dusty pushed him up and into the saddle. Dusty then pulled a knife and sliced free the rope, then was up and onto the horse behind Sam.

"Let's ride!" Dusty shouted.

The horse didn't wait to be told twice. It broke into a run toward the trees. It couldn't run at full speed because the ground was too uneven in the darkness, but they were moving at a fast trot.

Guns were fired from behind them. Dusty pulled his revolver and fired from the back of the horse. In the night and on the back of a running horse, he couldn't get a good view of what was going on behind him, but he saw flashes of gunfire from the prison roof and from somewhere near Sam's window, so that was where he tossed his shots. He felt one bullet sting the side of his face. Dusty didn't take time to even worry about it, and continued firing until his pistol was empty.

Sam lurched, and Dusty hoped it wasn't from a bullet.

Zack was in the saddle, a rifle up to his shoulder and he began squeezing off shots. The drawback of this was each gunshot created a flash that was easily seen in the night and would give the guards a target. But the benefit was that Zack was covering Dusty and Sam as they rode toward the trees.

Zack fired fast, jacking the Winchester and pulling the trigger and then jacking the gun again. Zack wasn't quite as good a shot as Johnny McCabe. Dusty figured few men were. But he was a good enough shot that he sent the guards running for cover.

"Let's ride!" Dusty called out to Zack.

They started off toward the north, cutting between trees. The moonlight was bright enough that they could see their way fairly well.

One problem about this plan was that Joe was still out there somewhere, on foot. Joe had said not to worry, that he would find them. Dusty only hoped Joe was right.

29

It turned out Sam had taken a bullet to the shoulder. They put a quarter of a mile behind them, then stopped to tend to him.

Dusty helped him out of the saddle, and checked the wound as much as he could in the moonlight.

"Looks like it might be in the shoulder muscle itself," he said. "Hard to tell out here. No bones seem broken, though."

Dusty wrapped a bandana around the wound as best he could.

As he worked, Sam said, "Looks like you got hurt, yourself."

A bullet had creased Dusty's cheekbone. It had stopped bleeding, but the side of his face was covered with drying blood.

"It'll take care of itself," Dusty said.

When he was done tying the bandana around Sam's shoulder, he said, "This will have to do for now. Slow down the bleeding."

Sam nodded. "It's all right. I can ride."

"Hold on," Zack said. He was looking off to a grove of trees, and drawing his gun.

Dusty stood up and did the same. He had reloaded his pistol, the first thing he had done when they stopped riding.

A man was stepping out of the shadows of the trees. He was holding his hands high in the air as he walked toward them.

He called out, "Hello, the camp."

It was Joe.

Zack handed him the reins to his horse and said, "This is hardly a camp."

Joe said, "It's the best we can do on short notice."

Dusty said, "How'd you get all the way out here so fast?"

"After I started the second fire, I ran in this direction. I was probably almost here before you even began riding."

"Sam's been hit," Zack said. "But he can ride."

"Then let's be going. We want to put as much distance between us and that there prison as we can. I say we head to that hacienda."

Two days earlier, when they were first scouting the area, they had found an old broken-down hacienda about ten miles north of the prison. It had been abandoned long ago. The roof had caved in and one adobe wall collapsed. But the barn seemed to be mostly intact. A few snakes and rats liked the shade, but Joe said they could be dealt with easily enough.

Dusty climbed into the saddle and Zack helped push Sam up behind him.

"Don't you go falling off," Dusty said to Sam.

"I'll hang on. You just turn this horse in the right direction.

Zack and Joe climbed onto their horses, and they started off into the night. Zack led the way and Joe rode behind Dusty and Sam, mindful of their back trail.

They were at the old hacienda an hour before sunrise.

Joe said, "I'll handle the varmints."

He slid off his deerskin boots and pulled on his riding boots.

"Harder leather," he said. "It can stop a snake bite."

"You hope, at least," Zack said.

Joe nodded. "I hope."

Joe found a broken, three-foot section of narrow timber from the wreckage of the hacienda. He pulled apart a cartridge and sprinkled black powder on one end, then struck a match and lit the end on fire. The powder caught immediately, and within a minute or so, the wood was burning. This provided him with a makeshift torch.

He then gathered some firewood from scraps of wood in the hacienda, and pulled some dry hay for tinder. He scraped away some of the debris on the barn floor—sticks and leaves and rocks, the kind of stuff that tends to gather in unattended buildings like this—taking it down to the bare earth. This barn had a dirt floor. With the scrap wood and tinder, he built a small fire at the center of the barn floor. He let the flames get no more than a foot in height. Not nearly high enough to present a danger to the barn roof, but enough to scare back the rodents and snakes.

"Come on in," he said. "We should be all right."

The boards that made up the barn walls were

crumbling with dry rot, and a couple of them had fallen entirely. This allowed enough ventilation so the barn didn't fill up with smoke.

Dusty looked about warily as he stepped into the place.

He said, "I never did like snakes or rats."

Joe shrugged. "I've dealt with worse."

Sam was able to get out of the saddle and walk into the barn on his own. Zack opened up his bedroll and Sam stretched out on it.

Joe went out to picket the horses behind the hacienda, and away from the trail.

"We've gotta wait here a while," Zack said. "Let Sam have some rest."

Dusty nodded. "If he dies, it would defeat the whole purpose of us being here."

"But by then, the Federales will have had time to spread out and begin searching the area. We won't be able to stay ahead of them anymore."

Dusty said, "We'll have to ride by night. Find places to hole up by day."

"How long do you think he'll be able to hold up like this?"

Sam said, "I survived five months in El Rosario. I'll hold up just fine."

Dusty said, "Even after we make it across the border, we may not be safe. Breaking a man out of prison is no small thing. The Mexican government might contact the American authorities, and we'll have American lawmen looking for us, too."

Joe was stepping back into the barn. "I know a place in Texas. The town where I worked as a deputy. It's only a couple days' ride north of the border. We might be able to cut down that a bit if we ride hard."

"You've told us about that lawman you work for. But would he break the law to help us out?"

"I wouldn't ask him to do that. But there's a ranch outside of town. The ramrod is an old Texian. He might."

30

Sam Wilson stood on the porch, breathing the nighttime Texas air. His mustache was thick and white. At his side was an old-school Colt .44 Dragoon. A cap and ball revolver. He was not a gunman but an old cowhand. He wore his gun high on his hip and not tied down.

Life had changed much in Wilson's lifetime. When he and Nathan Shannon had first come to this land, it had been empty. Just long, low hills covered with brown grass, and occasional long stretches of flat ground. There hadn't been a building within a day's ride. Now the ranch house stood tall and proud with adobe walls and a peaked roof. Off to the side was a barn. Beyond it was a corral. Out beyond that were miles of grassland, all claimed by the Shannon Ranch, with over a thousand head roaming and grazing.

Life had changed much, Wilson thought. And yet the breeze still smelled the same. Dry air. The scents of grass and sage.

He was about to go back into the house, but then he heard a sound from the barn. The sound of something being kicked over. Odd, he thought. The stalls should all be empty. There shouldn't be any activity in the barn.

Then he heard a horse nicker from the barn. There was at least one horse in there, after all. Even though he knew there should be none.

He drew his pistol and stepped down to the grass and covered the distance between the house and the barn in a few quick steps.

He stopped by the barn door and could see some pale light slipping through the gap between the door and the door frame. Someone was in there.

He was no gunfighter, but he could shoot straight. And he had been in more than one gun battle over the years. He and Nathan Shannon had defended this ranch against Comanche raiders a few times. They had exchanged shots with rustlers more than once.

With his pistol ready, he pulled open the door and stepped in.

A man was standing in front of him with a shotgun in his hands. A large, bushy beard and hair to his shoulders.

He looked much more trail worn than the last time Sam had seen him, but he would know this man anywhere.

"Joe," he said.

Joe lowered his scattergun. "Sam. Are you alone?"

Sam nodded. "Just me. Maddie's back in St. Louis visiting her mother. The hands are out with the herd. Why? What's going on? None of us were expecting you back so soon."

Joe said, "I'm not alone."

Two other men were there, and a third was lying on the barn floor.

One of the men had a thick, dark mustache, and his pistol was trailing low and tied down.

Wilson said, "Zack Johnson. You used to ride with the Texas Rangers. Your name is legendary in these parts. I met you once, years ago."

Zack stared at him a moment. "Sam Wilson."

They shook hands.

Zack said, "You and Nathan Shannon were building a ranch. Is this it?"

Wilson nodded. "This is the place. But Nathan's not here anymore. Caught a bullet a few years ago."

"Sorry to hear that. He was a good man."

"We got the man who did it, though. Or at least, the man who hired it done. Never got the man who actually fired the shot."

Josh introduced his nephew Dusty.

Joe said, "And this man on the ground is Sam Middleton."

Sam was awake. "I'm actually known by many names. But Sam is fine for now."

"He's caught a bullet," Joe said. "Which is why we're here."

Joe explained the situation. He left nothing out. Zack figured Joe must know the man well and trust him fully. That was good enough for Zack.

"We came here," Joe said, "because we know the law could be looking for us soon. I didn't want to put Tremain in the position where he had to pick between our friendship and the law."

"Well," Wilson said, "you're in luck. Tremain was called

away on Texas Ranger duties. He's not expected back for a while. Jericho's in charge while he's gone."

Joe nodded. "We need Doc Benson out here. Sam's lost a lot of blood, and that bullet might have to come out."

Wilson said, "I'll saddle a horse and ride into town and get Doc. You boys wait here. It'd be best if Jericho didn't see you. There's no one else at the house, so take Sam on in. Use one of the empty bedrooms upstairs. There's food in the kitchen. And whiskey, if you're of a mind."

"Much obliged."

Between the ride into town and the ride back, Wilson was gone three hours. The boys had moved Sam upstairs to one of the guest rooms. Between the three of them, Dusty was the one with the knack for cooking, so he put together a quick chicken soup for Sam, and fried up some steaks for himself, Zack and Joe.

Joe chewed into it. "Mmm-boy. Ain't tasted steak this good in a long time."

Zack said to Dusty, "I had almost forgotten how good you cook."

To Joe, he said, "One time a couple years ago, Dusty did some cooking for Hunter's saloon in town. You never tasted cooking so good."

They heard hoof beats outside. Most likely Wilson returning, hopefully with the doctor. But all three had pistols out, just in case.

Wilson came through the front door. "Just us, boys."

With him was a man taller than Zack, who was built like a boxer and wore his gun slung low and tied down. He was in a white shirt and a wide, black hat. He had a dark goatee and a square chin, and a nose that looked like it might have been broken once. Dusty guessed him to be maybe forty.

"This here is Doc Benson," Wilson said.

Dusty stared a moment.

"I know," the man said. "I don't look like a doctor."

"No offense," Zack said, "but you look more like a gunfighter."

The doctor smiled. "I'll take that as a compliment."

Dusty and Joe escorted him upstairs to see Sam.

"I've been shot worse than this before," Sam said.

Benson said, "I've seen worse wounds before, too. I know the conventional thinking is that all bullets have to come out, but I'm of the belief that sometimes you cause more damage trying to dig one out."

"What do you recommend?"

"I'll clean the wound out, and suture it shut. Give you some stitches. Then, you need to build back up the blood you lost. Get lots of rest. Drink plenty of fluids and eat some red meat. As long as infection doesn't set in, you should be back on your feet in a week or so."

Dusty glanced at Zack with a grin. "Oh we have a way of preventing infection."

"He ain't gonna like it," Zack said, returning the grin.

They held Middleton down while Wilson poured an ounce of whiskey into the bullet wound. Then Benson stitched it shut. Wilson tore up a bed sheet and Benson tied a bandage around it.

They left Middleton to sleep. Downstairs, Wilson offered Benson a glass of whiskey.

"I have to say," Benson said, "I've never seen anything like that done before. It really works?"

Zack said, "I learned it with the Texas Rangers, years ago. I've never seen an infection start up in a wound treated like that."

"Good to know." Then Benson said, "The Texas Rangers?"

Zack nodded. "Zack Johnson."

Benson's eyes widened with recognition. "I've heard the name before."

They shook hands.

Zack said, "This here's Dusty McCabe."

"McCabe," Benson said. "Because of the Texas Rangers connection, I must assume you're a relative of Johnny McCabe."

Dusty nodded. "His son."

Dusty had to admit, even after two years, he still liked the sound of being called Johnny McCabe's son. For so many years, he hadn't been the son of anyone.

Wilson poured whiskey and they sat in the parlor by

the cold, empty hearth.

Dusty said, "Judging by the way you wear that gun, I should know your name. But I can't make the connection."

"I was thinking the same thing," Zack said.

Doc Benson said, "Oh, I was known by another name. Long ago. Before my doctoring days. That's long behind me, though."

Dusty let it go. According to custom, if a man gave you a name, you accepted it at that and didn't pry into his past. As Dusty took another sip of whiskey, though, he found himself wondering about this gunfighter turned doctor.

After a time, Benson said, "I'd best be going."

Wilson said, "Want me to ride back with you, Doc?"

Benson grinned. "I think I can handle the ride back to town, Sam."

Wilson returned the grin. "There ain't much you can't handle."

Wilson stood with Dusty on the porch. In the moonlight they could see Benson riding away. They watched as he followed the trail in the moonlight, up a low grassy hill, then disappeared from sight.

"I feel kinda foolish offering to ride with him," Wilson said. "I was thinking of him as a doctor, not a gunfighter."

"What's his story?" Dusty said.

"Don't rightly know. Never asked. I do know this, though. He's a man to ride the river with. If anyone tries to give him trouble on the ride back to town, God help them."

PART SEVEN

Mahalia

31

It was July Fourth, late in the evening. The town had begun to quiet down. The lanterns that had been strung across the square were finally put out, and the square was deserted. Falcone decided to walk his rounds one more time before turning in.

He had discarded his tie hours earlier, and he left his jacket slung over the chair behind his desk. His badge was pinned to the lapel of his jacket, but he didn't bother to retrieve it. Everyone in town knew he was the marshal. Besides, he figured everyone in town was probably asleep by now, anyway.

His marshal's office had walls that were made of planks nailed upright. The office held two rooms, and three cells. It had two holding cells, with iron bars on each. There was a back room with a bunk, and this was where Falcone usually slept.

He hadn't seen the previous office, the one used by Jack McCabe. He was told it had been built of logs and had one cell.

Falcone had a shotgun, but he left it at the office. His only weapon was the pistol tied down to his leg. He wanted both hands free should he have to deal with any miscreants.

His primary concerns were alley ways and the three saloons. As he walked along, he found the alleys deserted, and in the saloons, men were bedding down on the barroom floors. To be expected, he figured, in a town where there was only one hotel, on a night when there was enough business for four.

He continued on from Hunter's, expecting to walk past the blacksmith's office and livery, when he noticed the livery door was ajar and a lamp was burning.

He stepped in and found Higgins, one of the thugs who usually followed Randall around. He had a horse saddled. A bedroll and saddlebags were tied to the back of the saddle.

"Where are you going?" Falcone said.

"Anywhere but here."

"You're riding out?"

Higgins nodded.

"Does Randall know?"

"He will, come morning. I'm not staying around for what's going to happen."

This had Falcone puzzled. He didn't know what Higgins was talking about. "What's going to happen?"

"You saw how he was around the McCabe girl tonight."

Falcone nodded.

"It almost made me sick, having to serve as his bodyguard while he was acting like that. I had to hold that boy back. Protect Randall. I wanted to knock Randall down myself."

Falcone rubbed at his chin. "You were telling me earlier that he has a problem."

Higgins nodded. "It's like I said. He like's 'em young. That's what's going on. And he doesn't care if they say no. He got into trouble in Chicago that way, a couple years ago. Same thing happened in Saint Louis, but he was able to buy his way out of it. Paid the family not to press charges. But it's different out here. Out west. Things ain't like they are back east. You go abusin' a woman here, you can get yourself lynched or shot. And that girl he's targeting now is a McCabe. What is he, suicidal?

"Besides, even I have *some* principals. That girl in Chicago was only fifteen. Randall's old enough to be her father, and then some."

Falcone nodded. This answered a few questions for him.

He said, "I was wondering why he chose this place, out in the middle of nowhere, to stage his gold rush."

"His lawyer said it might be good if he got out of town for a while. Find some small, out-of-the way place. But he can't stay away from the young girls."

Higgins led the horse from the barn. Falcone followed.

Falcone said, "So you're riding on."

Higgins nodded. "Don't know where I'm going. But it won't be here. I'll admit, just between you and me, I'm not the most honest man in the world. But Randall's set his sights on the McCabe girl, and he's out of his mind if he thinks he can stand against that family. I'm not gonna be here when the bullets start flying. I'm not gonna go up against Johnny McCabe or any of his sons for him. Not for this. I'm not out of my mind."

He stepped up and into the saddle. He said, "You'd better think long and hard about the man you're workin' for."

Falcone said, "I don't work for Randall. I work for the people of this town."

Higgins gave a bitter chuckle. "You collect a paycheck from him, don't you? And even if you didn't, it wouldn't matter. This town belongs to him. He gets what he wants. One way or the other. He always does."

Higgins turned his horse away and started down the street. He turned the corner from Main Street onto Randall Street, and rode past the hotel and was gone from Falcone's view.

Falcone blew out the lamp in the livery and shut the door, and stood a moment on the boardwalk.

He had some things to think about.

32

Falcone returned to his office. It was late. The town was asleep. Falcone sat at his desk with the lamp burning low.

He felt like he was reaching the end of a trail. Here he was, working for a man like Randall. The money was great, much better than he ever made as a raider. All he had to do was turn his back on some deplorable things Randall did, and maybe be willing to put a bullet in a man occasionally.

Could people really change? He had come to this town wanting...he didn't really know what he wanted. He just knew he had reached the end of a trail that he had begun riding back during the War.

He decided maybe the choice was simple. He reached into his desk and pulled out a bottle of whiskey, and stood it on the desk. He then drew his pistol and placed it beside the bottle. He would use one of them on himself tonight, he just wasn't sure which one.

He became aware of the sound of someone outside. Boot soles tapping their way down the boardwalk. He had thought the entire town asleep. He thought he could have a moment to himself. A moment uninterrupted. Falcone shook his head out of frustration and pounded the top of his desk with a fist.

The door to his office opened and the man stepped in.

It was Tom McCabe. The preacher with a gun.

Falcone said, "What are you doing here at this hour, preacher?"

Tom shrugged. "Couldn't sleep. Thought I'd take a walk."

"I'd like to be alone, if you don't mind."

Tom walked forward, and reached down to the desk and took the pistol.

He said, "Whiskey and a gun make for a dangerous combination."

"Maybe so."

"Did you know I took the job at the church? My wife and I have moved into the back room of the church building. We're going to live there until I can get a house built here in town. I'm a Methodist and the church is Baptist. But I suppose the parishioners were thinking any port in a storm." He smiled, but Falcone didn't. Tom shrugged and continued. "I talked them into letting me a run a sort of non-denominational service. After all, this town is growing fast, but there's only one church in town. We should try to welcome everyone, not just those belonging to one denomination."

"I see you're still wearing your gun."

Tom nodded. "Sort of a compromise I've made with myself."

Falcone was about to lecture him about wearing a gun against the town ordinance, but decided not to bother.

He said, "Preacher, this is not really a good time. Would you give me back my gun?"

Tom shook his head.

Falcone said, "I could take it from you."

"I doubt it. As my Uncle Johnny would say, we're both gunhawks. We could fight. One of us would win. But there's no guarantee it would be you."

Falcone said bitterly, "I'm no gunhawk. When your uncle uses that term, it's almost like it's weighted with honor. Like some sort of knight in buckskins. What I am is no gunhawk. What I am is just a killer."

"Do you believe in second chances?"

Falcone looked at him. "I'm not sure what I believe."

Tom said, "I was loaded with guilt for what I had done. The killings, and how I had felt about them. The fact that I found myself willing to shoot my own brother. And then I talked to you. And I realized I'm not necessarily the same man I was before all of that began. But this town is a new start for me. A new direction."

"I don't see what any of that has to do with me."

"Really? You don't? Look at you, Marshal. You're a man who hasn't touched whiskey in months. You're wearing a badge, now. You stand for something important to these people."

"I rode in here two years ago and attacked your uncle's ranch. One of my men put two bullets in him."

"That was before. Now you've come back to this place and you're wearing a badge."

Tom started pacing. "You know what a man said to me

once? The man who was the minister in town back in California, when I was growing up. The man who was my greatest inspiration in becoming a minister. He said to me that Jesus came here not only to teach us to forgive others, but to teach us to forgive ourselves."

"Why would I want to do that?"

"Because, my friend, God loves us. Even you. Even me. All of us. It's a simple as that."

"As simple as that."

Tom nodded. "Ultimately, it's as simple as that."

Tom set the pistol back on the desk.

He said, "Second chances, my friend. We all deserve one. Show us you're worthy of it. Show yourself that you are."

Tom headed toward the door. "I'm heading home. I'm feeling tired. I think I can sleep now."

He stopped in the doorway. "I'm coming by in the morning for coffee. I've joined the others at Hunter's a few times, but I think I'd rather have coffee here."

"Why?"

"Because I think we understand each other. Maybe more than anyone else here does. See you in the morning."

And Tom stepped out into the night.

Vic sat and looked at the gun and at the bottle.

He rose to his feet, and slid the gun back into his holster. In the morning, he would be taking the bottle back to the hotel.

With the bottle standing on the desk, almost like a silent reminder of days gone by, Vic headed outside.

He was tired. So very tired, weary all the way to his bones. And yet he wasn't sleepy. He wanted to breathe the night air, and to walk. And to think. To think about second chances.

33

Over breakfast, Ginny told Johnny and Jessica about the girl she had met the night before. The girl called Mahalia. Ginny talked about her, and Dusty's connection to her, to make sure Jessica was fully filled in on Dusty's story.

Jessica said, "And the girl's married, and with a baby?"

Ginny nodded. "That does seem to complicate things a little, doesn't it?"

Josh was standing by the stove, a cup of trail coffee in hand. He was planning a day in the saddle and didn't want to do any more sitting that he was going to need to.

He said, "Dusty and I traipsed all over Oregon looking for her, a couple winters ago. We hit the Willamette Valley, and then a few coastal towns both north and south of there. There's cattle in Oregon, and a lot of farming. The winters there are cool and rainy. Nothing like what we get here. They're just right for growing alfalfa during the winter, then put in a regular crop in the summer. Wherever we went, we asked about her and her father, but we never found anyone who knew their names."

Temperance was sitting at the table with a cup of tea and a muffin in front of her. She said, "And the poor girl's afraid of her husband. That's so sad."

Josh said, "A man who would hurt a woman ain't much of a man."

Ginny didn't correct him on the use of *ain't*. The situation was much too serious for that.

Temperance looked over her shoulder at Josh. He walked over to her and placed a hand on her shoulder, and she reached up with her hand to place it on top of his.

Bree said, "That man just needs to get a whallopin'."

Ginny gave her an admonishing look. "Now, Bree, none of this is our business."

Josh snorted a bitter chuckle. "Wait and see how long it stays that way once Dusty's home."

"I'll talk to Dusty," Johnny said.

Josh looked at his father. "Put yourself in his place. What would you do?"

Johnny nodded. "I know what I'd do."

Ginny glanced from Jessica to Johnny to Temperance. "This situation couldn't be any more explosive if it involved gunpowder and a match."

Fred saddled a couple of horses for Josh and Fat. Both boys had chaps strapped on over their jeans. You can't really tie down a pistol when you're wearing chaps, so Josh had tightened his gunbelt and his revolver was riding at his hip.

They were heading out specifically to check the cows that had been brought up from California. See if they were fattening up. Cattle lose weight on a long drive

Johnny was going to stay at the house today. Spend time with Jessica and Cora. Maybe take them on a small picnic and show them where the old Shoshone village had been, toward the center of the valley. Johnny had taken Josh, Jack and Bree there when they were younger. Josh remembered hunting the ground for arrowheads. He had found a couple.

Fred had already saddled a horse for Bree, and she was off for a morning in the hills, her rifle in her saddle and her revolver at her side.

Johnny caught up with Josh at the corral.

He had a tin cup of coffee in one hand. He said to his son, "I haven't done much work since I've been back. I've been letting you continue to run things."

"That's okay, Pa."

"I just want you to know why." Johnny let his gaze drift to the house, and then to the remuda grazing out back. "This place is yours, Josh. Yours and Bree's and Jack's and Dusty's. I built this place for all of you, so you'd have something. You're a good man, and I think it's time for you to take the reins. This place belongs to all of you, but from now on, you're the ramrod."

Josh was a little speechless. Johnny took advantage of the silence and kept speaking.

"On the ride back from California, Dusty and I talked a bit. I've already talked to Jack about this. I want you to know that we each cast our own shadows, and mine is no more important than yours or anyone else's. I don't want you to be like me, son. I want you to be like yourself.

"I'm not fully retiring. I'll still be around to help out

around here. And if you need advice, all you have to do is ask. But I want you to run this ranch your way. I want you to make your own mark on it."

The horses were saddled and Fat had mounted up and was waiting for him. "Hey, Josh. You comin'?"

Josh said to Johnny, "I won't let you down, Pa."

"You never have yet, son," and Johnny slapped him on the shoulder.

Johnny watched while Josh mounted up. Josh didn't stick his foot in the stirrup and swing into the saddle. Instead he grabbed the saddle horn with his left and leapt up and into the saddle. Funny, Johnny thought, how a vote of confidence can put a bounce in a man's step. Or into the way he mounts a horse.

He stood with his coffee in his hand, watching the boys ride off.

Josh and Fat rode in silence for a while. They followed the trail toward the center of the valley, then cut off and rode overland to a pass that would lead them out and to the foothills to the east.

Fat eventually said, "That's quite a thing, isn't it? That girl Haley."

Josh looked at him.

Fat said, "Bree was outside this morning, at the chicken house, gathering eggs. I talked to her a little, and she told me about Haley."

Josh chuckled to himself. Fat, always making sure he was in Bree's presence. If Bree went out to collect the eggs, he was somehow there. If she went to ask Fred to saddle a horse for her, Fat was somehow there and offering to do it himself. Fat was so stricken with Bree, and yet she found him amusing and a nice enough guy, but not husband material. Josh felt a little sad for Fat, because sooner or later Fat was going to realize this.

Fat was awkward. He was a little shy, and he didn't speak well. But he had more heart than most men Josh had met. Josh realized at that very moment that Fat was rich in the qualities he admired in a person. Josh had always been quick to laugh at Fat's awkwardness, but Fat deserved a lot better than that. Josh decided there would be no more laughs at Fat's expense.

Josh said, "Yeah, it's quite a thing about Haley. I don't really know what we're gonna do about it. But when Dusty gets back, I know what he's gonna do."

Fat reined up. Josh followed suit.

Fat said, "You know, Boss, I can handle this. Checkin' on them cows. You can trust my judgment about cattle and such."

"Yeah, Fat, I can."

"Then why don't you ride into town. Talk with Jack. Maybe check on that girl Haley. Maybe meet her husband and see what should be done."

Josh gave Fat a long look. He said, "You're a good man, Fat. Anyone ever tell you that?"

Fat shrugged and bobbed his head the way a shy man does when he gets a compliment and doesn't know what to do with it.

Josh said, "You're my top hand, Fat. You know that?"

"No, sir. I didn't."

"Well, you are. Pa made me officially the ramrod this morning, and until Dusty gets back, you're my right-hand-man. And even when he does get back, you're number two only to him. You ride on out and evaluate those cattle. The ones with the Swan brand on 'em. Maybe take a head count, too. I'll take your word."

"You got it, Boss," and Fat clicked his horse forward and rode on.

Josh turned his horse back, and headed toward Jubilee.

He found Jack at Hunter's. Even though a sort of peace had been made with Randall—an uneasy peace, but you take what you can get—Jack still felt the need to spend his days at Hunter's. *Protecting Aunt Ginny's investment*, he called it.

Darby was no longer around. He was working with Brewster on the family farm down the stretch a ways, learning what farming was all about. Josh knew Jack didn't fault him any for that. Darby had a wife and a child. He had made the decision to be a farmer. Darby's father had money, more than even Aunt Ginny, but the old man had cut him off and Darby had too much pride to go back begging. Josh liked Darby. And even more, he respected him.

Josh couldn't imagine a life working on your feet, though, planting crops and pulling weeds and such. But he respected Darby for doing what he had to do to take care of his family.

Josh found Jack working with Hunter to tap a keg they had just set up behind the bar.

Josh also found Bree at Hunter's.

"What are you doing here?" he said. "I thought you left this morning to do some riding in the hills."

"Apparently about the same thing you're doing. I thought you were riding out to work with the herd."

He gave a nod of surrender. "I guess it's hard to focus on other things when we know how hard it's going to be on Dusty to find Haley married to someone else."

Already, there were men at the tables. Not many. Josh did a quick head count and saw eight. They were sitting with coffee in front of them. A couple of them were engaging in what looked like a penny-ante game of poker. One cowhand was engrossed in a game of solitaire.

Jack was nursing along a cup of coffee. Chen had brewed up a cup of Chinese tea for Bree.

Chen was stationed behind the bar. He said, "Too early for a beer?"

Josh said "Why not. It's gotta be after twelve somewhere."

Chen poured him a warm one from the new keg.

"You know," Bree said. "Maybe we're getting all worked up over this for nothing. They might not be staying here long."

Jack shook his head. "She told Aunt Ginny her husband is here to try his hand at Williams Gulch."

"That doesn't mean he'll find gold. Maybe he'll give up before Dusty and the others get home."

Josh took a sip of beer. "I think Dusty could handle it if he knew she was married."

Bree said, "His heart'll be broken."

Josh nodded. "Yeah. But he'll get over that part of it. The part that's gonna be real trouble is if Aunt Ginny and Granny Tate are right. If she's afraid of her husband. That's the part Dusty won't sit still for."

"What do you think he'll do?"

Jack said, "You know Dusty. What do you think he'll do?"

"He'll go after that man."

Jack nodded grimly. "I know I would, if it was Nina. Now, it may not be any of Dusty's business, as Haley is married to that man. But it wouldn't stop me, and it won't stop Dusty. And he's capable of causing a lot more harm than I am."

Josh said, "Maybe they're both wrong. Granny Tate and Aunt Ginny."

Hunter had drifted over while they were talking. He said, "What do you think are the odds of that?"

Josh gave a deflating sigh. "Next to nothing."

They were quiet for a moment. Josh took another sip of beer. Bree took a sip of tea. Jack stood with one elbow on the bar, the cup of coffee idle in front of him.

Then Josh said, "So, have you seen her?"

Jack shook his head. "I keep finding myself going to the door and looking toward the hotel."

Josh shrugged. "I suppose we could just go over there and get their room number and knock on the door."

"What would you tell them?"

Josh grinned. "That we're the welcoming committee?"

Hunter said, "If you boys were the welcoming committee, I'd be high-tailing it out of town."

Jack nodded with a chuckle.

Chen said, "In my country, a man who would encourage fear in a woman is no man at all."

Josh said, "In that way, your country and ours are much alike."

Bree finished her tea, and started pacing. She said, "Well, we can't just do *nothing*."

Jack said, "I'd like to know what we could do."

"Maybe..." She was thinking while she paced. The morning was getting warm and Hunter had left the outer door open, so now only the swinging batwing doors separated the barroom from the street. Bree stopped her pacing in the doorway to enjoy the fresh, mountain air. "Maybe I can stay in town a while today. Kind of wander about. See if I can catch her in passing."

"So what are you gonna say?" Josh said. "Hi, I'm Dusty's sister. You might want to leave town before Dusty beats the life out of your husband?"

Bree shook her head, feeling a little defeated. "I can't really say that, can I?"

She idly let her gaze drift out the doorway, to the street beyond.

"Hey," she said. "I think that's her."

Josh and Jack left their drinks on the bar and hurried to the doorway.

Across the town square, at the foot of the hotel steps, was a girl. She had no hat and her hair was hanging free and looked a little wild. She had a baby cradled in her arms.

"Is that her?" Josh said. He hadn't gotten a look at her the night before.

"That's her," Bree said. "I saw her talking to Aunt Ginny."

They watched as the girl took a step. Then she took a staggering step. Then another. She was weaving as she walked, then stumbled backward and almost fell.

"She's hurt," Bree said, and burst out of the saloon at a dead run.

Jack and Josh were right behind her.

"Hey, are you all right?" Bree called to her, and came to a stop with her boots sliding on the gravel. The girl began to pitch over and Bree grabbed her by the shoulders.

"Whoa, now," Josh said. He also grabbed her by the shoulders, holding her upright while Bree took the baby from her arms.

"Are you all right?" Jack said.

The girl had a cut over one eye, and one cheekbone was swelling and turning purple. One lip was swollen.

Stepping fully into the role of doctor, Jack reached with one hand to move her hair out of her face and get a better look at the gash on her forehead.

"Who did this to you?" he said.

Her gaze was drifting. She wasn't really looking at any of them. *Concussion,* was his first thought.

Then her knees buckled, and Jack caught her. He slid one hand behind her knees and scooped her up.

Hunter was there with them. They hadn't seen him running up behind them.

"Get her inside," he said.

Jack carried her to the saloon. She was stirring to consciousness, so he gently placed her in a chair.

"Get her some water," Jack said.

Jack had asked Granny Tate one time why when someone was shaken up, she gave them water. Granny said because you have to keep water in the system. Dehydration makes any physical jolt more traumatic.

Hunter got a glass and filled it with water from the well he used out back. He had dug a well when he first built this place, and happened onto a natural spring. The water was cold and seemed clean.

Hunter handed the glass to Jack, and Jack brought it to Haley's mouth.

She drank a mouthful, then coughed, then drank some more. She opened her eyes.

"What happened to you, sweetie?" Bree said.

Josh stood back, staying out of Jack's way. He said, "Who did this?"

Chen stepped forward and began examining the head wound. He seemed to know what he was doing. Someday, Jack thought, he would have to ask Chen just how he knew all of the things he did.

Chen said, "This was done by an object with a dull edge."

"Like a club?" Jack said.

"Maybe when she was struck there," he indicated her cheekbone, "she fell against something."

Haley said, "I hit the corner of a table when I went down."

"Haley," Bree said "Did your husband do this?"

"Who are you?" she said. She spoke a little dreamily, like she was just waking up from a deep sleep.

"We're Dusty's family," she said. "Did your husband do this to you?"

She shook her head. "No. I just fell. That's all."

"That's one heck of a fall," Josh said.

"I'm all right."

"No, you're not," Bree said.

Chen said, "I think she has..." he was searching for the English word.

"Concussion?" Jack said.

Chen nodded quickly. "Yes. Concussion. Someone should go get Granny Tate."

"I'll go," Hunter said, and was out the door.

Haley opened her eyes with a frantic look. "My baby. Where's my baby?"

"Right here," Bree said. The baby was in her arms.

"As long as he's okay."

Bree looked at Jack and Josh. "Maybe someone should go and get Pa."

"No need," Josh said. "I'm gonna handle this myself."

And he strode for the door, driving his heels into the floor as he moved.

Falcone had slept very little the night before. He had spent much of it sitting on a bench on the boardwalk in front of his office, staring into the night and thinking, tossing the preacher's words back and forth. Forgiveness. Second chances. And the question, was he worth it? He got no answers, but he found the questions wouldn't let him sleep.

He decided to go *Johansen's* for breakfast. *Johansen's* was a new restaurant started up by a husband and wife from Missouri. They had left behind a life at a failing farm to set up shop here.

But before he went to the restaurant, he walked up a back street to a new building that was now serving as a rooming house. He pulled a pocket watch from his vest and checked the time.

He didn't have to wait long before the door opened, and she stepped out. Flossy. The one time saloon woman who had cavorted with him back in his outlaw days.

"Vic," she said, a little surprised to see him.

He tipped his hat to her, and said, "I thought I might walk you to the Johansen, if you don't mind."

She shrugged. "I walk it alone every morning."

"Well, a woman shouldn't have to walk alone. Especially with a town marshal available."

They walked a bit. There was much he wanted to ask her. Much he wanted to say. But he didn't know where to even begin. Rather than word something wrong, he decided to just remain silent.

He then said, "I heard word-of-mouth that you had quit the hotel."

"I didn't want to work for a snake like Randall. As soon as this restaurant started up, I asked Mister Johansen for a job."

"A snake like Randall, hmm?"

"I know men. One thing about my former life, I got to know men. He might be more civilized than the ones I knew, but he's a snake."

They walked to the hotel, and he took a seat and she put on an apron and asked him what he would have.

"I'll try the bacon and eggs," he said. "Sunny side up. And a coffee."

As he ate, he watched Flossy as she waited tables. And he thought about what he had been, and what he now was.

After breakfast, he left a sizable tip for Flossy and then walked down to the Main Street. Time to walk the rounds, he decided.

That was when he saw Josh McCabe running up the steps to the Jubilee Hotel.

This wasn't good, Falcone thought. He started running, but he was still a couple of blocks away. Josh was already through the front door before Falcone could clear one block.

Riding boots aren't the best things for running. The soles are smooth and you slip and slide on the gravel, which was what Falcone was now doing.

He got to the front steps and climbed them two at a time. Four steps from the boardwalk to the door. He then drew his pistol and went in.

The lobby was empty. No one was behind the counter.

Falcone stepped through a doorway and down a hallway, and then into Randall's office with his gun out in front of him, ready to fire.

Randall was at his desk, spectacles in one hand.

"Falcone?" he said.

Falcone blinked with surprise and lowered his gun. "I saw Josh McCabe head into the hotel, and he was moving like he meant business. I thought he was coming here for you."

That was when they heard a single gunshot. It came from above. The second floor.

Falcone had no idea what was going on. He hurried out the door, and back to the lobby and up the stairs, Randall behind him.

The second-floor hallway was empty, so Falcone figured the shots had to have been from one of the rooms. He had no way of knowing which room, but one door was open partway down the corridor.

The Jubilee had been built quickly and not very precisely, and the hallway floor creaked underfoot as Falcone moved down toward the open door. He was actually walking a little downhill as he moved along the hallway.

He stepped into a room and found it deserted. A double bed was at the center of the room, and the covers were pulled down and rumpled. The bed had been slept in. An empty crib rested quietly on the floor near the bed.

A door at a side wall was open, so Falcone stepped toward it, gun ready.

The door led to another hotel room. This one was a little larger, with a double bed toward the center, and a single twin bed near an open window.

A man was lying on the floor, and Josh was kneeling over him. Josh's gun was in his right hand, and with his left he was checking the man's neck for a pulse.

Josh looked up at Falcone and Randall. Josh said, "He's dead."

Falcone didn't know what was going on, but he aimed his pistol at Josh and said, "Put the gun down, boy. Don't make me use this."

Josh placed his gun on the floor.

Falcone said, "Stand up, hands in the air."

Josh said, "This isn't what it looks like. He pulled a gun on me and I had to defend myself."

Falcone knelt by the man on the floor and confirmed for himself there was no pulse in the neck.

Falcone said, "Where's his gun?"

Josh glanced at the body, then about the floor within reach. "Well, it was here. He shot at me."

"And you shot at him."

Josh nodded. "Yes. That's how he got my bullet in him."

Falcone looked at Josh with a little surprise. "We heard only one shot."

Falcone glanced at Randall for confirmation. Randall nodded.

"No," Josh said. "That's impossible. He aimed his gun at me and I had to draw mine. He shot and I shot. His missed, but mine didn't. The gun's gotta be here somewhere."

Falcone told Josh to wait while he searched the room. Josh did as instructed. Falcone searched under both beds, and under a small dresser that had a bowl and pitcher on top.

"There's no second gun here," Falcone said.

Josh thought a moment. "We shot in the other room. It all happened so fast. Maybe he dropped it there before he ran in here. I don't know."

Falcone didn't remember seeing a gun on the floor in the other room, but it was worth checking.

"Come on back to the other room," Falcone said. "Let's look."

There was no second gun in that room, either. Falcone checked under the bed and under the dresser. Even under the crib.

Randall said, "How are we even sure there *was* a second gun? We heard only one shot."

Josh glanced about. He spun around, toward the wall behind him, and said, "There. Look. A bullet hole in the wall."

Falcone walked over to the hole. He reached one finger up to touch it.

"Probably a forty-four or a forty-five."

Randall was growing impatient. "That bullet hole might have already been there. This is the frontier, and this hotel is not in very good repair. We heard only one shot, and the man lying dead in there doesn't have a gun. What happened is McCabe shot and killed an unarmed man."

Falcone looked at Josh.

Josh said, "I didn't. I would never shoot a man who wasn't armed and facing me, and trying to shoot me."

Randall said, "I want this man arrested. Right now."

Falcone ignored him and said to Josh, "Start from the beginning."

Randall said, "Falcone, I believe I just told you to arrest him."

Falcone glanced at him. "Which one of us is wearing the badge?"

Randall was furious, but said nothing.

Falcone said to Josh, "Let's hear it. From the start."

Josh told Falcone about Haley. How Dusty had fallen in love with her a couple of years ago, but her father had taken her to Oregon and Dusty didn't have the location. Dusty had searched through Oregon looking for her, and Josh had gone with him, but they couldn't find her. Then she showed up in town with a baby and a husband. Just minutes ago, she had been found outside beaten nearly unconscious by her husband.

Josh came here to the hotel to confront the man.

"To kill him," Randall said.

"To *confront* him," Josh said. "I intended to drive him out of town, before Dusty can get home. Because if the man was still here by then, Dusty *would* kill him."

"And where is Dusty?" Falcone said.

Josh couldn't very well say his brother was off helping break a man out of a Mexican prison.

What he said was, "He's gone on business. For the ranch. Don't know just when he'll be back."

Falcone said, "So, what happened when you came over here?"

"He was awake. This Gideon man. I don't know his first name. I told him I knew he had been beating his wife, and he was leaving town right now. He took exception to that, and pulled a gun. I drew mine. I'm not fast like Pa or Dusty, but I'm fast enough. He fired and I fired. His bullet missed me by a couple of inches and landed in the wall behind me, but mine caught him square in the chest.

"He staggered a couple steps, then turned and ran through the doorway to the adjoining room. I ran in. He had fallen on the bed. The smaller one, by the window. I tried to pull him to his feet, but he just fell to the floor."

"Don't you find this just the least bit hard to believe?" Randall said to Falcone. "I didn't see any blood on the front of that man's shirt."

Falcone said, "A gunshot wound doesn't always start bleeding immediately. Sometimes there's a minute or two before it really starts flowing. And that man didn't live long after the shot. Dead men don't bleed."

"Am I to believe that a man fatally shot with a bullet in his chest was able to turn and run into another room before he dropped?"

Josh said, "I've seen a deer take a bullet like that and run half a mile through the woods before it drops."

Falcone was rubbing his chin thoughtfully. "All sorts of unpredictable behavior can happen once a bullet is in a man."

Randall said, "I don't care. I want this man arrested.

Now."

Falcone looked at Josh. "I'm afraid I have no choice."

35

Bree rode hell-bent-for-leather back to the ranch to tell Pa and Aunt Ginny that there had been a killing and Josh was in jail.

Johnny had Fred saddle Thunder for him.

Bree met him out at the corral. "Pa, I want to ride back with you."

"No, I'd like you to stay here. Help Jessica keep your aunt from having Fred hitch up the buggy for her. I want to check things out for myself. We don't need her riding in, with her temper, and making things worse."

What he really meant was he didn't want Bree riding in and making things worse. Josh was known for his temper, but among his children, it seemed to Johnny that Bree was the most volatile if she got worked up.

She said, "Okay, Pa."

A short while later, Johnny rode down the main street of the town on Thunder. He didn't know what he was going to say to Falcone, but he knew in his gut there was going to be a confrontation sooner or later. Looked like it was going to be sooner.

This was the Fifth of July—the celebration had dimmed down a lot from the previous day, but there were still a lot of people in town. Folks were walking along the boardwalks and crossing the street. Cowhands and prospectors, going from one saloon to another. One man walking arm-in-arm with one of Miss Alisha's girls. They all stopped to stare at Johnny as he rode up to the marshal's office and swung out of the saddle and gave Thunder's rein one turn about the hitching rail.

He didn't look at them. He just kept his gaze fixed straight ahead as he opened the office door and walked in.

Falcone was at the desk. He rose to his feet.

First thing Johnny said was, "You rode out to my ranch to tell me you didn't want trouble. But now you do this."

"I'm just following the law. There seems to be enough reasonable circumstantial evidence to call for an inquest. I'm riding down tomorrow to Bozeman to send a wire for the circuit judge."

Falcone glanced down to the holster tied down to Johnny's leg. Falcone said, "I talked earlier about an order I issued that guns aren't to be worn in town."

"You want to take it from me?"

Falcone gave him a long look. Finally he said, "If I make an exception for you, I'll have to make it for everyone."

"This would require that I take you seriously as a lawman. I doubt many around here do."

Johnny walked up to the cell. "Josh. Are you all right?"

Falcone said, "I can't allow any interactions with the prisoner."

Johnny glanced at him. "You want to try and stop me?"

Falcone shook his head wearily. "I really doubt there's a man alive who could stop you."

"You go for that gun, and they'll be carrying you out of here feet-first. Believe that. I still owe you for two bullet holes one of your men put in me. I never shot a man who didn't need it, but from where I stand, I'm looking at a man who does."

Falcone held his hands up in resignation, and sat at the edge of the desk. "You have five minutes."

"I have all the time I want to take."

Falcone nodded. "All right. You have all the time you want to take."

Johnny looked at Josh, but positioned himself sort of sideways so Falcone was in his peripheral vision.

Johnny said, "Tell me what happened, son."

Jack was standing in the doorway. He had seen his father riding up to Falcone's office, and thought he might join him.

Josh told Pa what had happened. How they had found Haley beaten and collapsing in the street. Josh had gone into the hotel to confront her husband. Her husband pulled a gun and Josh drew, and they both fired. Gideon's bullet went into the wall, and Josh's went into Gideon.

Gideon then turned and ran into the adjoining room, and Josh followed him. Gideon had collapsed, half on the bed by the window and half on the floor. Josh tried to lift him to his feet, but the man fell fully to the floor. He was dead.

Johnny said to Falcone, "So, why's he behind bars?"

Falcone said, "I was in the hotel at the time, and heard only one shot. And we couldn't find a second gun. We couldn't find any indication that Gideon was carrying one."

"Wasn't he wearing a gunbelt?"

Falcone shook his head no.

Josh said, "He had the gun tucked into the front of his belt. He wasn't wearing a gunbelt."

Johnny noticed Jack standing in the doorway. Jack said, "Granny Tate's with Haley. Granny said she should be all right. There's a concussion."

Johnny nodded. "Does she have a place to stay?"

"The hotel room. Her husband had it paid up through the end of the week."

"We can't leave her there alone, in this condition. Especially with a baby to take care of. Let's take her back out to the ranch."

He and Johnny stepped out onto the boardwalk.

Johnny said, "I'll ride back to the ranch and get the buggy. A girl beaten-up like you said she was shouldn't be forced to sit on a horse."

Jack nodded. "I've been thinking, about the two gunshots. Why no one seemed to hear a second shot."

"Any ideas on that?"

Jack shook his head. "I'd like to take a walk around town. Ask a few questions."

36

Falcone was at the restaurant when it closed up and Flossy stepped out the door to begin her walk to the boarding house.

"Vic," she said. "What're you doing here?"

He shrugged. "Just thought I might walk you home. If you don't mind the company."

"You forget, Vic. I know you. You never do anything just for the sake of doing it. You always have these other plans. Plans you don't share with anyone."

"Ulterior motives?"

"Yeah. Them."

"Don't you believe people can change?"

"I don't know. I'd like to believe it. I've seen people want to change. But in the end, they don't really."

"Are you saying you don't want me walking you home?"

She gave a sigh of resignation and started walking. "Walk along if you want to. I don't care. But that's all that's gonna happen. You ain't comin' inside."

"Walking you home is all I intend." He stepped into pace beside her.

She said, "I heard about the arrest you made today. Ain't you afraid to leave your prisoner alone?"

Falcone shook his head. "He'll be all right. He's not going anywhere. I didn't really want to make the arrest, anyway. He didn't do it."

"How do you know?"

"By the look in his eyes. He's not a murderer. It takes a certain something inside you to look a man in the eyes and just gun him down in cold blood."

"You should know."

He was silent a moment. Then he said, "Yes. I should know."

She stopped walking after a bit, and looked him in the eye. "What are you doing here? Hiding behind that badge? Who are you trying to fool? I know what you are. We *all* know what you are. The McCabes know what you are. You might have somehow got all the charges dropped, but that don't mean you're not guilty."

"You said you don't believe a man can change."

She shook her head. "Nope. Not really."

"How about second chances? Do you believe in them?"

"Do you really think you deserve one?"

"I don't know." He started walking again, and she fell into place alongside him.

She said, "You know, the McCabes ain't gonna let that boy rot in jail. They'll be comin' for him. You might end up facing the old man, himself. You think you're up to that?"

"I faced him already. This afternoon. He came by the jail."

She stopped again and looked at him. "You faced Johnny McCabe, and you're still alive?"

"We didn't draw on each other. We just talked."

"I'd like to have been a fly on the wall for that one." They started walking again.

They reached the rooming house.

Vic took his hat completely off. He said, "You asked what I'm doing here. I guess I don't completely know."

"You want my forgiveness for the way you treated me?"

He shook his head. "I don't know."

"Good night, Vic," she said, and stepped inside.

He placed the hat back on his head, and walked away.

37

Falcone stepped into his office. Josh McCabe was standing by the barred window in the cell, looking off into the night. He glanced over his shoulder toward the office as Falcone walked over to his desk.

"I see you're still here," Falcone said.

"You're lucky I am. I don't know how smart it is, leaving a prisoner alone like that."

"You won't go anywhere. You're a man of honor."

Josh chuckled. "Is that what I am?"

Falcone was sliding open a desk drawer, but then he stopped and looked fully at Josh.

Falcone said, "I think that's exactly what you are. I've fought against you people three times now. I think 'a man of honor' describes you and your father and brothers better than any other description."

"Even still, I'd leave a deputy here to watch the place while I was gone."

"One problem with that. I can't find anyone willing to be my deputy."

"Can you blame them?"

Falcone shook his head. "Honestly? No."

He returned to his desk drawer, and pulled out two envelopes.

He said, "I have another errand to tend to. Watch the shop, will you?"

"Where are you off to now?"

"I was asked a question tonight, and I found I didn't really know the answer. But now I think I might."

Josh looked at him. "I have no idea what you're talking about."

Falcone gave a chuckle and a half-grin. "I'm not sure I do, either."

He started for the door, stuffing the envelopes into his jacket pocket. "I won't be gone long."

"I'll be counting the seconds."

The lamps in the hotel lobby were turned up. Randall left the hotel open until nine o'clock, just in case any wayward travelers arrived and needed a room.

A clerk was standing idly, leaning his elbows on the desk and reading a newspaper. Now that the stage was coming through town three times a week, they got the weekly paper out of Helena.

"Is he in his office?" Vic said.

The clerk said, "Nope. Gone up to his room."

Vic started up the stairs.

Aloysius Randall used Room Number One upstairs as his own personal quarters. Falcone found the door shut, and he knocked.

Randall's voice was slightly muffled by the closed door. "What is it?"

"It's Falcone. I need to talk a minute."

"Come on in."

Vic stepped in. This room had a small roll-top desk in one corner, and Randall was sitting there with his feet up on the desk and a glass of scotch in his hand.

"Falcone," Randall said. "Come on in. Have a scotch."

Vic shook his head. "Thanks, but I haven't touched it since the night you hired me. I don't think I ever will again."

Randall looked at him with pity, and with an air of condescendence. "I've known men who try to stay away from it. They can only do it for so long."

"That's because they try to stay away from it. I'm not trying. I just don't want it anymore. The longer I'm away from it, the more I see what it did to me. What I let it do to me. What I found myself capable of doing, as long as I could hide in whiskey afterward."

Randall rolled his eyes. He was quickly becoming bored with this. "What is it you want, Falcone?"

"What I want is to tell you I quit."

Randall blinked with surprise. "You quit?"

"I'm officially resigning from the position you offered me."

"Who else am I going to find to be marshal of this town? I could offer the job to Jack McCabe, but I wouldn't be able to control him."

"I'm not quitting as marshal. I'm just resigning from the position you offered me back in Wichita."

"You smug, ungrateful..."

"Oh, I'm grateful. Believe me. You picked me up out of

the gutter. Gave me money to survive. If not for you, I probably would have drunk myself to death by now. You see, a drowning man doesn't question who is throwing him a rope. He just grabs the rope."

"And yet you can walk away from me."

"I think I have to. For my own sake."

"Well, I paid you a good deal of money. And I paid you in advance, so you're still mine till the end of the month."

Falcone reached into his jacket and pulled out two envelopes, and dropped them both on the desk.

He said, "My advance pay for the month. And last month's pay."

Randall looked at him with disbelief. "You're really walking away. If you'd stayed with me, you could have been a rich man."

Falcone nodded. "Could have been. But I'm starting to see there are some things that are more important."

"Whatever that means." Randall looked away, as though he was done with this conversation. "Oh, by the way, have you seen Higgins? He's been missing all day."

Falcone decided to say nothing. It was Higgins' choice to ride away unannounced. "Haven't seen him since yesterday."

Not entirely a lie.

"Well, *marshal*," Randall said the word with the full weight of sarcasm, "if you're done with me, could you leave me in peace?"

Falcone nodded. "I do want to thank you, though, for all you did for me."

"You imbecile. I didn't do anything for you. I did it for myself. You were a man of unique capabilities, and you were in a position that made you easy to control."

"I guess I'm not so easy to control, am I?"

"Get out."

Falcone nodded. He turned away and was out the door, and pulled it shut behind him.

He walked down the stairs to the lobby, thinking that he hadn't felt this free in a long time.

Johnny sat by the fire, a scotch in his hand.

He said, "I hate leaving Josh in that jail overnight. I hate the thought of any of my sons being in jail."

Ginny sat in her rocker. She said, "Hopefully we'll have him out of there, soon."

"We may have to get a lawyer. The nearest one is down in Bozeman. But I don't think he's much more than a half-drunken bumpkin who does wills and deeds."

"No. We need a real defense attorney, if this is to go to court. I'll spend some money and bring one up from San Francisco. I know of a good one. A young man, but he's been making a lot of noise. Winning a lot of cases. He has an office in the city, and one in Stockton, too."

Jack was standing, leaning one elbow against the mantel. In his other hand was a glass of bourbon.

He said, "If only we could find that other gun."

Bree was on the sofa. "Josh says both guns were fired. But everyone seems to think they heard only one shot."

Jack nodded. He had asked people in the street. He had talked with the bartender downstairs in the hotel lounge. "I don't know what to think about that."

"What I do know," Johnny said, "is that Josh is no murderer, and he's not a liar."

Ginny said, "Correct on both counts."

Jack took a sip from his glass. "What are the chances that this is somehow political? We know Falcone is in Randall's pocket. Could this be some sort of move to pressure Aunt Ginny's vote on the Town Council?"

Ginny said, "Or to get me to resign from the Council entirely."

Bree said, "Or it could just be some sort of twisted attempt at revenge on the part of Falcone."

As Johnny sat thinking about this, Haley sat at the far end of the sofa. The night had turned off a little cool, and she was wrapped in a quilt. Johnny knew that if you were injured or had taken a beating, you tended to get chilled easily.

The bruise on her cheekbone had now spread outward, turning the side of her face purple. Granny had tied a bandage around her head to cover the gash over her eye.

She looked so small, Johnny thought, sitting there. So lost. So afraid.

Johnny said to her, "Haley, does it strike you odd at all that your husband would go for a gun like that? With no real provocation?"

She shook her head, and said in a small voice, "No."

Temperance was walking into the parlor from the kitchen. She had been puttering around, doing some final cleaning from dinner. Shutting things down for the night. She took an upright chair upholstered in velvet that Ginny had shipped from the house in San Francisco the previous fall.

Ginny said to Haley, "It doesn't surprise you that your husband would pull a gun on a man like that? Like the way Josh described?"

Haley said, "He killed a man in Oregon. That's why we're here. It's not because the farm failed. The farm wasn't doing good, so that's the reason we gave for leaving and folks believed it. But it wasn't the real reason."

"He killed a man?" Johnny said.

She nodded.

"Did you see it?"

"No. He told me about it. He would go into town and get liquored up. He was gone long into the night sometimes. But he showed up one night with a body in the back of the wagon. I didn't see the body, but I saw something was wrapped up in canvas. He said it was a body. He said the man had cheated him at cards and he confronted the man about it in an alley and shot him. It was two in the morning. He went out there with a shovel and dug a grave by moonlight at the edge of the yard and buried the man there.

"He then decided maybe we should leave the area, in case anyone started asking questions. He said he'd heard about a gold strike here, so we came here."

Ginny said, "I think in the morning, I'll take a ride down to Bozeman and send a telegram to San Francisco."

Johnny took a sip of coffee from a cup he held in one hand. "Ginny, I hate seeing you spend your money this way. It feels a little bit like charity. Maybe we can sell some beef to pay for the lawyer."

"Nonsense. It's not charity. It's family helping family. If

you want, if it makes you feel better, you can sell some beef to pay me back. After this is over."

Johnny nodded. He supposed that was good enough for him.

Jessica came down the stairs.

She said, "Cora's asleep. And the baby's sleeping too."

She perched on the arm of Johnny's chair with one foot still touching the floor.

He said, "Come morning, Jack, I'd like you to drive your aunt down to Bozeman."

Jack shifted his feet a little. "If it's all the same, Pa, I'd like to go into town. I want to check the crime scene again. We've got to find that gun, and the longer we wait, the less likely it's going to turn up."

Ginny said, "The boy has a point."

Bree said, "I can drive you in. We can get Fat to come along, if you'd like."

Jack grinned. "I'm sure Fat would like that."

Bree rolled her eyes.

Most of the conversation had drifted its way upstairs while Jessica was putting Cora to bed.

She said, "Is there a possibility this Falcone person somehow hid the gun?"

Johnny shook his head. "Not that I'd put it past him, but I don't see how it would be possible."

Jack said, "From what Josh told us, Falcone came into the room immediately after the shots were fired."

Bree said, "According to Josh, he was standing in the other room, with the dead man." She glanced at Haley, realizing she had spoken crassly about the girl's husband. "I'm sorry."

Haley didn't react. She was just sitting, staring into the fire.

Bree said, "Falcone and Randall ran into the first room, then through the door into the second room, where they found Josh. When the man was shot, if he had dropped the gun he used to shoot at Josh, then it would have been on the floor when Falcone and Randall came in."

Ginny said, "One of them could have grabbed it."

Johnny shook his head. "That would require some awfully fast thinking."

"Men like Randall don't rise to the top by thinking slowly."

Johnny nodded. Good point.

He looked at Jack. "All right. But I'm going to be the one to drive your aunt to Bozeman. Just in case Randall is really trying to get her off the Council. We don't really know how far he'd go, but we do know how far Falcone would. You go into town and try to find that gun."

Bree said, "What do you want us to do?"

"Stay here, out of trouble. No riding in the hills, tomorrow. I want you here at the house. Help Temperance take care of Haley."

Bree nodded. "Yessir."

Haley said, "I'm so sorry to have brought this all onto you."

Ginny said, "You just get yourself well. Hopefully all of this will be behind us by the time Dusty and the others are home."

39

Early the next morning, Johnny left for Bozeman with Aunt Ginny. Matt had caught wind of what was happening, and joined them for the drive. It might be good to have another gun along. No one expected to see them again before late afternoon.

Jessica and Temperance sat in the kitchen having one more cup of coffee.

Jessica said, "We don't know if they'll run into trouble on the way to Bozeman or back. If Randall will try to have them killed."

Temperance shook her head.

Jessica said, "So, we just sit here and wait?"

Temperance nodded and took a sip of coffee. "That's what we do. Aunt Ginny told me in this family, when something like this is happening, there's a lot of sitting and waiting. And in this family, this kind of thing seems to happen a lot."

Haley sat on the sofa in the parlor and nursed the baby, and then set the baby down in a bassinet within reach. The bassinet was made of wicker. It had been a gift to Johnny and Lura from Aunt Ginny, when Josh was born.

The morning was a little cool, so Bree had started up a small fire in the hearth. Bree added a piece of wood to the fire, then settled back in Aunt Ginny's rocker.

Haley said, "I am so glad Dusty found you all. The last I had seen him was at the little way station my father and I ran in Nevada. He was on his way to a little town, trying to find his mother. All he had was her name. I think the little town was called Baker's Crossing."

"A lot has changed in Dusty's life over the past couple of years."

Haley nodded. "Changed for the good, it looks like. When I knew him, he didn't even know his last name. And now, to think his father is Johnny McCabe. It's easy to believe, though. He did some shooting that was really astounding. Saved my life from two outlaws who tried to take over the way station."

Bree said, "Yeah. Dusty told us about that. He said it was touch-and-go for a few seconds, and he was forced to kill both men."

"He's being modest. He did some of the most outstanding trick shooting I've ever seen. And he did it while bullets were being fired at him."

Bree nodded with a smile. "That's Dusty."

Bree looked over to the bassinet. "And that's a beautiful baby you have."

"I so wish it was Dusty's. I know I shouldn't feel that way. I shouldn't think those things. Just because I feel a certain way for Dusty doesn't mean he feels the same, and I sure wouldn't want him burdened with us."

Bree said, "Oh, he feels the same. There's a certain light comes on in his eyes whenever he mentions you."

"He still talks about me?"

Bree gave a quick nod. "Sometimes."

"I've said it before, I know, but I am so grateful for all you and your family are doing for little Jonathan and me."

Bree shrugged. "Dusty would do anything for you. That makes you automatically welcome here."

Jack left his horse at the hitching rail in front of Hunter's. He visited with Hunter and Chen for a bit and had the last of the coffee in that morning's pot, then headed to the hotel. He wanted to check the two hotel rooms. The one where the guns were fired, and the one where Gideon died on the floor.

He found Falcone already there. Falcone was standing in the center of the first room, looking like he was in deep thought.

Jack said, "I didn't expect to find you here."

"I'm still trying to piece things together."

"Why?"

Falcone looked a little annoyed. "Because I'm the marshal. That's why."

Jack almost said, *No really. What are you really doing here?* Jack doubted there was anyone in town who believed Falcone was here to actually work as a lawman. He must have had some plan he was in the process of putting together while hiding behind the badge. He was going to rob the bank, or some other such thing.

But what Jack said was, "Did you find anything?"

Falcone shook his head. "I really don't believe your brother shot Gideon down in cold blood, if that means anything. I had to arrest him because he's a suspect and the circumstantial evidence is reasonably good. I'm going to have to ride down to Bozeman and wire the Territorial Governor about it, but he's probably going to agree to an inquest. He'll send in a territorial judge."

"Josh said there were two shots, but everyone I've talked to seem to hear only one. What do you make of that?"

Falcone rubbed his chin thoughtfully. "Have you ever heard two guns go off at once? It's sometimes a little hard to realize it was two guns, and not one. Especially if you're standing a little ways away."

Jack said, "Or downstairs, or out on the boardwalk."

Falcone nodded. "But of course that's just a theory. And it holds no water at all if we can't find that second gun."

"*We?*"

"I could sure use your help."

This surprised Jack a little. He said, "Why? I studied medicine. How would that help you here?"

"Because you're a college man. You're taught to think analytically. I could use a second pair of eyes in going over this room and the next one."

Falcone drew a breath and continued. "Look, if your brother says there was a second gun, then I'm going to believe there was one, unless I find seriously compelling evidence to the contrary. Yet there doesn't seem to be one. Which means I'm missing something."

Jack asked himself, *Could this man be sincere?* He didn't think so. He doubted a man like Falcone had had a sincere moment in his entire life. Yet he could find no ulterior motive in having Jack help him search for the missing gun. In fact, he couldn't imagine why Falcone was even bothering to search.

Jack said, "All right. We'll work together."

They searched the room. They searched the next one. The bed in the first room was still unmade and rumpled, so they searched through it. They found nothing.

Jack said, "Maybe we should bring Josh up here. Have him walk us through it step-by-step."

Falcone nodded. "I'll go get him."

Haley and Bree moved to the front porch. The baby was awake and had to nurse again. Haley wasn't sure the front porch would be the best place for privacy, but when they got there, Bree said, "Look around you."

Ahead of them was a view that stretched to the small stream and the wooden bridge a quarter mile away, and beyond that the land stretched off toward the center of the valley. What looked to Haley like miles of grass with stands of trees scattered here and there.

Bree said, "If anyone rides up from the valley, we'll see 'em coming long before they're close enough to see us here on the porch."

To the right, not far from the house, was a thick tangle of trees and bushes. Briars and brumbles.

Bree said, "No one could get through that. Well they could if they tried, but they'd make so much noise trying that we'd hear them long before they saw us."

To the left were the barn and the bunkhouse. Further back and beyond their line of sight was the corral, and beyond the corral was the open grassy acreage Fred used for the remuda.

Bree said, "The bunkhouse is empty. Fat and Kennedy and Old Ches and Danny are all off with the herd. Josh and Jack are in town. Fred's the only one here, and he hardly ever comes around to the front of the house."

Haley took an old rocker Aunt Ginny kept on the porch during the warmer months, and then dropped a towel over her shoulder and down over the baby for privacy. Bree took an old wooden straight-back chair.

Haley said, "I really appreciate all you and your family are doing for me. I really do. But I can't stay here. It just wouldn't be right."

Bree said, "You're welcome to, as long as you like."

Haley nodded. "Mister McCabe has said the same thing, and Miss Ginny. But I have family back east. A grandmother, and two uncles and their families. I want Jonathan to know his family, especially since he'll be raised without a father. I was thinking of maybe sending a telegram to my Uncle Emmett. He said to Pa and me when we went west that if it doesn't work out to let him know. He said if we need to come back east, he has room for us if we needed a place to stay for a while."

"Where do they live?"

"Uncle Emmett runs a farm just outside of Brighton, New York."

Bree gave a slow, thoughtful nod. "I'd hate to see you go, but I think I understand."

"Maybe I can write something and we can get Jack or Josh to ride down to Bozeman and send it off as a telegram. If they wouldn't mind. I could write a letter, but the way the postal service is out here, it may not arrive for months. After all that's happened, I want to get there. Get settled in before winter."

Bree said, "It would be a real shame if you left before Dusty is back. I know he'd love to see you."

Haley was silent a moment, staring off toward the center of the valley. "I'd like to see him, too. But at the same time, maybe it's not for the best. We didn't really know each other all that long, and so much has happened since then. So much time has passed. I'm not the same girl I was when he knew me."

She drew a breath, and said with some wistfulness, "I used to wonder what it would have been like, though. If Dusty had come back for me before Pa and I left for Oregon. I wrote him a letter. I wonder if he got it."

Bree said, "He did. He still has it."

"It wasn't all bad, being married to my husband. It was never good. Not like you see with your father and Jessica. Just the way they look at each other. Even if it's just a casual glance, it's never really just a casual glance. You can see the love in their eyes. You can feel it in the room when they're both there. It's the same with Josh and Temperance. Or Jack and Nina. With Alexander, the best it every got was maybe somewhat pleasant. He only got violent sometimes. Not very often. He was gone much of the time. Working in the fields by day, and drinking in town at night. My life was mostly just lonely. But there was always a little fear, because you never knew just what would set him off.

"I would lay in bed sometimes and just wonder what it would have been like, had Dusty come back to the way station before I had left. But it was just a dream, really. I'm not the same girl anymore. So much has happened. He's going to want to reunite with that girl from the way station. I'm afraid what he'll find in me is a stranger."

They heard the shoe soles hitting the pinewood floor inside before the door opened and Temperance stepped out.

She said, "We've got a problem. Ants. They're all through the sugar."

Bree's mouth fell open. "You were going to make that apple cobbler of yours."

Temperance nodded her head.

Bree said to Haley, "Temperance makes the best apple cobbler."

Temperance said, "Well, I guess not today."

"No. There's got to be a way." Bree got to her feet. "Maybe I can just ride into town for some sugar."

Haley was laughing. "You must really like that cobbler."

Bree looked at her, wide-eyed with enthusiasm. "Oh, they're just the absolute best."

Temperance said, "You know what Pa said. He wants us all to stay home today."

"I won't be gone long. And it's just to town. I'll be back before you know it. I'm gonna go have Fred get me a horse."

And she skipped down the steps and ran off to find Fred.

Josh's hands were cuffed in front of him.

"For what it's worth, I don't believe this is necessary," Falcone said. "But if the townspeople saw me letting a prisoner virtually run free, I'd have no chance of winning the upcoming election."

"Election?" Josh said. "Are you serious?"

"More than I've ever been."

They found Jack in the room. He hadn't left.

He said, "Is everything here just as it was when you came in to confront Gideon?"

Josh looked about. "Seems to be."

"Walk us through it," Falcone said.

Josh went to the open doorway. "I opened the door and stepped in. He was standing over there. By the bed."

Jack stepped over to the bed. "Here?"

"Over a few inches more. He was standing sideways."

Josh took a step to one side, and then turned sideways to Josh.

Josh said, "Yeah. Like that. Then he turned his head to look at me."

Jack turned his head toward the doorway.

Josh said, "Just like that."

"Then what happened?" Falcone said.

"I said to him, *You're Haley's husband. I saw what you did to her.* Or something close to that. I didn't see the pistol tucked into the front of his belt. He started turning to me, pulling the pistol out as he did so."

Jack turned toward Josh, pointing toward Josh with his index finger, as though his finger was a gun. "Like that?'

Josh nodded. "When I saw the gun, I began drawing mine. He was faster than I would have thought. He didn't look like a gunfighter, but he handled his gun like he knew how to use it. He fired a shot and I fired mine."

"Could both guns have been fired at the same time?" Falcone said.

Josh nodded. "Maybe. I don't know. It all happened so fast."

Jack said, "So, what happened next?"

"My bullet caught him square in the chest. He was knocked back a couple of steps but kept his footing. I cocked my gun in case I needed a second shot, but he turned and ran through that door," Josh's gaze swept from Jack to the doorway leading to the adjoining room. "It was ajar, and he just pushed his way through. I started following him."

Falcone said, "Let's go."

They stepped into the adjoining room. It was warm and stuffy. The room had been closed up, and the day was turning off hot.

Josh said, "I stopped in the doorway. He was sort of laying across that bed by the wall."

Jack went over to the bed and stretched out on it. "Like this?"

Josh shook his head. "No. His knees were on the floor. Only his shoulders were on the bed. Kind of like he was trying to get down to pray, but fell forward."

Jack maneuvered himself around so his upper torso was on the bed, but his butt was hanging off the side and his knees were on the floor.

He said, "Like this?"

"Yeah. I stood here a few seconds, expecting him to roll over and fire at me. But he didn't. So I went over to the bed and pulled him off."

Falcone said, "Show us how."

Josh went over to the bed and grabbed the back of Jack's shirt collar with his left hand. He held his right hand up and out, as much as he could with cuffs on his wrists.

He said, "I had my gun in my right hand, so I grabbed him with my left."

Josh then gave Jack's collar a yank, and Jack let himself be pulled upright.

Josh said, "Except, he didn't come all the way upright. His knees kind of buckled, and he went down over backwards. Landed on the floor, and he just laid there. I didn't think he was breathing. I knelt down by his side to check for a pulse, and there wasn't any."

He looked at Falcone. "That was when you and Randall came in."

Jack said, "Where was his gun at this point?"

Josh shook his head. "He didn't have it. It was in his right hand when he came into the room, but both hands were empty when I pulled him off the bed."

The bed was neatly made, the covers in place.

Jack said, "Was the bed made?"

Josh nodded. "I think it was."

Falcone went to the doorway, then turned to face the bed. "So, somewhere between here and there, the gun disappeared. Like it somehow vanished into thin air."

Josh nodded. "I'm in real trouble, ain't I?"

Fat was riding in from having spent a night at the line cabin.

He had done as Josh asked, checking the cows with the Swan brand, evaluating their condition and taking a head count. Then he had decided to check in with the floaters, the men Josh had hired to patrol the outer reaches of McCabe range and make sure the stock didn't roam too far.

Every so often, Josh's Pa thought they should make a presence there. Either he or Josh, or Dusty when he was home, would do this. But Fat decided he was going to take his position as Josh's right-hand-man seriously, so he had taken it upon himself to do this.

The floaters usually bunked at the line cabin. It was late when Fat got there, so he had spent the night.

He was a bit rumpled from sleeping in his clothes and needed a shave, and his floppy hat had a thin layer of trail dust on it. The day had really turned off hot, especially outside the valley. He was thinking a deep drink from the well would be in order. Or even better, a quick ride into town for a deep drink of cold beer at Hunter's.

He saw Bree by the corral. She was stepping up and into the saddle.

He reined up beside her.

"Miss Bree," he said, touching the brim of his hat.

"Fat," she said. "I'm heading into town. Ants got into the sugar, so I'm taking a quick ride in and get another five pounds. Pa wants us to stay close to home today, but I won't be gone long."

"Would you like me to come along?"

She smiled and shook her head. "I'll be fine. I'll take the horse trail."

He nodded, and she turned her horse and was off.

Fred came walking over. He said, "I don't like her riding off like that. But she has her own mind and you can't talk her out of anything."

Fat said, "Something's wrong, isn't there?"

Fred quickly told him about Josh being arrested the day before. Fat had ridden out in the morning, so he hadn't known.

Fred said, "Johnny and Aunt Ginny are off to Bozeman. She's gonna send a wire to an attorney she knows of in 'Frisco. Johnny wanted all the women to stay close to the house today."

Fat swung out of the saddle. "Fetch me a fresh mount. I'll ride after her."

Fred gave him a look that said, *you've got to be kidding.* "You gonna risk her getting peeved at you? You know her temper."

"Mister McCabe wouldn't want her to stay close to home if there weren't a reason."

Fred nodded and grabbed a rope that was coiled up and hanging off a fence post, and went to drop a loop on a fresh horse.

Fat supposed the cold beer at Hunter's would have to wait.

Falcone said to Josh, "I've done some bad things in my life. More than I could ever make up for. But one thing I won't do is let a man hang for something he didn't do."

Josh said, "What makes you so sure I didn't do it?"

"Because I know you. I've fought against you. You get to know a man fast that way. I just don't believe you have it in you to shoot a man down in cold blood. You don't have it in your eyes."

Jack said, "But without that gun, it might be hard to convince a jury."

Josh said, looking about the room quickly, "Sure is hot and stuffy in here. I don't remember it being this way yesterday."

Falcone nodded. "The window was open yesterday."

Then he and Jack looked at each other, the idea occurring to both of them at the same time.

Jack said, "Are you thinking what I'm thinking?"

Falcone nodded.

Jack climbed over the bed and flipped open the latch and pushed the window wide open.

Josh said, "That's the way it was."

Jack looked outside. Falcone was there behind him, looking over his shoulder. Below the window was a patch of thick junipers, and just beyond it some pines.

"Let's get down there," Falcone said.

Down below, they rummaged through the bushes. It was Falcone who found the pistol.

"That's it," Josh said.

"We had a light rain last night. It's still wet." He flipped open the loading gate and turned the cylinder one notch at a time. He dropped a spent cartridge into his hand. "It's been fired once. It hadn't been cocked again, because this was still in front of the firing pin."

He looked at Josh and smiled. "Now I don't think it'll

even go to a jury."

Jack slapped Josh on the shoulder.

Falcone said, "I do have to talk to Mrs. Gideon, though. Get her statement."

Jack said, "That means riding out to the ranch. I don't think, under these circumstances anyone'll mind."

They were heading for the livery when they saw Bree riding through the alley between Hunter's and the blacksmith, and out onto the main street. Josh's cuffs were gone, and he was once again wearing his gun.

"What're you doing in town?" Jack said.

She told him.

"Didn't Pa say to stay close to home?"

"Temperance wants to make apple cobbler for desert tonight. We need sugar."

Josh grinned. "If Temperance wants to make apple cobbler, nothing should stand in her way."

Bree said, "My thoughts exactly. I'll get the sugar and I'll be right home."

Randall was in his office when Torgeson stepped in. He had a dark and swollen brow from the punch he had taken from Jack in the ring a couple of days ago. The swelling had spread down into his eye, and now the eye itself was swollen shut and dark. But he was functional.

Torgeson said, "Mister Randall. She just rode into town."

Randall was at his desk going through mail. He looked up eagerly and said, "Is she alone?"

"Her brothers are in the livery saddling up and riding out. Falcone is with them. Looks like she's heading for Franklin's."

"Go and invite her here to see me. I'll be upstairs in my room."

"Yes, sir."

Bree swung out of the saddle and gave the rein a couple of tugs around the hitching rail in front of Franklin's. She stepped up onto the new boardwalk that ran the length of the street, and into Franklin's.

The place was deserted.

She called out, "Mister Franklin?"

He called from his back room. "I'll be right there."

She decided to make herself content with browsing about while she waited.

The front door opened, and two men stepped in. One of them she recognized. One of Randall's men. The one Jack had knocked out in the ring.

"Miss Bree?" he said. "We need you to come with us."

She looked at him like he had lost his mind. "I'm not going anywhere with you."

"Mister Randall needs to see you."

"I don't want to see him."

The one with the black eye stepped in front of her. The other grabbed her by the arms.

"You're coming with us right now," the black-eye man said.

Her rifle was in her saddle, but she had left her gunbelt home. She hadn't thought she would need it on a simple ride to town. *Foolish*, she thought. Now she understood why Pa never left the house without his.

The other one said, "Out the back door. Don't want any witnesses."

Bree made to struggle, but the one with the black eye grabbed her by the chin. Hard.

He said, "You're coming to see Mister Randall. We can do it the easy way, or the hard way. But either way, you're going to see Mister Randall."

40

Fat came out from the horse trail behind Hunter's, and saw Bree's horse tethered in front of Franklin's. He rode over and left his horse beside hers, and stepped up and onto the boardwalk. Bree was going to be so furious with him, but he didn't think Mister McCabe would mind. Ultimately, if Mister McCabe gave you an instruction, or if he even just asked you to do something, you did it.

He stepped in, but Bree wasn't there. Charlie Franklin was down by the back door, looking out into what was now the alley behind his store.

"Mister Franklin" Fat said. "Is Bree McCabe here?"

Franklin looked at Fat with fear in his eyes.

He said, "Mister Cole, I saw two of Randall's thugs escort her out of here. They took her through the alley to the hotel."

Fat knew he was alone in this. He had passed Josh and Jack and Vic Falcone on the horse trail. They were heading for the ranch. If Fat was going to handle this, he would have to do it alone.

For a second, he thought of running across the street and getting Hunter. But then it might be too late. Whatever Randall wanted to do to Miss Bree, it wasn't going to be good. Fat had seen the look in Randall's eye at the dance.

Fat pulled his pistol and quickly checked the loads. He had seen Mister McCabe and Josh do this. He then thumbed a sixth cartridge into the cylinder. Something Mister McCabe had said once that he did if he was expecting trouble. Fat then put his gun back in his holster.

He said to Franklin, "Go across the street and get Hunter. Tell him I'm going to the hotel to get Bree. Tell him to bring his rifle."

And Fat was out the door and running down the boardwalk.

Falcone reined up. They had gone only about half a mile from town.

Jack said, "What's wrong?"

Falcone said, "You're going to think I'm insane. But I

just don't feel right about leaving your sister in town."

Josh said, "She'll be all right. She can handle herself. And besides, Fat's there."

Falcone nodded. He looked at Josh and Jack gravely.

He said, "Maybe so. But there are things I know about Randall."

Josh said, "Like what?"

"Come on," Falcone said, and wheeled his horse around and started back toward town.

With the black-eye man pulling Bree by one elbow, and the other man behind her and his hands on her shoulders and pushing her, they got her up the stairs. They then pushed her into the open doorway of Randall's room.

"Here she is, Boss," Torgeson said.

"Thank you, men, "Randall said. "That'll be all."

They shut the door, leaving Bree alone in the room with Randall. He was standing in the center of the room.

She said, "What do you want?"

Randall smiled. "Why do I have to *want* anything? Maybe I just wanted to talk. To get to know you a little better. After all, you're the daughter of a prominent local family, and I'm probably the most prominent local business man."

She said, "I have nothing to say to you."

Randall began advancing toward Bree. He said, "Miss McCabe, I have to admit, I've been intrigued with you from the start. Taken with you, really. I know I am a lot older than you, but that doesn't mean we can't be..." he searched for the words, "friendly to each other."

She began backing up. "Mister Randall..."

He held a hand up, like he was signaling her to stop. "Now, please just hear me out. I have money. And I have powerful friends. And I have ambitions. And you are a young woman of extreme capabilities. We could go far together."

"Mister Randall..." Her back bumped into the wall. She could back up no further. "We can't go anywhere together."

He shook his head. "Now, now. I'm not used to taking *no* for an answer."

"Well, I'm afraid you're going to have to."

"No, I'm not."

He was now inches from her. She could smell the

tobacco smoke from his last cigar.

"Mister Randall, you're not acting like a gentleman."

He smiled. It wasn't his usual, practiced theatrical smile. It was like a wildcat that had just caught its dinner.

"Miss Bree, there is a time to be a gentleman, and there is a time not to be. This is a time not to be."

"You're going to have to accept my answer as what it is. No."

He shook his head. "No I'm not."

"My father will kill you. And my brothers."

"You forget. I am right now the most powerful man in this state. I'm friends with the governor. I have the local circuit judge in my pocket. I am going to have you, and there is not anything you can do about it. So you might as well comply."

He grabbed her hard around the back of the neck.

"Now," he said. "I don't want to hurt you. But a man like me, I get what I want."

She reached around with her hand to his wrist, and dug her thumb into a spot between the man's wrist and thumb. A place Mister Chen had shown her.

He yelped and pulled his hand away, and then with his other hand he delivered a hard backhand slap that caught her in the mouth. She fell back against the wall and then to the floor.

She looked up at him with a trickle of blood making its way from the corner of her mouth.

But she was not looking at him like a scared girl, about to become prey to this man. She was looking at him like she was going to kill him.

He stopped in his tracks. He hadn't been expecting this from her. A man like Randall wanted his victim afraid. He wasn't looking for a contest.

She raised her boot, about to drive it not into his groin, which would have been obvious, but into his knee. Again, like Mister Chen had taught her.

But then the door opened and with a roaring shout, Fat Cole came charging in at the man, tackling him, slamming him into the wall.

Fat swung a fist into Randall's face. Once. Then again. But Fat was a cowboy, not a fighter. He knew how to drop a loop over a steer at a full gallop, but he punched like he wasn't used to punching. His fists made contact, but not with maximum efficiency. Randall's head bobbed with both punches, but they weren't enough to stop him.

Fat went to throw a third punch, but Randall raised an arm to intercept the punch, then delivered a solid right cross to Fat's face.

Randall has boxed before, Bree realized. She had seen the way her father fought, and the way he had taught Josh and Jack. Pa had done some boxing, back in Pennsylvania when he was growing up.

Fat was knocked back two steps by the punch. Randall stepped in and drove a low uppercut into Fat's stomach, doubling the cowboy over. Randall then grabbed him by the shoulders, straightening him up, and delivered another right cross. This one caused Fat's knees to buckle, and he hit the floor.

Bree was not going to wait around and be anyone's victim. She was a McCabe, and it was time Randall learned what that meant.

He turned to face her and found her already on her feet. He stood a whole head taller than she did, but to her this meant nothing. She smacked him in the face with the palm of her left hand—again, Mister Chen's teaching. It caught him in the nose. He hadn't been expecting this, and a shot to the nose has a way of stopping your momentum.

She advanced on him as he was stepping back. She raised her arm, bending it fully as she did so, and drove an elbow in this eye. Then it was time for a knee to the groin, and she did so with gusto.

He fell to his hands and knees, and she reached into his coat and pulled out his revolver. A larger caliber than hers, so she held it with both hands as she hauled back the hammer.

"Time for you to learn a valuable lesson," Bree said. "You don't mess with a gunhawk."

She heard footsteps rattling up the stairs, and Victor Falcone charged into the room. He was in his tie and jacket, and his badge was catching the lamplight in a sort of dull, yellow gleam.

Fat was now sitting up, but was holding onto his

stomach.

Bree said, "Are you all right?"

He nodded, but he hadn't yet recovered enough wind to speak.

Randall was now sitting up. Blood was streaming from his nose where Bree had struck him, and his eye was already blackening and swelling from where she had elbowed him.

"I want these two arrested," Randall said to Falcone. "They tried to rob me. She lured me in here, trying to seduce me, and her cowboy friend tried to attack me."

Falcone grinned. "I don't think so. You see, I actually know where Mister Higgins is. He and I had a talk before he rode out. He told me about Chicago, and Saint Louis."

Randall closed his eyes for a moment. He apparently hadn't been expecting this.

There were more rapid footfalls out on the stairway, and Josh and Jack came running in.

"It's all right, boys," Falcone said. "I just had to save Mister Randall from your sister Bree. I think she would have killed him."

"You're dang right on that," Bree said.

Randall said, "My statement is that those two tried to rob me."

Fat now had the wind to speak. "That ain't true. He tried to have his way with Miss Bree."

Falcone nodded. He said, "Aloysius Randall, you are under arrest for assault on these two."

"You fool. I own the local judge. I'll be out of jail in no time."

Falcone shook his head. "I'd pity you, if that's the case. Because the jail is probably the only way I can keep these two boys and their father away from you. They have another brother, too. He's away right now, but I wouldn't want any of them on my trail."

Randall got to his feet. "You're out of your mind if you think you can stand against me."

Falcone shook his head. "It's not me standing against you. It's the law standing against you."

"You fool. I put that badge on you, and I can take it off."

"Maybe so. But not until the next meeting of the Town

Council. And until then, you're under arrest."

Falcone reached into his jacket for the handcuffs he had taken off of Josh, and snapped them onto Randall's wrists.

He said to Bree, "You might want to get your friend to Granny Tate. Make sure he isn't too badly hurt. And yourself, too."

She nodded. "Thank you."

"No need to thank me. I'm just a servant of the people."

He led Randall away.

PART EIGHT

Early Autumn

41

  Johnny awakened at the sound. He was lying in bed. Jessica was curled up beside him. He could tell by the gentle rhythm of her breathing that she was asleep.
  What sound had he heard? He hadn't been sure. It had happened while he was asleep, but it had awakened him. Probably the house settling, he thought. He was trying to calm these battlefield instincts that kept him forever on edge. And yet, the instincts seemed to survive as if they had a mind of their own.
  He reached in the darkness to the chair beside the bed. His pistol was there. Six full cartridges loaded. But he didn't take it in his hand, as much as he wanted to. He forced his hand away and he settled back into his pillow.
  But he didn't let himself go back to sleep. He wouldn't until he was sure that the sound was nothing to be concerned about.
  Then he heard it again. A sort of muted *thunking* sound from down below. He knew this house well enough to know what the sound was. A boot accidentally kicking the leg of a kitchen chair. Someone was downstairs in the kitchen, and had bumped into a chair. If it had been someone from this household, they wouldn't be bumping into chairs. They would have turned up a lamp so they could see.
  He grabbed the gun and sat up in bed, and reached for his levis. If you're going to be in a gunfight, you at least want your pants on.
  In his bare feet, with his levis on and his pistol in his hand, he went down the hall to the room Jack was using. Now that Matt and Peddie were living on their own section of land and putting up a house of their own, a bedroom was free and Jack had moved back in from the bunkhouse.
  Johnny stepped into Jack's room and laid a hand on his shoulder. Jack stirred a moment, then was awake.
  Johnny whispered the words. "Someone's downstairs in the kitchen."

While Jack was pulling on his pants, Johnny stepped out and into Josh's room. Johnny shook Josh's shoulder, and his son was awake.

Johnny said in barely a whisper, "Someone's rummaging around downstairs in the kitchen. Get your gun and follow me."

Johnny started down the hall, gun ready. He didn't cock it because that would be a recipe for disaster. Cocked guns tended to go off when you weren't ready for them to do so. He didn't cock his gun until he was ready to shoot.

He started down the stairs, keeping as close to the edge of each step as possible so the boards underfoot would be less likely to creak. He glanced back and saw Jack was right behind him. Josh had his pants on and his gunbelt draped over one shoulder, and was at the head of the stairs, about to start down behind Jack.

Johnny touched down on the parlor floor, and he saw Ginny in the darkness. She was standing in the doorway to her room.

She whispered to him, "Someone's in the kitchen."

A lamp in the kitchen had now been turned up, and the pale glow made its way into the parlor.

"Stay here," Johnny said to her. "The boys and I'll check it out."

Johnny crossed the floor, touching each foot down silently, heal-to-toe. A lot of folks thought when you wanted to walk quietly, you went up on your toes. But Johnny had learned from the Shoshone that you touched the heel of your foot down first, silently placing the foot down rather than just dropping it, then let your weight roll from heel to toe in a fluid motion.

He crossed the parlor as such. He had shown this sort of walking to the boys, and they were demonstrating at the moment that they were good students.

Johnny stepped into the kitchen, his gun ready, but then he broke into a grin.

"Dusty," he said. "Zack. Joe."

Jack breathed a sigh of relief behind Johnny, and lowered his gun.

Dusty was in a linen Mexican-style shirt that had been white once, but was now stained forever by sweat and trail dust. His hat was floppier than the last time Johnny had seen him, and he now had a beard that was thin with youth, and maybe an inch long.

Zack was there, looking equally trail worn. And Joe. And sitting in a kitchen chair was the man Johnny was hoping he would see with them.

"Sam Middleton," Johnny said, extending his hand. "It's mighty good to see you."

Sam looked at him with a weary grin. "It's mighty good to be here. Believe me."

Sam's left arm was in a sling.

Sam said, "I caught a bullet when we were escaping from the prison."

Johnny set his pistol down on the table. Dusty was extending a hand to him, but Johnny bypassed the hand and took his son in a hug. Then Jack and Josh were shaking hands with Dusty.

Johnny grasped Zack's hand and then Joe's, and he then he looked over his shoulder to the parlor doorway and called out, "Ginny! Come on out! They're home!"

Johnny said to the man in the chair, "Sam, let me introduce my other sons. Jack, Josh, this is Sam Middleton. The man who saved all of our lives back in California."

Sam was about to extend a hand to Jack, but then his eyes landed on the doorway to the parlor, and the woman standing there.

His mouth fell open, and he rose from his chair. Johnny glanced back to Ginny to see that she was staring at him the same way.

He said, "Virginia? Virginia Brackston? Is that really you?"

That was when two things happened.

Ginny said, "Addison?" And she fainted dead away.

And Dusty saw in the doorway behind her a girl he had started to think he would never see again, and certainly didn't expect to see here.

"Haley?"

42

Ginny somehow managed not to hurt herself when she went down to the floor, and quickly came around. It was Sam who was at her side, one hand under her head.

Jessica was there. She said, "Should we go for Granny Tate?"

Bree said, "I'll go get Fred to saddle a horse."

Ginny shook her head. "No. I'm all right."

Then she looked into Sam's eyes.

She said, "Addison? Is it really you? How can it be? You died so many years ago."

He said, "I'm so sorry, Ginny."

Johnny was looking at both of them. He had to admit, he was about as puzzled as he had ever been. How was it possible Ginny knew Sam Middleton? But she apparently did. She was using the name Sam had said was his real name.

Then it dawned on Johnny. Over the years, she had mentioned a young man she had been in love with. Was going to marry. She talked very little of him, and even then it was only after a couple glasses of wine. She had never given his name.

Could it be? Johnny wondered. *Could this be the man?*

She said, "But you died in that storm at sea."

He shook his head. "The ship went down, yes. But I wasn't on board. There's so much we need to talk about."

Johnny saw Dusty standing and staring not only at his aunt, but also at Haley.

Johnny said to Dusty, "Go talk to her."

Dusty hesitated. After all, Aunt Ginny had just collapsed to the floor.

Johnny said, "Go ahead. We'll take care of your aunt."

Dusty stepped into the parlor and said to Haley, "I can't believe you're here."

He pulled her in for a long hug. She wrapped her arms around him too, but after a moment she pulled away.

She said, "We have a lot to talk about. Come on, upstairs. There's something I have to show you."

Jessica got Ginny a glass of water, and then Ginny

was strong enough to stand.

Johnny said, "Come on outside, everyone. Let's give them room to talk."

Ginny gave him a *thank you* glance.

Cora was at the foot of the stairs. "Mommy? What's going on?"

Jessica said to Johnny, "I'll get her back to sleep and wait for you upstairs."

Johnny headed out the back door along with the others.

Johnny said, "Doesn't look like you had an easy time."

Zack shrugged. "I suppose the fact that none of us were killed breaking him out of prison could count as an easy time."

Joe and Zack told them about the prison. El Rosario, and how they broke Sam out of it.

Zack said, "Breaking him out of there the way we did would have been impossible if it had been a regular prison. But it wasn't well fortified. They were relying on the secrecy of the place, and were more concerned with trying to keep the prisoners in than defend against an attack from outside."

Joe said, "It has a dark reputation. From what Sam was saying about the way the prisoners are treated there, the reputation is deserved."

Johnny said, "I've heard about El Rosario. Mentions of it here and there, over the years. But I never thought it really existed."

Joe said, "Men go in there, but they don't come out."

Johnny grinned. "Except for Sam."

Joe nodded. "Except for Sam."

They moved around to the front porch.

Zack said, "I'm worn out, right to the bone."

He dropped into Ginny's rocker. Joe took the straight-back. Josh sat on the steps, and Johnny stood and leaned against one post that held up the porch roof. Jack paced about on the porch.

Johnny dug into his vest for his pipe. "So tell me about the ride north."

Zack shook his head. "It wasn't good. Word got out fast about the prison break. Sam's name is on reward posters probably all the way north to the Canadian border. His real name."

Joe said, "I'm not sure how long we're gonna be able to stay around here. The Feds suspect our family had something to do with the break-out."

Zack nodded. "We found that out in Cheyenne. A marshal there who knows Jack."

Jack smiled. "Jubal Kincaid. A good man."

Joe nodded. "He is that. He gave us some information. Unofficial, of course. And told us our meeting with him never happened."

Zack said, "Sam caught a bullet in the shoulder when we were getting away from the prison. We rode north to Texas."

"A ranch I know there," Joe said. "They put us up while Sam recovered. The local doctor took care of his shoulder."

"But then going north was a problem. We stopped at a way station in Colorado and found a federal marshal there with a small posse. There was a shootout. We had to kill at least two of 'em."

Johnny winced at this. It was going to make matters much worse.

Zack said, "So they know we're heading north. It's only a matter of time before they figure out we're here."

Johnny said, "No one has ever taken a man off this place. It's not gonna change now."

Zack shook his head. "We can't ask you to do that, old friend."

"You're not asking."

Joe held up his hand in a stopping motion. "Johnny, we already talked about this. We're stopping here just for a little while. Sam apparently knows Aunt Ginny. After they're done talking, then we're riding out. Heading north for the border."

Jack said, "Dusty's just been reunited with Haley. Now he's got to ride away."

Zack shook his head. "I don't see the point of that." He said to Josh, "Apparently that little girl in there is the one you and Dusty rode to Oregon to find."

Josh nodded.

Zack said to Joe, "I say, once Sam is done talking with

Aunt Ginny, that the three of us just ride on. Don't tell Dusty about it."

Joe nodded. "According to Kincaid, the law suspects our family was involved. They don't know which ones. There's no way they can prove it was specifically Dusty."

"Especially once word gets out that Sam is north of the border. They'll be looking there, not here."

Ginny sat on the sofa. Sam was beside her, his hand in hers.

He explained about the Mexican general's son. The price on his head. His years on the run.

He said, "I never wanted to leave you. But if the law found me, then I would have been taken away from you, anyway. And back in those days, Marshal Aikens was only one step behind me."

"But you could have told me the truth."

He shook his head. "I was afraid you wouldn't love me anymore if you knew I was something of a rogue."

"Oh, Addison. How could you think that?"

He shrugged. "I don't know. I was young."

"Well, we're together now."

He drew a weary breath.

She said, "What is it?"

He told her about the Mexican prison, and the ride north.

"We can't stay long," he said. "We're headed for the Canadian border. We only came this way so Zack and the boys could visit with everyone here before we continued on. I had no idea when they mentioned an 'Aunt Ginny' that it was the girl from my past."

She said, "You've just arrived, and now fate pulls us apart once again."

"Only for a time," he said. "I'll return as soon as I can."

She shook her head. "It might be asking too much."

"What might be?"

"Addison, I'm not the same young girl you knew years ago. Years have passed. More than twenty of them. In many ways, we're like strangers."

He reached a hand to touch the side of her face. "In the ways that count, you're the same Virginia Brackston. And once this is done, will you be here waiting for me? I know it's a lot to ask, but..."

She said, "Oh, Addison. There has never been anyone but you. I can wait a little while longer."

When they stepped out to the front porch, they found Fred had saddled three horses. Joe and Zack were waiting for them.

Sam said, "What about Dusty?"

Zack shook his head. "He's staying here. He doesn't know it yet. But he's staying."

Sam said to Ginny, "I suppose it's goodbye. For now."

She nodded. "Only for now."

He then bent down to her—she was a lot shorter than he—and lightly kissed her. Then the kiss turned deeper.

Johnny turned away. They all did.

When they pulled apart, without a word, Sam went down the steps, and all three climbed into their saddles.

With a flair of the debonair that Ginny remembered being so strong in her Addison, he removed his hat and made as much of a sweeping bow as he could from the saddle. She smiled, and affected a curtsey.

Johnny said, "Keep your powder dry, you three."

Zack nodded. "And you."

Josh said, "Ramon has been doing a fine job watching over your ranch. And we'll stop in from time to time and make sure everything's all right."

Joe said, "Aunt Ginny, good to see you again."

She smiled. "And you, Josiah. I wish we could have had longer to visit."

"Next time."

She nodded. "Indeed. Next time."

Joe said to Zack and Sam, "Come on. Let's ride."

With the moon high in the sky, they turned their horses and rode down toward the center of the valley.

Johnny walked over to Ginny and said, "Are you all right?"

Tears were streaming down her face. She made no effort to hide them. But she nodded and said, "I will be."

They all stood and watched as the riders grew distant in the moonlight. The iron-shod hooves of their horses clattered against the wooden bridge, and then the riders were past the bridge and gone into the night.

The baby was sleeping in a wooden crib. Dusty stood by the crib, looking down in wonder.

He said, "This is yours?"

Haley nodded. She wiped back a tear. "Things are so different than I ever wanted them to be."

They sat on the bed. Because the baby was asleep, they didn't turn up the lamp. The only source of light was what drifted in from the moon outside.

He said, "I went to Oregon and searched for you for three months. Josh came with me. But Oregon is a big place."

"But you're here now."

He nodded. "I wish I smelled better. We've been on the trail a long time."

She shook her head with a smile. "I'm just glad you're here."

She told him of how her father had died shortly after they got to Oregon, and she had married Alexander Gideon. She told Dusty about how Alexander treated her. And how Josh had gone to confront him and shot the man.

She said, "But he did give me one thing. He gave me a beautiful baby boy."

Dusty took her hand. "I can't stay long. We broke a man out of prison, and the law's coming for us. But once it's done, once the dust has settled, I'll be back."

"Oh, Dusty." She looked at him sadly. "I won't be here. I'm leaving in two days. I'll be catching the stage for Cheyenne. Little Jonathan and me. I'm moving east, to live with an uncle. After all I've been through I just need to go home."

"You won't be here?"

She shook her head. Tears were forming in her eyes. She reached up to wipe them away before they could begin streaming.

She said, "I'm not the same girl you knew back in Nevada. So much has happened. I need time to just catch my breath. My aunt will help me with Jonathan. And you belong here. You have a family, now. You belong with them."

He said, "Life isn't fair, is it?"

She shook her head again. "Not that I ever noticed."

Dusty heard a sound that he recognized as riders on the wooden bridge out beyond the ranch. Their iron shod hooves rang out in the night. He went to the window and in the moonlight saw the three he had ridden in with riding off into the darkness.

He hurried out to the hallway and down the stairs and out to the porch.

Pa and Aunt Ginny were standing there. And Jack and Josh and Bree.

"They didn't wait for me," Dusty said.

"No," Aunt Ginny said. "And I, for one, am glad. We need you here with us, not gallivanting off to Canada."

"If I hurry, I can catch up to them."

He charged down the steps, shouldering past Jack as he did so, and began running toward the barn.

He found the stalls empty. Didn't matter. He would go out back and fetch himself a horse. He grabbed a rope, but when he stepped from the barn, he found Pa standing there.

Dusty said, "Out of my way, Pa."

Johnny said, "No, Dusty. I want you to take a minute and listen to me."

Dusty wanted to move. He wanted to run to the remuda out back with a rope in his hand and grab himself a horse. But this was Pa, so he stood his ground and waited.

Pa said, "You want to ride after them."

Dusty nodded. "Yes, Pa. I want to share the burden with them. I rode with them all the way. I don't want to be let off the hook."

"It's just what I would have wanted when I was your age. But they're doing you a favor, son."

"They're trying to spare me. But they don't need to."

Johnny drew a breath, pausing a moment while he tried to find the words. "A father wants to give his children a better life than he had. Everything about my life that's good, I want to share with you all. But everything that's bad is something I want to help you avoid. If you can learn from my mistakes, then maybe you don't have to make the same ones."

Dusty stood patiently.

Johnny said, "You know what life on the run is, from growing up with the Patterson gang. If you ride out to catch up with Zack and Joe and Sam, you'll be going right back to that life. Do you really want that?"

Dusty hesitated. He hadn't really expected the question. He found himself saying, "No. Not really."

"This is your chance to walk away. You're young and have your whole life ahead of you. Zack and Joe are giving you a chance to live that life. It's not that they're not letting you share the burden. It's that they're giving you the opportunity they would hope would be given to them, if they were in your place."

Dusty stood silently.

Johnny said, "You're Aunt Ginny has missed you terribly, and has worried about you every step of the way. She knew what you boys had ridden to Mexico to do. She knew there was a possibility you might get shot in the attempt. Spend some time with her. And spend some time with that girl in there, the girl you rode to Oregon to try to find."

Dusty said, "She's leaving in a couple of days. Going back east to live with her family."

Johnny nodded. He knew this. "Then spend every second you can with her."

Dusty stood a moment. This was a lot to think about. Then he held up the rope and said, "I guess I'd better put this back."

Johnny smiled. "You do that."

44

Bree was thinking about Fat Cole, and how he so often seemed to make a pest out himself around her. If she stepped out of the house, he would somehow try to find his way over to her and ask how she was doing. Or comment on the weather. Or ask if he could saddle a horse for her. Her brothers had teased her about it more than once. Josh had said once that if Fat was trying to shoe a horse and Bree walked by, he would likely drive the nail into his own leg.

And yet, she no longer saw Fat. He seemed to be making himself scarce. A few weeks had passed since Randall had tried to get violent with her, and since then she had caught only a couple glimpses of Fat.

The night before at dinner, Josh had said to Pa, "Strange thing. Fat has asked to join the floaters out at the line cabin."

"Didn't expect that," Pa said.

"I don't want to tell him no, if that's what he wants, but I'd like to keep him here at headquarters. He's turning into our top hand. A man I can really depend on."

Bree was thinking about all of this while she was curled up on her bed with a book. She was in her nightgown, and had decided it was time to visit Tolstoy again. With all that had been going on lately, she hadn't done much reading.

But she found herself staring at the pages. Staring but not reading. Her mind kept going to the events of the past few weeks. Not just Fat Cole or Aloysius Randall, but also to Dusty and Haley. A love that seemed to be just beyond their reach. Haley was heading back east to live with family. Haley and her little son.

And she thought of Aunt Ginny and the man she had thought lost at sea all those years ago. Addison Travis. The man who now called himself Sam Middleton. Where Dusty's love with Haley seemed to be ending before it could really begin, Aunt Ginny and Addison were possibly finding a new beginning.

And she thought of Pa and Jessica. Bree had never thought Pa would love again, not after losing Ma. But she was glad to be wrong. And now Bree had a little sister in Cora.

Her thoughts returned to Fat. He had always been something of a pest, but she never thought poorly of him. And she thought about how he had attacked Randall like a madman, just to try to save her.

She got to her feet and glanced out the window. From her bedroom she had a view of the open meadow behind the house, where the remuda often grazed.

In the fading light, she could see a man was out there. Tall and narrow. She realized it was Fat.

He's not going to avoid me this time, she thought.

She shouldered into her robe but didn't even bother to grab her slippers.

She ran down the stairs and through the parlor and into the kitchen in her bare feet, her robe open and trailing behind her.

Aunt Ginny and Jessica were sitting at the table, sharing a cup of tea.

"Bree?" Aunt Ginny said.

"Gotta run," Bree said, as she charged across the kitchen toward the back door. "Something I've gotta take care of."

And she was out the door.

"Land sakes," Ginny said. "That girl."

Bree ran across the long grass to the back meadow. Fat Cole had dropped a loop on a horse and stopped as he realized Bree was between him and the ranch yard. He looked like he wanted to escape, but there was nowhere to go.

"Evenin', Miss Bree," he said uncomfortably. He was looking downward, not at her.

"What's going on?" she said. "You've been avoiding me for weeks."

"No, I haven't. I..."

He stopped talking because he was trying to lie, and she wasn't buying it. And she didn't think a man like Fat was comfortable lying, anyway.

He raised his gaze to meet hers. "I tried to fight for you. To protect you. To keep you safe. That's all I've ever wanted since I first saw you is to keep you safe."

She couldn't believe she was hearing these words. He had never said anything like this before. He had stammered and stumbled around her, but never really said anything.

She felt like something inside her was melting.

He said, "But I failed you. I couldn't stop him. You winded up having to stop him to save both of us. I don't know why I didn't draw my gun. I guess in the heat of the moment, I didn't think about it."

"Pa always said I was a hellcat."

"Do you know how that makes me feel not to be able to protect the girl I..." He left what he was going to say hanging in the air.

She stepped toward him. "You fought him. You tried to defend me. Do you know how that makes me feel?"

"I don't know. But I've gotta saddle this horse and be going." He tried to step around her, but she stepped into his way.

It was then that she saw the saddle lying in the grass, and the bedroll tied to the back of it.

"What's going on?" she asked.

"I'm quittin'. I left a note for Josh in the bunkhouse."

"Why are you quitting?"

"Because every time I see you, it's gonna be a reminder to me of how much I failed you. You, the one person in the world I don't want to fail."

She found herself saying, "I don't want you to go."

"This horse is mine. I rode in on him. I'll be riding out on him."

He started to walk forward, but she didn't move. He stopped and she stepped forward, and placed a hand on the side of his face.

She said, "I can't call you Fat. I just can't bring myself to call you that, anymore. I never liked it. I always thought that was a horrible nickname."

He looked a little surprised, like he hadn't expected her to say that. He shrugged his shoulders and said, "It's all right. I don't mind. It's short for Jehosaphat."

She grinned. "I don't know if I could call you that, either."

He returned the grin. "It *is* a mouthful."

"What's your middle name?"

He said, "Charles."

"Charles Cole. That's what I'm going to call you from now on. You're too good a man for a name like *Fat*."

"Well, I gotta be riding."

"No you don't. You're staying here."

"I got no reason to."

She said, "Yes you do. The reason is because I don't want you to go. Charles."

"Why?"

She then sprang at him, wrapping her arms around the back of his neck and pressing her mouth against his. He staggered back a step, then let go of the rope and took her in his arms, lifting her fully off the grass.

Josh and Jack stood leaning against the back of the house. Josh's arms were folded, and Jack had a length of straw in his teeth.

Jack said, "You see that?'

"Mm-hmm," Josh said.

"You owe me a dollar."

Jack held out his hand. Josh gave a sigh of defeat, reached into his vest and pulled out a silver dollar and dropped it into Jack's hand.

Jack said, "Nice doing business with you."

It was late when the restaurant closed. Then cleaning the place up took about an hour. Washing dishes. Cleaning the kitchen. Sweeping the floors. Pulling off the table cloths and replacing them with clean ones. Johannes had said to Flossy that it was important the place smell fresh and clean to the customers when they walk in.

She was tired when it was finally time to leave. Bone weary. It sure beat the life she had before, though.

Johannes let her out the front door and then locked it behind her. She found Vic Falcone waiting for her.

When she had first met him, he had struck her as handsome in a dashing sort of way. A way that made the breath catch in her chest. He had stood tall, with an impossibly well-groomed handlebar mustache. He spoke elegantly, and yet there was almost a savage power about him.

Then, as the years went by and he gradually lost his battle with whiskey, he somehow seemed to wilt. The mustache became less groomed and his jaw became covered with stubble. His shoulders seemed to sag and he stood less straight, and the savage power seemed to fade. He went from a man she believed could be defeated by no one, to a man who she wasn't sure could even stand up to a strong wind.

At the end of it, when Two-Finger Walker beat the stuffing out of him and placed him on a horse backwards and sent him riding away down the side of a mountain, all she had felt for him was pity.

And yet now he was standing here before her. A black hat and a black jacket. A checkered vest and a string tie. His shoulders filled out the jacket with what seemed like renewed strength and he stood tall and straight again.

And, of all things, a badge was pinned to his lapel.

He wore his gun hanging low at his right side and tied down. Just like the old days. And when she stepped out of the hotel and saw him standing there, her breath caught in her chest once again.

He took off his hat. "Miss Flossy," he said. "Would you please do me the honor of allowing me to walk you home?"

She shrugged and had to hold back a giggle. "If you

like."

And so they walked. He asked her about her day, and seemed to listen with earnest interest as she talked about waiting tables and how her feet hurt, but how excited she had been to get a huge tip from one prospector who had struck a small claim.

She said, "According to him, the assayer said he had two hundred dollars' worth of ore. He gave me a twenty dollar tip. Can you imagine that? His whole meal cost a dollar."

She then asked him about his day, and he told her about coffee in the morning with the preacher, and then walking his rounds. He would like to hire a deputy, but couldn't find anyone who was willing to work with him.

He said, "The preacher finally told me if I was in a pinch and needed someone, to call on him."

"The preacher with a gun," she said, letting the contradiction roll over in her mind.

He said, "He wears his gun like he knows how to use it. Like a McCabe. But when he speaks from that pulpit, he speaks like a man who knows. Like a man who has faced evil and won."

"You've gone to listen to a preacher?"

He nodded. "A few times. And he joins me in my office most every morning for coffee. Miah Ricker has joined us a few times, too."

She said, "Has Randall caused any trouble?"

"Not yet. I hope he doesn't. But with a man like him, it's best not to turn your back."

Two weeks ago, there had been an inquest regarding charges against Randall for assault and battery on Bree McCabe and Jehosaphat Cole. But the circuit judge was owned by Randall, and the charges were dismissed without it having to go trial. Randall was now once again running his hotel and selling lots of land.

Flossy said, "What are you going to do if the McCabes come for him?"

"I'll deal with it if and when it happens."

"Won't that put you kind of between a rock and a hard place?"

He nodded. "That comes with wearing the badge, I suppose."

Flossy and Vic made their way along one boardwalk, then crossed an empty street and walked up another. Eventually they arrived at the boarding house.

Flossy figured sooner or later he was going to want to come in with her. And she was thinking tonight might be the night she said yes.

But instead, he stood and said, "Miss Flossy, there's something I would like to ask you."

She was curious. "What's that?"

"I would like to see you."

She shrugged. "You've done a lot more than that, over the last few years."

He shook his head. "I'm asking your permission to court you, proper. The way it should have been done in the first place."

She didn't know what to say. Finally, the words came out. "Vic, I'm just a whore."

He shook his head again. "I've been thinking a lot lately about second chances. I think maybe we all deserve one. Some might say we don't. Some might hate me forever for the man I was, and it's their right, I suppose. But I believe in second chances. You're not a whore, Flossy. You're a waitress. And I'm the town marshal. At least until the next election. And I'm asking permission to court you."

She looked at him in silence for a long moment. Felt like forever. She truly didn't know what to think.

Finally, she said, "Second chances, hmm?"

He nodded.

She found herself also nodding. "Yes, Marshal Falcone. I think I would like it very much if you courted me."

She was smiling, from her heart outward. She didn't think she had truly smiled since she didn't remember when.

46

Johnny was still dressed but sitting on the bed and leaning his back against the headboard. He had made the headboard himself of narrow pine logs. It formed a sort of rectangle, and in the center the logs formed the letter M.

Johnny's gunbelt was draped over one corner of the footboard, easily three feet out of reach. He was letting it remain where it was. He was thinking of trying to sleep tonight without his gun on the chair by the bed.

Jessica was in her nightgown and was sitting in front of the mirror brushing out her hair. She had let it out of the bun it was usually in, and it fell nearly to her waist.

Johnny said, "Your hair has gotten long since we left California."

"I'm thinking of cutting maybe four inches off it."

"Really? I kind of like it this way."

She looked at him with a smirk, raising her brows a smidgen. "Really? Does it give me a wild Shoshone woman look?"

He was returning the smirk. "And how."

This was when Cora came running in and jumped onto the bed and landed on Johnny's lap.

Johnny said, "What are you doing up, sweetie? We put you to bed an hour ago."

She nodded her head. "I couldn't sleep."

"You think you can sleep in here?"

She smiled and snuggled into him, using his chest as a pillow. She said, "Mmm-hmm."

Johnny said, "So how do you like it here?"

"I really like it good."

"You do, huh?"

Jessica was smiling. "This makes two of us."

Cora said, "Did you really live with a bunch of Indians on that spot where you showed us?"

Johnny nodded. "Sure did. For a whole winter. For a while, Joe and Zack and I called this place Shoshone Valley. The name sort of faded away, though."

"What do you call it now?"

Johnny shrugged. "I don't think we call it anything, really. Just the valley."

Jessica said, "You probably should come up with a name for it before Aloysius Randall starts calling it Jubilee Valley."

Johnny laughed. "Very true."

Cora said, "How about McCabe Valley?"

Johnny thought about that for a moment. "Oh, I don't know."

"I think it's a good name."

"So do I," Jessica said, and went back to brushing out her hair.

Johnny said, "Cora, I'm going to take you back to bed."

She said, "I'm happy here."

Her voice was getting a sort of dreamy tone, like she was fading off.

Jessica said, "All right, Cora. You can stay a few more minutes. But when I'm done here, I'll take you back to bed."

Jessica continued running her brush through her hair.

She said, "So, Bree and Fat are now a couple."

Johnny nodded. "Who saw that coming?"

She gave him a look that said, *are you serious?* She said, "You could see that coming a mile away."

He returned the look to her. "I knew he was taken with her. That much was obvious. But I didn't know she had any feelings for him."

"She did. She just didn't know it, yet."

Johnny was silent, trying to digest that one.

She said, "We women really are a mystery to you men, aren't we?"

"Well, you are to this man."

She set the brush down on the dresser and got to her feet.

Johnny said, "And now we have to call him Charles."

"Well, you can't really call your future son-in-law Fat, can you?"

"Future son-in-law?" He had a pained sound to his voice.

She was enjoying this, as she climbed onto the bed. "Just think. There could be a Fat, Junior one day."

He was shaking his head. "Let's just take it one step at a time."

Jessica looked at Cora, whose eyes were shut.

Jessica said, "Is she asleep?"

Johnny nodded. "Out cold."

"We'll have to carry her to bed."

Johnny shrugged. "She can stay here. There's enough room."

He slid Cora off of him, and she buried the side of her face into a pillow.

Jessica said, "For a fearsome gunfighter, you really are a big softie, you know that?"

47

This was the day Haley was leaving. Dusty had driven her and the baby into town to catch the stage. From there, she would board the train in Cheyenne for points east. Dusty had asked that no one else come along. He wanted to be alone with Haley on her final day here.

Jack and Josh were in the kitchen. Jack was at the table with a cup of coffee in front of him. Josh was on his feet, his own cup of coffee on the table, abandoned.

Josh didn't agree with Jack, and Josh was never one to express his disagreement quietly.

Jack said, "Aunt Ginny agrees with me, and so does Pa."

"Well, I think you're all wrong." Josh wasn't really shouting, but he might as well have been. His voice had the subtlety of a trombone.

Jack held up his hand in a sort of *slow down* motion. "Josh, when was the last time both Pa and Aunt Ginny were wrong about something?"

Josh gave him an incredulous look. "Are you kidding me? Were they right about sending you off to college?"

Jack turned away. Now he was feeling a little miffed.

"All right," Josh said. "I'm sorry. I shouldn't have said that. But it's true. They were wrong then, and they're wrong now. Both of 'em."

"When it comes right down to it, it doesn't matter what either one of them thinks. Or you or me or Bree, for that matter. What counts is what Dusty and Haley think. It's their lives. She's making the decision she needs to, and Dusty's trying to be supportive. You should consider how hard this on him, and try to be supportive of him."

Josh shook his head and spun on his heel and pulled open the door. "I'm going for a ride."

"Like that'll solve anything."

Josh ignored him. "You want to find me, I'll be at Hunter's."

He slammed the door shut, rattling the glass panes.

Ginny and Temperance stepped in from the parlor.

"What was that all about?" Temperance said.

"Where were you, in the parlor hiding?"

"Well," Aunt Ginny said, going to the cupboard for a tea cup. "We weren't going to come in here with all that noise going on."

"Josh just thinks we're all wrong about Haley and Dusty. He thinks Dusty should tell her he wants her to stay."

Ginny had the cup, and went to the stove and the water kettle that was still hot.

She said, "That would just make it harder on Haley to do what she feels she has to do. Leaving is not going to be easy on her."

"Josh says that if it was Temperance, he wouldn't just let her ride off."

Temperance sat across from him. With a smile, she said, "That's sweet of him. But it's not the same situation. Haley has a baby to consider."

Jack nodded. "I'm in full agreement. It's just that Josh isn't."

Ginny had gotten a tea ball out of a drawer and was filling it with some China black.

She said, "Josh will come around. He usually does."

Jack shrugged. "Maybe."

Temperance said, "He has a stubborn side to him. That's part of what I love about him."

Jack gave her a look like he thought she was crazy, and she laughed. Ginny chuckled, too.

Ginny said, "Well, you boys have fall roundup starting in a couple of days. Maybe Josh can work off his steam then."

Temperance said to Jack, "So, now that you're not wearing a badge anymore, are you going to work here as a cowhand?"

He looked to his aunt. "Actually, there's something I was thinking about."

This had Ginny's attention.

He said, "I know I said I didn't want to go to school. All I really wanted was to be here, raising cattle and such."

Ginny nodded.

He said, "Times are different, now. Things have changed. The town has grown. There's a population of over a six hundred now, just three miles from here. I suppose it's sort of made me face the reality that civilization is coming west. Mile by mile. With every year that passes, this land is less and less the remote wilderness Josh and Bree and I grew up in."

Ginny nodded again, and said, "Change is one of the constants of life."

Temperance said, "Are you thinking of going back to school?"

He said, "Not medicine. I'm grateful for the education I received, and if not for that, Nina's father would have lost his leg last summer. But I don't think medicine is where I want to spend my life."

"Then, where?" Ginny asked.

"I've put a lot of thought into the role I played in helping Falcone find the gun. The gun that proved Josh didn't murder Alexander Gideon. And I put a lot of thought into what might have happened if we hadn't found that gun. How everything, Josh's freedom and maybe his very life, would have hinged on how good that lawyer from San Francisco would have been. The one you sent for. I've also put a lot of thought into something Pa said a little while ago. About shadows."

Ginny's brow dropped a bit. She didn't quite know what he was talking about, but she didn't ask. She let him continue.

He said, "I'm thinking law school."

Ginny said, "Have you thought about where?"

"Harvard has an eighteen month program in place. They're one of the only schools in the country that requires an undergraduate degree to qualify for their law school. But it's the best law school in the country. Unfortunately, the most expensive."

Ginny said, "That's not an issue. You know that."

"Aunt Ginny, I couldn't ask you to foot the bill for this, too."

"You're not asking. I insist."

"Maybe, if you wouldn't mind, I could pay you back after I'm settled in as an attorney."

Ginny said, "I'll tell you what. I'll pay for law school, and then you can pay me back if that's what you feel you need to do."

"The problem is, I now have Nina in my life. I have been thinking about proposing to her."

Temperance was all smiles at this. "Really?"

Ginny said, "It was inevitable, the way things are going between you two."

"But it wouldn't be fair to either one of us for me to be gone for eighteen months. And I don't want to go that long without seeing her."

Temperance said, "Get married, and then she can go with you. You can both live in Boston while you go to school."

Ginny smiled. "Problem solved."

"Just like that?" Jack said.

"Often the important things in life are really quite simple, once you allow yourself to stop complicating things."

"Just like that," he said.

"Just like that."

He took a sip of coffee, and said to his aunt, "How about that? I'm going to law school."

48

Old Hank shut the stage door and then climbed up to the driver's seat. Dusty stood on the boardwalk as Hank snapped the reins and gave a *giddyup!* The stage lurched forward.

Haley looked out the window, watching him with brows that were raised in the way a woman does when she's about to cry. She didn't wave. She just stared at him.

Dusty was about to raise his hand for a final wave, but didn't. He just stood, his hat hanging against his back and his gun tied down to his leg. He never felt so helpless or so empty.

Haley. The love of his life. He had lost her once two years ago, and now he was losing her again.

The stage turned the corner of the street, past the Jubilee Hotel, and then was gone. Dusty stood, looking off at the empty street. He drew a breath, trying to gather strength inside.

He turned away and saw Josh standing a block away, leaning against the building. Josh's arms were folded and he had raised one leg with his knee bent, and his foot was placed against the wall.

Dusty walked over. "How long have you been here?"

"Long enough. I didn't think you should be alone right now."

"Didn't I say I wanted to spend the morning alone with Haley?"

Josh nodded. "And you did."

Dusty decided to say nothing. Haley was gone, and being angry with Josh wouldn't change this.

He thought about wandering down to Hunter's for a beer, but then decided not to. Pa had said once over the past year or so that you shouldn't turn to alcohol to help you cope. That's when it starts to get ahold of you.

Dusty instead climbed into the buggy he had used to drive Haley and little Jonathan in to town. Josh's horse was tethered nearby, and he swung into the saddle.

The buggy could never handle the horse trail, so they began out of town by heading down Main Street. Past the new livery. Past the marshal's office, and the new houses that had popped up. Past the Freeman home. At one point, this house had stood off alone, a short distance from the town. Now the town had swelled out to overtake it.

"Hard to believe," Josh said. "Last spring, this was the little town of McCabe Gap. Not even a town, really. Just a little community. Now that community is gone and the town of Jubilee stands in its place."

Dusty said nothing. He reached around to his back and grabbed his hat and pulled it up and onto his head.

"Fat has decided he doesn't want to go out and join the floaters," Josh said. "Fine with me. I didn't want him to, anyway."

Dusty continued to ride along in silence.

"You missed breakfast this morning."

Dusty finally spoke. "Didn't think I'd be very good company."

"Bree tells us we're not supposed to call him *Fat* anymore. We have to call him *Charles*. Can you believe that?"

Dusty went back to riding along in silence.

Josh said, "I'm thinking of cutting my hair. I've had it long like Pa for a lot of years. I was thinking of maybe cutting it short like Jack's."

Dusty said, "You'd look like a chicken."

Josh cracked a grin and was going to give a shot back to Dusty. The little banter they often fell into when it was just the two of them. But Dusty had no grin. He was just riding along on the buggy seat, staring at the trail ahead, the reins in his hands.

Josh decided to say nothing more, and began riding in silence himself. Dusty kept the single horse pulling the buggy to a walk. Josh kept Rabbit to a walk, to match Dusty's pace.

The land was open about them, with a scattering of trees here and there. Mostly pines. To the right, by a small creek, stood a stand of maples.

Josh and Dusty followed the trail as it curved right, and through the open area between ridges that was still called McCabe Gap.

Then Josh gave Rabbit a light tug of the reins and the horse came to a stop, and Josh said, "Okay, I've got something to say."

Dusty continued along, and said, "I don't want to hear it."

"Well, you're gonna. Stop that buggy or not, you're gonna hear what I have to say."

Dusty pulled the horse to a stop. "I suppose it can't be avoided."

Josh nudged Rabbit forward until he was sitting beside the buggy.

"I kept quiet through all this. I figured it's your business. Aunt Ginny said once sometimes a person has to walk his road alone. Okay. I understand all of that. But I've got to say this."

Dusty looked away with resignation, like he truly was not in the mood for Josh right now.

Josh said, "Maybe you're doing the right thing. Taking the high road. Letting Haley go because it's what she thinks she needs right now. But I think you're wrong."

Dusty finally turned to look at him. "You don't know what it's like until you've walked in my shoes."

"All I know is if it was Temperance on that stage, and my son, I'd be high-tailing it after them."

Dusty said, "It's not my son. It's *his* son."

"You love that girl, don't you?"

Dusty nodded.

Josh said, "Any child of hers is a child of yours. Family isn't determined by blood. It's determined by love. You've been here for a couple of years now. Haven't you gotten that through your head yet?"

Dusty stared at him.

Josh said, "You came up with all the logical reasons for letting her go. But there's one good reason for asking her to stay. A man is lucky to find in his life, even once, the kind of love I see in your eyes when you look at her. And in her eyes when she looks at you. It's like what I have with Temperance. Haley might think going back east to be with her family is what she needs right now. But think about it. If the situation was reversed. If it was Temperance on that stage, what would you be telling me?"

Dusty said nothing.

Josh said, "She has no place to stay but with us, and we don't really have the room. But you'd tell me not to worry about any of that. It'll all work out. That's what you'd say. We'll figure it all out once she and the boy are back here. She and Jonathan can have your room and you can sleep on the sofa. I'd let you sleep on the floor in my room if I could stand your snoring. It'll all work out. What's meant to be will be. Aunt Ginny has said that more than once."

Dusty was silent, the way a man is when he is reconsidering something he thought he had already figured out.

Josh said, "You know these hills. You know the way the trail from here down to the Bozeman snakes along. You cut directly southwest, you'll catch up to the stage. If you get moving now."

Dusty looked at him. Then looked off toward the southwest.

Josh said, "Here. Take Rabbit. He's a mountain horse, born and bred. He can navigate these ridges better than any horse I've ever seen. Except maybe Thunder."

Josh swung out of the saddle.

Dusty didn't even take the time to climb out of the buggy. Rabbit was standing only about five feet away. He leaped from the buggy to Rabbit, grabbed the reins and clicked Rabbit into a gallop.

Josh was grinning. He climbed up into the buggy and clicked the horse ahead.

He said, as though Dusty could still hear him, "I'll tell Temperance she should set two more places for dinner tonight."

Dusty caught up with the stage eight miles south of Jubilee. He brought Rabbit to a sliding stop on the trail.

Rabbit could sure run, he thought. They had taken five miles overland at a full gallop, without stopping once. Rabbit was covered with lather and his nostrils were flaring, but even now as they stopped on the trail, the horse still wanted to run. He pranced about in a full circle and started kicking at the ground before Dusty could get him to settle down.

The stage was approaching, the horses moving at a light run. Dusty raised one hand for Old Hank to stop. Hank hauled on the reins and gave out a "Whoa!"

"Sorry about this, Hank," Dusty said. "I gotta talk to one of your passengers."

Dusty swung out of the saddle and left the rein trailing. Rabbit shook his head back and forth a couple of times, letting his opinion be known. He didn't want to stand around here. He wanted to run.

The horse was headstrong and impatient. Dusty had the brief thought that it was no wonder Josh liked this horse so much.

Haley was looking out the window at him. "Dusty?"

He opened the stage door. "Haley, can you come on out? I need to talk to you."

The baby was in the wicker basket on the seat beside Haley. A man and a woman were on the stage, sitting across from her. They were somewhere between forty and fifty and dressed for traveling. The man was in a jacket and a string tie, and the woman was in a dress with a high-buttoned collar and a hat pinned to her hair.

The woman said, "Go ahead, dear. We'll look after little Jonathan."

Haley climbed out of the stage, Dusty taking her hand as she stepped down.

She said, "I don't know what else we can say, Dusty. We've already been over this."

"I know it makes perfect sense for you to go back east and raise Jonathan with your family's help. It makes all the sense in the world, except for one thing. I love you. And you love me. We belong together, right here. You and me and Jonathan."

She shook her head sadly. "He's not yours, Dusty."

"Yes he is." He reached one hand to the side of her face and let it gently trail along her jaw. "Any child of yours is a child of mine. I was a little slow in seeing that, but it's the way of it. We'll raise him together. You and me. Husband and wife. Like it's meant to be."

Haley was shaking her head, like a little stab of common sense within was telling her not to be impulsive. To think things through. But it was only a little stab. As she shook her head, she was smiling and tears began running down her cheeks.

The woman said through the open door, "I'd seriously

think about saying yes, dear."

Haley turned the head shaking into a quick nod. "Yes. Yes. Absolutely yes."

The man said, "Are you gonna kiss her boy, or what?"

Dusty took her in for a kiss and wrapped his arms around her, and lifted her feet from the ground and twirled her around.

Haley was laughing. He was laughing. The man and woman in the stage were clapping their hands together. Old Hank was watching from the top of the stage and smiling.

Dusty set Haley back on her feet, and she said, "Mister Hank, can you toss down my trunk?"

Dusty tied the trunk to the back of the saddle. Rabbit shifted his feet a little and rolled one eye at Dusty, letting Dusty know he wasn't too pleased about this. Dusty then helped Haley up and onto the saddle. Haley wasn't much of a rider and she held onto the saddle like she was afraid she would fall off any second. Her dress billowed out behind her. Dusty got her feet securely in the stirrups and then handed the baby up to her.

Old Hank waved to them and then the stage was off.

Dusty was on foot, and with Rabbit's rein in one hand, they started back toward town.

He glanced up at Haley and saw the tears were gone, and she was giving a glowing smile.

She said to Jonathan, "That's your daddy. And he's bringing us home."

Hunter sat on the bench in front of his saloon and took in the October air. It had been downright cold the night before. A layer of ice had formed on the trough by the hitching rail in front of the saloon. But now the sun was shining warm. Might be one of the last warm days, Hunter thought. There was already snow in the mountains.

In his hand was a tin cup filled with coffee. It was Thursday, not normally a busy day of the week. Chen had the afternoon off, and though the saloon was open, there were no customers yet. *Nice time to sit a bit, and enjoy the afternoon,* Hunter thought.

A maple that stood in front of Miah Ricker's smithy shop was fully awash in autumn red. The air was clean and with the dry scents of fall.

The street was mostly empty, but Hunter saw a man walking along toward him. A gray jacket and a string tie, and a wide-brimmed cattleman's hat. Worn low against his right leg was a gun.

"Afternoon, preacher," Hunter said.

Tom nodded. "Beautiful one, isn't it?"

Hunter nodded. "Days like this make you thankful to be alive."

"Sure do."

"Great afternoon for thinking. I've got to find me a name for my saloon."

Tom said, "Most folks just call it 'Hunter's.'"

Hunter nodded. "But I need a sign that's fitting for a town this size. We have us an actual town here, now. I used to have a sign up over my door, but it rotted and came apart a while ago. I have a plank of wood inside now, and thought I might paint a name on it, and have the sign up for the weekend. It's pay week, and the cowhands'll all be in, whooping it up."

Hunter's gaze drifted to motion across the street and down a ways. Vic Falcone was walking hand-in-hand with the waitress from Johannes's restaurant, Flossy.

Hunter said, "Hard to believe he's still here."

Tom nodded his head. "He's announced he's running in the election next month."

"He'll never win. Not that one."

"Oh, I don't know. I'll be voting for him."

"You?"

Tom nodded. "Indeed. I've gotten to know him."

Hunter shook his head. "I'll never trust that man. He can wear a badge all he wants, but he's a killer."

"He was a killer, true. But now he's a marshal. Just like the woman he's with. Used to be a saloon woman, but now she's a waitress."

Hunter looked at him. "Do you really believe anyone can change that much?"

Tom shrugged. "I've been thinking a lot about second chances lately. The marshal and Flossy. Even myself, for that matter. And my Uncle Johnny and Jessica. They're both getting a second chance at love. And look at Dusty and Haley. Look at Aunt Ginny and Sam Middleton. Who would have foreseen that? And Harland Carter. It seems to me that maybe this place is a place for second chances."

Hunter was looking at him. "That's not what the Good Book preaches, is it? I thought it preached forgiveness."

Tom said, "Indeed. But isn't part of forgiveness giving someone a second chance?"

This gave Hunter something to think about. "Second chances, hmm?"

Tom nodded. "Second chances."

Tom continued on his way down the boardwalk.

Hunter sat for a few minutes, drinking is coffee. Then it occurred to him that he had found the name for his saloon.

He went back into the barroom, and the long, wide plank that was laid across two tables. With some black paint and a brush, he painted the sign in block letters.

Once the paint was dry, he mounted the sign above the front door. He then stepped out into the street so he could see how it would look to customers.

In block letters facing the other buildings on Main Street were the words SECOND CHANCE SALOON.

From behind him, a man spoke. "Looks good."

Hunter looked over his shoulder to see Vic Falcone and Miss Flossy standing there. Vic was squinting upward at the sign, and the sunlight was glinting from his badge.

Vic said, "It's a very appropriate name. This place has

turned out to be one of second chances for a lot of us."

This was sure the place for them, Hunter thought. There had been a time when he was on the run, himself, with a price on his head that wasn't entirely undeserved. But Johnny McCabe had given him a second chance and asked no questions.

Hunter said, "Would you two like a drink?"

Falcone grinned. "Thanks for the offer, but I think I've touched my last drop of alcohol. I wouldn't say no to a cup of coffee, though."

"Then come on in. It's on the house."

Made in the USA
Middletown, DE
31 March 2025